MIDNIGHT TALES

The Dream in the Dead House

Bram Stoker

MIDNIGHT TALES

Edited and with an Introduction by
Peter Haining

Peter Owen
London and Chester Springs

PETER OWEN PUBLISHERS
73 Kenway Road, London SW5 0RE

First published in Great Britain 1990
© Peter Haining 1990
This paperback edition published 2001

Permission to use quoted material in this book has been
granted by courtesy of the following:
Unwin Hyman Ltd for an extract from
Henry Irving and the Victorian Theatre by Madeleine Bingham;
Faber & Faber Ltd for extracts from
Henry Irving: The Actor and his World by Laurence Irving

ISBN 0 7206 1134 2

A catalogue record for this book is available from the British Library

Printed and bound in Great Britain by MPG Books Ltd, Cornwall

CONTENTS

A number of the stories in this collection have been edited for modern readers, while those which were first published in American periodicals have been anglicized to facilitate easier reading. A few of the stories also appear under the titles which Bram Stoker intended for them rather than those which were substituted by the editors of the magazines in which they originally appeared.

P.H.

'The Midnight Side'

Christopher Lee talking to the Editor

Every one of us has his or her dark side and I believe we all recognize this fact from our own experiences – and in any event, all the psychiatrists and psychologists can't be wrong! We all harbour in ourselves what Shakespeare calls the 'secret, black and midnight' aspects of our character, which means that we all react in one way or another to the morbid, the occult, the fantastic, the strange, the weird – the list of adjectives to describe this area of human experience is virtually endless.

It is certainly an element I have commented on many times during my professional career and I have also felt it in my own personal life. I am convinced, in fact, that the majority of cinema audiences – like the majority of people – enjoy a jolt from time to time, and therefore a well-made terror picture (I prefer that term to 'horror film') has an enduringly popular place in film entertainment. The same can also be said of television, radio, the stage and, of course, books.

I can still remember the impression Bram Stoker's novel *Dracula* had on me. It was unforgettable. And I am sure I am no exception. I read the book as a fourteen-year-old schoolboy, before the Second World War, and I recall vividly the fears it inspired in me. The effect on an adolescent mind was startling – but certainly the thought never occurred to me that one day I would bring the character of Dracula to life in the cinema!

Just as I have played a great many other roles on the screen, so Bram Stoker wrote other books and short stories of which the general public as a whole is unaware. This fact was bought home to me when I met

Bram's granddaughter and great-grandson while I was making a long-playing record of his short story 'Dracula's Guest'.

I now have copies of most of Bram Stoker's works in my library and I do not think I am overstating the case when I say that there are certainly several more among them which deserve to be dramatized.

Introduction

The story of how Bram Stoker found the inspiration for his great vampire novel, *Dracula*, was one that the amiable, red-bearded Irishman delighted in telling in the years following the book's first publication in 1897, and, indeed, continued to tell right up to the time of his own death some fifteen years later.

'The idea came to me in a nightmare', he would say, the laughter-lines gathering around his eyes. 'One evening I was dining with Henry Irving when I ate a little too much dressed crab and I spent all night long dreaming these weird dreams about a dead–alive man preying on the living!'

It was a good story and one that Stoker was happy to relate when being interviewed, or attending a literary function, or more particularly when dining with the great actor – whom he served as manager – and a circle of his friends. In truth, it was little more than a story, beyond the fact that the idea *had* first begun to take shape in his mind at one of the many evening meals he shared with Irving. Indeed, it is now evident that not only does literature owe one of its greatest fantasy novels to a supper-time conversation, but that a number of Bram Stoker's other tales of fiction also owe their origins to these convivial meals, sometimes attended by just Irving, Stoker and a few others, sometimes by a dozen and more guests.

Though Irving and Stoker did occasionally dine at the most fashionable restaurants in London, more often than not after an exhausting performance they would eat in Irving's own private dining-room at the rear of the Lyceum Theatre, of which for the last two decades of the Victorian era he was the actor-manager and lessee. This ornately furnished private restaurant, served by its own chef and well-stocked cellar, was known as 'The Beefsteak Room' and occupied the self-same premises as an earlier meeting-place of a group of theatrical people who had called themselves 'The Sublime Society of Beef-steaks'.

The Beefsteaks had been inaugurated at the start of the nineteenth century by Samuel Arnold, the composer and champion of English opera, who had been responsible for restoring the Lyceum Theatre. He had turned what had formerly been some old lumber rooms into an exclusive night-time club which was dedicated to excellent food and good conversation. Among those who joined Arnold in this pursuit were various stage-struck members of the nobility, the leading actors of the day, playwrights such as Richard Brinsley Sheridan and composers such as Thomas Perry, the prolific writer of melodramatic oratorios. As the name of the order implied, vast beefsteaks were the main dish, washed down with equally large quantities of beer and port.

When Henry Irving took over the Lyceum in 1871, the Sublime Society had, however, long since ceased to exist, and the grandiloquent rooms where it had met had fallen into disrepair. Irving, a lover of good meals and conversation, ordered the rooms restored and redecorated, and was soon afterwards entertaining equally colourful parties of up to thirty-six people at a time. He insisted on a much more varied menu, though, and also plied his guests with champagne and brandy. There were few nights when Bram Stoker did not sit at the same table as 'The Chief' (his sobriquet for Irving) and in his *Personal Reminiscences of Henry Irving* (1906), he offered these observations of the room which had had such an important influence on his own life and work:

The ordinary hospitalities of the Beefsteak Room were simply endless. A list of the names of those who supped with Irving there would alone fill chapters of this book. They were of all kinds and degrees. The whole social scale has been represented from the Prince to the humblest of commoners. Statesman, travellers, explorers, ambassadors, foreign princes and potentates, poets, novelists, historians – writers of every style, shade and quality. Representatives of all the learned professions; of all the official worlds; of all the great industries. Sportsmen, landlords, agriculturists. Men and women of leisure and fashion. Scientists, thinkers, inventors, philanthropists, divines. Egotists, ranging from harmless esteemers of their own worthiness to the very ranks of Nihilism. Philosophers. Artists of all kinds. In very truth the list was endless and kaleidoscopic.

My dear friend Stoker
"God bless you!
God bless you!"
Hy Irving

Dublin
3 Dec 1876

Small wonder, then, that a man like Bram Stoker, gregarious and imaginative by nature, a published writer himself as well as being Irving's manager, should have found inspiration for his literary work in the conversations that ebbed and flowed all around him at such cosmopolitan gatherings. Nor, as I shall describe in due course, is it surprising that he should have contemplated collecting the short stories inspired by these dining-room conversations into a book entitled *Midnight Tales*, which is now published almost eighty years after the author's death.

The story of the association of Bram Stoker and Henry Irving has already been told in several biographies of the two men, but there are certain details relevant to this collection which should be noted here.

Abraham 'Bram' Stoker was born in Dublin in 1847 where his father was one of the officials in the Chief Secretary's Department in Dublin Castle. He was educated at Trinity College, winning honours in oratory and composition as well as distinguishing himself as a sportsman. For a number of years Bram worked in the Irish Civil Service where he eventually became an Inspector of Petty Sessions. But the monotony of the work turned his thoughts towards journalism and in particular drama criticism, for he had already fallen in love with the theatre.

It was while seated in the stalls of the Theatre Royal, Dublin on the evening of Wednesday 28 August 1867 that Bram saw Henry Irving for the first time. It was a performance that had an indelible effect upon him and, though he had no way of knowing it then, was to change the whole course of his life.

The young theatre-goer was, in fact, so impressed by Irving in the role of Captain Absolute in Sheridan's *The Rivals* that when it was poorly reviewed in the *Dublin Mail* he wrote a spirited defence of the actor for what he saw as his 'distinguished, dashing and buoyant' playing of the part. When the article was accepted by the editor, Bram offered to contribute reviews of other productions to the *Mail* – without payment – and this work undoubtedly helped nurture his understanding and appreciation of the stage.

Bram saw Henry Irving again when he returned to Dublin in May 1871, but it was not until the actor appeared in the city for a third series of performances in December 1876 that the critic at last had the opportunity to meet the man he had grown to idolize. This meeting followed another laudatory review he had written of Irving's inter- pretation of Hamlet at the Theatre Royal. Irving's grandson, Laur- ence, has described the first encounter of the two men in his biography *Henry Irving: The Actor and His World* (1951):

> Irving expressed a wish to meet this enlightened critic. That night, before the play began, John Harris, the theatre manager, brought to Irving's dressing-room a ruddy, bearded gentleman of about thirty with something of the appearance of Sir Francis Drake, whom he introduced as Mr Bram Stoker. As there was little time for con- versation, Irving asked Stoker to join him at supper after the play. Over supper Stoker explained that he was a civil servant who, in the course of duty, was at that time engaged in writing a textbook on *The Duties of Clerks in Petty Sessions*, but by the way of recreation wrote articles and dramatic criticisms for the *Mail*. His robust appearance and hearty ebullience did not suggest a clerical bookish- ness. Irving was naturally attracted to Stoker's emotional enthusi- asm, particularly when he talked of the theatre. He was extremely well read and had already written a number of short stories.

An immediate friendship developed between the two men, and Stoker dined again several times with Irving before the actor returned to London. As they parted, the actor gave his admirer a signed photograph bearing the inscription, 'My dear friend Stoker – God bless you!'

The tie binding the pair was now forged, and when Irving came once more to Dublin in the winter of the following year, he im- mediately made contact with his Irish friend. Now, though, he had a proposition to make, as Laurence Irving has also recorded:

> During his stay, Stoker was constantly in Irving's company, sup- ping with him off hot lobsters at Corless's restaurant or escorting him to wrestling matches in Phoenix Park. Towards the end of the week they supped together in Stoker's rooms. Irving then disclosed in guarded terms the situation in which he found himself. His success was opening up enormous opportunities and it was possible before long he would be forced to make a change from his current

partnership arrangement and become his own master. He would need a loyal friend to share the burden of management. Already he was able to leave the details of stage-management in the capable hands of Harry Loveday. A business and front-of-the-house manager was harder to find. Such a post would allow a man of varied talents plenty of scope and was infinitely preferable to the dusty drudgery of the civil service. No more was said; Irving merely ruminated on his recent problems and his future hopes. Stoker, however, thought that by this time he knew his man. When Irving left, he wrote in his diary: 'London in view!'

Almost exactly a year later, with his weighty tome on the duty of clerks at last completed, Bram Stoker quit his job in Dublin, and on 9 December 1878, accepted the job he was to fill with enormous enthusiasm and dedication until the day of Irving's death.

Bram quickly learned what a demanding taskmaster Irving could be – and was soon suffering from his wicked sense of humour. As Madeleine Bingham has written in her book *Henry Irving and the Victorian Theatre* (1978):

Irving's way of life was entirely bounded by his profession, but he made himself into a splendid and respected public figure. His private character, when the curtain was rung down, is more difficult to define. With his friends and cronies he would sit up till dawn smoking cigars, drinking, and relaxing after the play. He had a mordant humour when he wished to use it. Yet all agreed that no one could be more raffish and mischievous than he in his off-duty hours. He would joke and tease his assistants, Bram Stoker, and especially Loveday, who followed him like a dog.

Bram, however, accepted the Chief's late-night activities, writing in his biography:

I well understood even then, though I understand it better now, that after a hard and exciting day or night – or both – the person most concerned does not want to go to bed. He feels that sleep is at arm's-length till it is summoned. I did not like to thwart him when he felt that a friendly chat of no matter how exaggerated dimensions would rest him better than some sleepless hours in bed.

Those who stayed up chatting with Irving – or joined him for supper – could also vouch for the pleasures of the conversations to be had in his company, and how easily he could dominate any group. The actor Graham Robertson years later vividly recalled a dinner party he attended in the Lyceum's back-stage restaurant. 'The bright candle-lit table among the shadows of the Beefsteak Room – the beautiful ivory face of our host against the dark panelling – remains in my memory', Robertson said. 'Round that pale face which seemed to absorb and give out light, the rest of the scene grows vague and out of focus. . . .'

Other diners recalled the variety and liveliness of the talk at Irving's table; often it was about the theatre, perhaps Irving's current produc-tion or maybe those of other leading actors in London and the provinces. But just as often, the subjects were as wide-ranging as the professions and interests of those gathered around the great man. Walter Herries Pollock, the editor of the *Saturday Review* and a long-time friend of Irving, wrote in 1908:

> There was always good conversation around Irving: anecdotes of the stage; stories of public figures; tales of far distant places; of high adventure and wild imagination. As long as the tale was worth the telling and the teller had the command and wit to tell it he could be sure of a good hearing. Journalists like myself, and writers like Hall Caine and Bram Stoker, the actor's manager, on many a night rose from Irving's table replete in appetite and inspired in mind.

Stoker, indeed, found at the Beefsteak table the inspiration for the most famous of his literary creations, *Dracula*. The success of this novel has come to overshadow the name of its author, creating one of the most enduring myths of the twentieth century. The powerful story of the vampire has been retold in all the mediums of entertainment including the theatre, radio, cinema and television, as well as being frequently utilized in art and literature. Indeed, the figure of Count Dracula is now as universal as that of Robinson Crusoe, Sherlock Holmes, James Bond and, of course, Frankenstein's Monster.

Sadly, Bram Stoker died before his novel began to enjoy its huge commercial success and he would probably be amazed to learn that it has now been translated into forty-four languages and has provided the inspiration for well over 200 films. On the screen it has also made the reputations of several actors, most notably the American Bela Lugosi in the thirties, and more recently the British film star, Christopher Lee. Though the two men interpreted the role in very different ways, neither has left audiences in any doubt about the spine-chilling power of Stoker's creation.

But it is equally true that the success of *Dracula* has tended to obscure Bram Stoker's other works, in particular his short stories. Though one collection of his tales, entitled *Dracula's Guest*, was assembled posthumously in 1914 by his widow, Florence, a number of other stories have remained forgotten in the magazines to which Stoker sold them during his lifetime. It is these tales which form the major part of this collection.

In his obituary published in *The Times* on 22 April, 1912, Bram Stoker was described as a fluent and flamboyant writer who had managed to find the time amid much arduous and distracting work to write a good deal. He was, the newspaper added, 'a master of a particularly lurid and creepy kind of fiction represented by *Dracula*'. According to his obituarist, however, 'his chief literary memorial will be his *Reminiscences of Irving*.' How that remark must have since caused *The Times* to squirm!

Not all the tales which are included in this volume are lurid and creepy, however, though they are all marked by those elements of the strange and the mysterious which are hallmarks of Stoker's writing. More particularly, they are stories inspired by the conversations around Henry Irving's dinner table. Indeed, the manner in which many of them are told has the style of actual conversation, and in the pages which follow the reader may well experience the uncanny feeling of being transported back a century to the candle-lit Beefsteak Room and of finding himself seated alongside Bram Stoker in that fascinating circle of men talking away the midnight hours. . . .

Peter Haining
Boxford, Suffolk
August 1989

The Dream in the Dead House

There is no question that the most famous of Bram Stoker's stories to have been inspired by a candle-lit dinner amidst the Gothic splendour of the Beefsteak Room was *Dracula*. The famous novel was not, in fact, the result of eating too much crab as Stoker liked to fantasize. It developed from a conversation about the vampire tradition in Transylvania which Stoker had with an acknowledged expert on Romanian folklore named Arminius Vambery, a professor at the University of Budapest. Vambery, a much-travelled and widely respected scholar, had come, appropriately, to see Irving in *The Dead Hand* on the night of 30 April 1890 and was invited to supper afterwards. There he regaled Irving and Stoker with stories of his researches in Transylvania. One tale which particularly fascinated them was that of a man who claimed to have been attacked by a wolf-like creature which drank his blood. It may have been a vampire, Vambery said, for these dead–alive beings were known throughout the country and were greatly feared by the peasants. The actor and his manager sat almost in silence as Vambery talked away through the night, and Stoker later wrote, 'He was most interesting and Irving was delighted with him.'

The idea of a vampire caught Stoker's interest at once, and in the following months as *Dracula* took shape in his mind, he corresponded with Professor Vambery, picking his brain for more information to be used as background detail. The story of the blood-drinking wolf Stoker decided to use as part of the very first chapter of the book, but later when the manuscript was finished and the publishers, Arnold Constable & Company, asked for some cuts on the grounds that it was too long, Stoker, always enormously busy, found it easiest just to withdraw this section. (A suggestion that he took it out because his wife found it too gruesome, and believed it would offend readers when they had hardly begun the book, is difficult to substantiate.) The dramatic episode, restored just as Stoker intended it to appear in his novel, now follows as the first story in this collection.

While the facts I have given about the creation of *Dracula* are well documented, the model for the character of Count Dracula is less certain. Some experts believe that Stoker based the Count on the gaunt figure of Irving himself, and in particular the actor's inter-pretation of the role of Mephistopheles, complete with flashing eyes and whirling scarlet cloak. However it is also true that he met a man who sounds to me the very image of Dracula at another dinner in the Beefsteak Room. The man was a Greek actor, Jacques Damala, then married to the great tragedienne, Sarah Bernhardt, who came regularly to dine with Irving when she was in London. Stoker wrote of Damala in his diary, 'He looked like a dead man. I sat next to him at supper, and the idea that he was dead was strong on me. His eyes, staring out of his white waxen face, seemed hardly the eyes of the living.' Damala/Dracula? – the reader must decide for himself!

I SHALL ENTER HERE some of my notes of my journey from London across Europe to Transylvania as they may refresh my memory when I talk over my travels with my darling Mina.

Even before I reached my destination I had a foretaste of what lay ahead. For one night during my journey I did not sleep well – though my bed was comfortable enough – and I had all sorts of queer dreams. There was a dog howling all night under my window, which may have had something to do with it; or it may have been the paprika, for I had to drink up all the water in my carafe, and was still thirsty.

Be that as it may, the dreams concerned a Dead House at Munich and grew more strange and terrible whenever I thought of them. Indeed, it all seemed so strange and mysterious. . . .

I had decided to go for a drive and when we started the sun was shining brightly in Munich and the air was full of the joyousness of early summer. Just as we were about to depart, Herr Delbrück (the *maître d'hôtel* of the Quatre Saisons, where I was staying) came down, bareheaded, to the carriage and, after wishing me a pleasant drive, said to the coachman, still holding his hand on the handle of the carriage door: 'Remember you are back by nightfall. The sky looks bright but there is a shiver in the north wind that says there may be a sudden storm. But I am sure you will not be late.' Here he smiled, and added, 'For you know what night it is.'

Johann answered with an emphatic, 'Ja, mein Herr,' and, touching his hat, drove off quickly. When we had cleared the town, I said, after signalling to him to stop: 'Tell me, Johann, what is tonight?'

He crossed himself, as he answered laconically: 'Walpurgis Nacht.' Then he took out his watch, a great, old-fashioned German silver thing as big as a turnip, and looked at it, with his eyebrows gathered together and a little impatient shrug of his shoulders. I realized that this was his way of respectfully protesting against the unnecessary delay, and sank back in the carriage, merely motioning him to proceed. He started off rapidly, as if to make up for lost time. Every now and then the horses seemed to throw up their heads and sniffed the air suspiciously. On such occasions I often looked round in alarm. The road was pretty bleak, for we were traversing a sort of high, wind-swept plateau. As we drove, I saw a road that looked but little used, and which seemed to dip through a little, winding valley. It looked so inviting that, even at the risk of offending him, I called Johann to stop – and when he had pulled up, I told him I would like to drive down that road. He made all sorts of excuses, and frequently crossed himself as he spoke. This somewhat piqued my curiosity, so I asked him various questions. He answered fencingly, and repeatedly looked at his watch in protest. Finally I said: 'Well, Johann, I want to go down this road. I shall not ask you to come unless you like; but tell me why you do not like to go, that is all I ask.'

For answer he seemed to throw himself off the box, so quickly did he reach the ground. Then he stretched out his hands appealingly to me, and implored me not to go. There was just enough of English mixed with the German for me to understand the drift of his talk. He seemed always just about to tell me something – the very idea of which evidently frightened him; but each time he pulled himself up, saying, as he crossed himself: 'Walpurgis Nacht!'

I tried to argue with him, but it was difficult to argue with a man when I did not know his language. The advantage certainly rested with him, for although he began to speak in English, of a very crude and broken kind, he always got excited and broke into his native tongue – and every time he did so, he looked at his watch. Then the horses became restless and sniffed the air. At this he grew very pale, and, looking around in a frightened way, he suddenly jumped forward, took them by the bridles and led them on some twenty feet. I followed, and asked why he had done this. For answer he crossed himself, pointed to the spot we had left and drew his carriage in the direction of the other road, indicating a cross, and said, first in German, then in English: 'Buried him – him what killed themselves.'

I remembered the old custom of burying suicides at crossroads: 'Ah! I see, a suicide. How interesting!' But for the life of me I could not make out why the horses were frightened.

Whilst we were talking, we heard a sort of sound between a yelp and a bark. It was far away; but the horses got very restless, and it took Johann all his time to quiet them. He was pale, and said: 'It sounds like a wolf – but yet there are no wolves here now.'

'No?' I said, questioning him; 'isn't it long since the wolves were so near the city?'

'Long, long,' he answered, 'in the spring and summer; but with the snow the wolves have been here not so long.'

Whilst he was petting the horses and trying to quiet them, dark clouds drifted rapidly across the sky. The sunshine passed away, and a breath of cold wind seemed to drift past us. It was only a breath, however, and more in the nature of a warning than a fact, for the sun came out brightly again. Johann looked under his lifted hand at the horizon and said: 'The storm of snow, he comes before long time.' Then he looked at his watch again, and, straightway holding his reins firmly – for the horses were still pawing the ground restlessly and shaking their heads – he climbed to his box as though the time had come for proceeding on our journey.

I felt a little obstinate and did not at once get into the carriage.

'Tell me,' I said, 'about this place where the road leads,' and I pointed down.

Again he crossed himself and mumbled a prayer, before he answered: 'It is unholy.'

'What is unholy?' I enquired.

'The village.'

'Then there is a village?'

'No, no. No one lives there hundreds of years.' My curiosity was piqued: 'But you said there was a village.'

'There was.'

'Where is it now?'

Whereupon he burst out into a long story in German and English, so mixed up that I could not quite understand exactly what he said, but roughly I gathered that long ago, hundreds of years, men had died there and been buried in their graves; and sounds were heard under the clay, and when the graves were opened, men and women were found rosy with life, and their mouths red with blood. And so, in haste to save their lives (aye, and their souls! – and here he crossed himself) those who were left fled away to other places, where the living lived, and the dead were dead and not – not something. He was evidently afraid to speak the last words. As he proceeded with his narration, he grew more and more excited. It seemed as if his imagination had got hold of him, and he ended in a perfect paroxysm of fear – white-faced, perspiring, trembling and looking round him, as if expecting that some dreadful presence would manifest itself there in the bright sunshine on the open plain. Finally, in an agony of desperation, he cried: 'Walpurgis Nacht!' and pointed to the carriage for me to get in.

All my English blood rose at this, and, standing back, I said: 'You are afraid, Johann – you are afraid. Go home; I shall return alone; the walk will do me good.' The carriage door was open. I took from the seat my oak walking-stick – which I always carry on my holiday excursions – and closed the door, pointing back to Munich, and said, 'Go home, Johann – Walpurgis Nacht doesn't concern Englishmen.'

The horses were now more restive than ever, and Johann was trying to hold them in, while excitedly imploring me not to do anything so foolish. I pitied the poor fellow, he was so deeply in earnest; but all the same I could not help laughing. His English was quite gone now. In his anxiety he had forgotten that his only means of making me understand was to talk my language, so he jabbered away in his native German. It began to be a little tedious. After giving the direction, 'Home!' I turned to go down the crossroad into the valley.

With a despairing gesture, Johann turned his horses towards Munich. I leaned on my stick and looked after him. He went slowly along the road for a while: then there came over the crest of the hill a man tall and thin. I could see so much in the distance. When he drew near the horses, they began to jump and kick about, then to scream with terror. Johann could not hold them in; they bolted down the road, running away madly. I watched them out of sight, then looked for the stranger, but I found that he, too, was gone.

With a light heart I turned down the side road through the deepening valley to which Johann had objected. There was not the slightest reason, that I could see, for his objection; and I daresay I tramped for a couple of hours without thinking of time or distance, and certainly without seeing a person or a house. So far as the place was concerned, it was desolation itself. But I did not notice this particularly till, on turning a bend in the road, I came upon a scattered fringe of wood; then I recognized that I had been impressed unconsciously by the desolation of the region through which I had passed.

I sat down to rest myself, and began to look around. It struck me that it was considerably colder than it had been at the commencement of my walk – a sort of sighing sound seemed to be around me, with, now and then, high overhead, a sort of muffled roar. Looking upwards I noticed that great thick clouds were drifting rapidly across the sky from North to South at a great height. There were signs of coming storm in some lofty stratum of the air. I was a little chilly, and, thinking that it was the sitting still after the exercise of walking, I resumed my journey.

The ground I passed over was now much more picturesque. There were no striking objects that the eye might single out; but in all there was a charm of beauty. I took little heed of time and it was only when the deepening twilight forced itself upon me that I began to think of how I should find my way home. The brightness of the day had gone. The air was cold, and the drifting of clouds high overhead was more marked. They were accompanied by a sort of far-away rushing sound, through which seemed to come at intervals that mysterious cry which the driver had said came from a wolf. For a while I hesitated. I had said I would see the deserted village, so on I went, and presently came on a wide stretch of open country, shut in by hills all around. Their sides were covered with trees which spread down to the plain, dotting, in clumps, the gentler slopes and hollows which showed here and there. I followed with my eye the winding of the road, and saw that it curved close to one of the densest of these clumps and was lost behind it.

As I looked there came a cold shiver in the air, and the snow began to fall. I thought of the miles and miles of bleak country I had passed, and then hurried on to seek the shelter of the wood in front. Darker and darker grew the sky, and faster and heavier fell the snow, till the earth before and around me was a glistening white carpet the further edge of which was lost in misty vagueness. The road was here but crude, and when on the level its boundaries were not so marked, as when it passed through the cuttings; and in a little while I found that I must have strayed from it, for I missed underfoot the hard surface, and my feet sank deeper in the grass and moss. Then the wind grew stronger and blew with ever increasing force, till I was fain to run before it. The air became icy-cold, and in spite of my exercise I began to suffer. The snow was now falling so thickly and whirling around me in such rapid eddies that I could hardly keep my eyes open. Every now and then the heavens were torn asunder by vivid lightning, and in the flashes I could see ahead of me a great mass of trees, chiefly yew and cypress all heavily coated with snow.

I was soon amongst the shelter of the trees, and there, in comparative silence, I could hear the rush of the wind high overhead. Presently the blackness of the storm had become merged in the darkness of the night. By-and-by the storm seemed to be passing away: it now only came in fierce puffs or blasts. At such moments the weird sound of the wolf appeared to be echoed by many similar sounds around me.

Now and again, through the black mass of drifting cloud, came a straggling ray of moonlight, which lit up the expanse, and showed me that I was at the edge of a dense mass of cypress and yew trees. As the snow had ceased to fall, I walked out from the shelter and began to investigate more closely. It appeared to me that, amongst so many old foundations as I had passed, there might be still standing a house in which, though in ruins, I could find some sort of shelter for a while. As I skirted the edge of the copse, I found that a low wall encircled it, and following this I presently found an opening. Here the cypresses formed an alley leading up to a square mass of some kind of building. Just as I caught sight of this, however, the drifting clouds obscured the moon, and I passed up the path in darkness. The wind must have grown colder, for I felt myself shiver as I walked; but there was hope of shelter, and I groped my way blindly on.

I stopped, for there was a sudden stillness. The storm had passed; and, perhaps in sympathy with nature's silence, my heart seemed to cease to beat. But this was only momentarily; for suddenly the moonlight broke through the clouds, showing me that I was in a graveyard, and that the square object before me was a great massive tomb of marble, as white as the snow that lay on and all around it. With the moonlight there came a fierce sigh of the storm, which appeared to resume its course with a long, low howl, as of many dogs or wolves. I was awed and shocked, and felt the cold perceptibly grow upon me till it seemed to grip me by the heart. Then while the flood of moonlight still fell on the marble tomb, the storm gave further evidence of renewing, as though it was returning on its track. Impelled by some sort of fascination, I approached the sepulchre to see what it was, and why such a thing stood alone in such a place. I walked around it, and read, over the Doric door, in German –

COUNTESS DOLINGEN OF GRATZ
IN STYRIA
SOUGHT AND FOUND DEATH
1801

On the top of the tomb, seemingly driven through the solid marble – for the structure was composed of a few vast blocks of stone – was a great iron spike or stake. On going to the back I saw, graven in great Russian letters:

The dead travel fast

There was something so weird and uncanny about the whole thing that it gave me a turn and made me feel quite faint. I began to wish, for the first time, that I had taken Johann's advice. Here a thought struck me, which came under almost mysterious circumstances and with a terrible shock. This was Walpurgis Night!

Walpurgis Night, when, according to the belief of millions of people, the Devil was abroad – when the graves were opened and the dead came forth and walked. When all evil things of earth and air and water held revel. This very place the driver had specially shunned. This was the depopulated village of centuries ago. This was where the suicide lay; and this was the place where I was alone – unmanned, shivering with cold in a shroud of snow with a wild storm gathering again upon me! It took all my philosophy, all the religion I had been taught, all my courage, not to collapse in a paroxysm of fright.

And now a perfect tornado burst upon me. The ground shook as though thousands of horses thundered across it; and this time the storm bore on its icy wings, not snow, but great hailstones which drove with such violence that they might have come from the thongs of Balearic slingers – hailstones that beat down leaf and branch and

24

made the shelter of the cypresses of no more avail than though their stems were standing-corn. At the first I had rushed to the nearest tree; but I was soon fain to leave it and seek the only spot that seemed to afford refuge, the deep Doric doorway of the marble tomb. There, crouching against the massive bronze door, I gained a certain amount of protection from the beating of the hailstones, for now they only drove against me as they ricochetted from the ground and the side of the marble.

As I leaned against the door, it moved slightly and opened inwards. The shelter of even a tomb was welcome in that pitiless tempest, and I was about to enter it when there came a flash of forked-lightning that lit up the whole expanse of the heavens. In the instant, as I am a living man, I saw, as my eyes were turned into the darkness of the tomb, a beautiful woman, with rounded cheeks and red lips, seemingly sleeping on a bier. As the thunder broke overhead, I was grasped as by the hand of a giant and hurled out into the storm. The whole thing was so sudden that, before I could realize the shock, moral as well as physical, I found the hailstones beating me down. At the same time I had a strange, dominating feeling that I was not alone. I looked towards the tomb. Just then there came another blinding flash, which seemed to strike the iron stake that surmounted the tomb and to pour through to the earth, blasting and crumbling the marble, as in a burst of flame. The dead woman rose for a moment of agony, while she was lapped in the flame, and her bitter scream of pain was drowned in the thundercrash. The last thing I heard was this mingling of dreadful sound, as again I was seized in the giant-grasp and dragged away, while the hailstones beat on me, and the air around seemed reverberant with the howling of wolves. The last sight that I remembered was a vague, white, moving mass, as if all the graves around me had sent out the phantoms of their sheeted-dead, and that they were closing in on me through the white cloudiness of the driving hail.

Gradually there came a sort of vague beginning of consciousness; then a sense of weariness that was dreadful. For a time I remembered nothing; but slowly my senses returned. My feet seemed positively racked with pain, yet I could not move them. They seemed to be numbed. There was an icy feeling at the back of my neck and all down my spine, and my ears, like my feet, were dead, yet in torment; but there was in my breast a sense of warmth which was, by comparison, delicious. It was as a nightmare – a physical nightmare, if one may use such an expression; for some heavy weight on my chest made it difficult for me to breathe.

This period of semi-lethargy seemed to remain a long time, and as it faded away I must have slept or swooned. Then came a sort of loathing, like the first stage of sea-sickness, and a wild desire to be free from something – I knew not what. A vast stillness enveloped me, as though all the world were asleep or dead – only broken by the low panting as of some animal close to me. I felt a warm rasping at my throat, then came a consciousness of the awful truth, which chilled me to the heart and sent the blood surging up through my brain. Some great animal was lying on me and now licking my throat. I feared to stir, for some instinct of prudence bade me lie still; but the brute seemed to realize that there was now some change in me, for it raised its head. Through my eyelashes I saw above me the two great flaming eyes of a gigantic wolf. Its sharp white teeth gleamed in the gaping red mouth, and I could feel its hot breath fierce and acrid upon me.

For another spell of time I remembered no more. Then I became conscious of a low growl, followed by a yelp, renewed again and again. Then, seemingly very far away, I heard a 'Holloa! holloa!' as of many voices calling in unison. Cautiously I raised my head and looked in the direction whence the sound came; but the cemetery blocked my view. The wolf still continued to yelp in a strange way, and a red glare began to move round the grove of cypresses, as though following the sound. As the voices drew closer, the wolf yelped faster and louder. I feared to make either sound or motion. Nearer came the red glow, over the white pall which stretched into the darkness around me. Then all at once from beyond the trees there came at a trot a troop of horsemen bearing torches. The wolf rose from my breast and made for the cemetery. I saw one of the horsemen (soldiers by their caps and their long military cloaks) raise his carbine and take aim. A companion knocked up his arm, and I heard the ball whizz over my head. He had evidently taken my body for that of the wolf. Another sighted the animal as it slunk away, and a shot followed. Then, at a gallop, the troop rode forward – some towards me, others following the wolf as it disappeared amongst the snow-clad cypresses.

As they drew nearer I tried to move, but was powerless, although I could see and hear all that went on around me. Two or three of the soldiers jumped from their horses and knelt beside me. One of them raised my head, and placed his hand over my heart.

'Good news, comrades!' he cried. 'His heart still beats!'

Then some brandy was poured down my throat; it put vigour into me, and I was able to open my eyes fully and look around. Lights and shadows were moving among the trees, and I heard men call to one another. They drew together, uttering frightened exclamations; and the lights flashed as the others came pouring out of the cemetery pell-mell, like men possessed. When the further ones came close to us, those who were around me asked them eagerly: 'Well, have you found him?'

The reply rang out hurriedly: 'No! no! Come away quick – quick! This is no place to stay, and on this of all nights!'

'What was it?' was the question, asked in all manner of keys. The answer came variously and all indefinitely as though the men were moved by some common impulse to speak, yet were restrained by some common fear from giving their thoughts.

'It – it – indeed!' gibbered one, whose wits had plainly given out for the moment.

'A wolf – and yet not a wolf!' another put in shudderingly.

'No use trying for him without the sacred bullet,' a third remarked in a more ordinary manner.

'Serve us right for coming out on this night! Truly we have earned our thousand marks!' were the ejaculations of a fourth.

'There was blood on the broken marble,' another said after a pause – 'the lightning never brought that there. And for him – is he safe? Look at his throat! See, comrades, the wolf has been lying on him and keeping his blood warm.'

The officer looked at my throat and replied: 'He is all right; the skin is not pierced. What does it all mean? We should never have found him but for the yelping of the wolf.'

'What became of it?' asked the man who was holding up my head, and who seemed the least panic-stricken of the party, for his hands were steady and without tremor. On his sleeve was the chevron of a petty officer.

'It went to its home,' answered the man, whose long face was pallid, and who actually shook with terror as he glanced around him fearfully. 'There are graves enough there in which it may lie. Come, comrades – come quickly! Let us leave this cursed spot.'

The officer raised me to a sitting posture, as he uttered a word of command; then several men placed me upon a horse. He sprang to the saddle behind me, took me in his arms, gave the word to advance; and, turning our faces away from the cypresses, we rode away in swift, military order.

As yet my tongue refused its office, and I was perforce silent. I must have fallen asleep; for the next thing I remembered was finding myself standing up, supported by a soldier on each side of me. It was almost broad daylight, and to the north a red streak of sunlight was reflected, like a path of blood, over the waste of snow. The officer was telling the men to say nothing of what they had seen, except that they found an English stranger, guarded by a large dog.

'Dog! that was no dog,' cut in the man who had exhibited such fear. 'I think I know a wolf when I see one.'

The young officer answered calmly: 'I said a dog.'

'Dog!' reiterated the other ironically. It was evident that his courage was rising with the sun; and, pointing to me, he said, 'Look at his throat. Is that the work of a dog, master?'

Instinctively I raised my hand to my throat, and as I touched it I cried out in pain. The men crowded round to look, some stooping down from their saddles; and again there came the calm voice of the young officer: 'A dog, as I said. If aught else were said we should only be laughed at.'

I was then mounted behind a trooper, and we rode on into the suburbs of Munich. Here we came across a stray carriage, into which I was lifted, and it was driven off to the Quatre Saisons – the young officer accompanying me, whilst a trooper followed with his horse, and the others rode off to their barracks.

When we arrived, Herr Delbrück rushed so quickly down the steps to meet me, that it was apparent he had been watching within. Taking me by both hands he solicitously led me in. The officer saluted me and was turning to withdraw, when I recognized his purpose, and insisted that he should come to my rooms. Over a glass of wine I warmly thanked him and his brave comrades for saving me. He replied simply that he was more than glad, and that Herr Delbrück had at the first taken steps to make all the searching party pleased; at which ambiguous utterance the *maître d'hôtel* smiled, while the officer pleaded duty and withdrew.

'But Herr Delbrück,' I enquired, 'how and why was it that the soldiers searched for me?'

He shrugged his shoulders, as if in depreciation of his own deed, as he replied: 'I was so fortunate as to obtain leave from the commander of the regiment in which I served, to ask for volunteers.'

'But how did you know I was lost?' I asked.

'The driver came hither with the remains of his carriage, which had been upset when the horses ran away.'

'But surely you would not send a search-party of soldiers merely on this account?'

'Oh, no!' he answered; 'but even before the coachman arrived, I had this telegram from the Boyar whose guest you are,' and he took from his pocket a telegram which he handed to me, and I read:

BISTRITZ

Be careful of my guest – his safety is most precious to me. Should aught happen to him, or if he be missed, spare nothing to find him and ensure his safety. He is English and therefore adventurous. There are often dangers from snow and wolves and night. Lose not a moment if you suspect harm to him. I answer your zeal with my fortune – Dracula

As I held the telegram in my hand, the room seemed to whirl around me; and, if the attentive *maître d'hôtel* had not caught me, I think I should have fallen. There was something so strange in all this, something so weird and impossible to imagine, that there grew on me a sense of my being in some way the sport of opposite forces – the mere vague idea of which seemed in a way to paralyse me. I was certainly under some form of mysterious protection. From a distant country had come, in the very nick of time, a message that took me out of the danger of the snow-sleep and the jaws of the wolf.

The Spectre of Doom

The custom of telling stories during their evening meals together was one that Bram Stoker and Henry Irving began to develop even before Stoker had become the actor's manager. Describing Irving's visit to Dublin in September 1878 – three months before he threw in his lot with the English thespian – Stoker wrote:

> I was with him a great deal, not only in the theatre during rehearsals as well as at the performances, but we drove almost every day and dined and supped at the house of my brother; at my lodgings or his hotel; at restaurants or in the houses of other friends. There we would sit talking over the events of the day or telling stories of the past and the many things which had befallen us in our respective spheres of life.

Early on in their association, Irving told his new friend that he had always been intrigued by the supernatural and indeed had appeared in several plays which capitalized on the public's love of being made to shiver in their seats. It was a topic to which he found an immediate response from Bram, who had been steeped in Irish folklore by his mother ever since his childhood. So, while Irving would reminisce about the famous Gothic novels he had read and the stage parts he had played (such as D'Aubigné in *The Man in the Iron Mask* in 1858; Prince Piombino in *Frankenstein* the following year; and Earl Percy in *The Castle Spectre*, which he had brought to the Queen's Theatre, Dublin in March 1860), Stoker would talk about the banshees, leprechauns and pookas of Irish legend.

One of Bram's stories which particularly interested Irving was based on the recollections of his mother and concerned the terrible outbreak of cholera in Sligo in 1832. Stoker told this tale with a relish which suggests that it was a key factor in his early fascination with the weird and the strange, a fascination which he later developed as a writer. On hearing this story, Irving felt that while such terrible events could never be portrayed on the stage, they could surely be utilized in fiction. Bram replied that he had already begun sketching out an allegorical fantasy based on his mother's description of having 'seen' the approach of the cholera plague like some enormous spectre of doom. Intended primarily for younger readers, it was first published in the *Dublin Mail* in November 1880, complete with a superb macabre illustration by W. V. Cockburn which is also reprinted here.

FAR AWAY THERE IS a place known as the Country Under the Sunset. Time there goes on much as it does here. Once it had been a beautiful land and there had been love and reverence towards the King, but this was no more. No longer was there perfect peace.

The people of the Country Under the Sunset had become more selfish and more greedy, and had tried to grasp all they could for themselves. There were some very rich and there were many very poor.

Most of the beautiful gardens in the land were laid to waste. Houses had grown up close around the King's palace; and in some of these dwelt many persons who could only afford to pay for part of a house.

All the beautiful country was sadly changed, and changed was the life of the dwellers in it.

The spirits that guarded the land were very, very sad. Their great white shadowy wings drooped as they stood at their posts at the portals of the land. They hid their faces, and their eyes were dim with continuous weeping, so that they heeded not if any evil thing went by them. They tried to make the people think of their evil-doing; but they could not leave their posts, and the people heard their moaning in the night season, and said, 'Listen to the sighing of the breeze; how sweet it is!'

So it is ever with us also, that when we hear the wind sighing and moaning and sobbing round our houses in the lonely nights, we do not think that our angels may be sorrowing for our misdeeds, but only that there is a storm coming. The angels wept evermore, and they felt the sorrow of dumbness – for though they could speak, those they spoke to would not hear.

Whilst the people laughed at the idea of giants, there was one old old man who shook his head, and made answer to them, when he heard them, and said: 'Death has many children, and there are giants in the marshes still. You may not see them, perhaps – but they are there, and the only bulwark of safety is in a land of patient, faithful hearts.'

The name of this good old man was Knoal, and he lived in a house built of great blocks of stone, in the middle of a wild place far from the city.

In the city there were many great old houses, storey upon storey high; and in these houses lived much poor people. The higher you went up the great steep stairs the poorer were the people that lived there, so that in the garrets were some so poor, that when the morning came they did not know whether they should have any thing to eat the whole long day. This was very, very sad, and gentle children would have wept if they had seen their pain.

In one of these garrets there lived all alone a little maiden called Zaya. She was an orphan, for her father had died many years before, and her poor mother, who had toiled long and wearily for her dear little daughter – her only child – had died also not long since.

Poor little Zaya had wept so bitterly when she saw her dear mother lying dead, and she had been so sad and sorry for a long time, that she quite forgot that she had no means of living. However, the poor people who lived in the house had given her part of their own food, so that she did not starve.

Then after a while she had tried to work for herself and earn her own living. Her mother had taught her to make flowers out of paper; so she made a lot of flowers, and when she had a full basket she took them into the street and sold them. She made flowers of many kinds, roses and lilies, and violets, and snowdrops, and primroses, and mignonette, and many beautiful sweet flowers that only grow in the Country Under the Sunset. Some of them she could make without any pattern, but others she could not, so when she wanted a pattern she took her basket of paper and scissors, and paste, and brushes, and all the things she used, and went into the garden which a kind lady owned, where there grew many beautiful flowers. There she sat down and worked away, looking at the flowers she wanted.

Sometimes she was very sad, and her tears fell thick and fast as she thought of her dear dead mother. Often she seemed to feel that her mother was looking down at her, and to see her tender smile in the sunshine on the water; then her heart was glad, and she sang so sweetly that the birds came around her and stopped their own singing to listen to her.

She and the birds grew great friends, and sometimes when she had sung a song they would all cry out together, as they sat round her in a ring, in a few notes that seemed to say quite plainly: 'Sing to us again. Sing to us again.'

So she would sing again. Then she would ask them to sing, and they would sing till there was quite a concert. After a while the birds knew her so well that they would come into her room, and they even built their nests there, and they followed her wherever she went. The people used to say: 'Look at the girl with the birds; she must be half a bird herself, for see how the birds know and love her.'

From so many people coming to say things like this, some silly people actually believed that she was partly a bird, and they shook their heads when wise people laughed at them, and said: 'Indeed she must be; listen to her singing; her voice is sweeter even than the birds'.'

So a nickname was applied to her, and naughty boys called it after her in the street, and the nickname was 'Big Bird'. But Zaya did not mind the name; and although often naughty boys said it to her, meaning to cause her pain, she did not dislike it, but the contrary, for she so gloried in the love and trust of her little sweet-voiced pets that she wished to be thought like them.

Indeed it would be well for some naughty little boys and girls if they were as good and harmless as the little birds that work all day long for their helpless baby birds, building nests and bringing food, and sitting so patiently hatching their little speckled eggs.

One evening Zaya sat alone in her garret very sad and lonely. It was a lovely summer's evening, and she sat in the window looking out over the city. She could see over the many streets towards the great cathedral whose spire towered aloft into the sky higher by far even than the great tower of the King's palace. There was hardly a breath of wind, and the smoke went up straight from the chimneys, getting fainter and fainter till it was lost altogether.

Zaya was very sad. For the first time for many days her birds were all away from her at once, and she did not know where they had gone. It seemed to her as if they had deserted her, and she was so lonely, poor little maid, that she wept bitter tears. She was thinking of the story which long ago her dead mother had told her, how Prince Zaphir had slain the giant, and she wondered what the Prince was like, and thought how happy the people must have been when Zaphir and Bluebell were King and Queen. Then she wondered if there were any hungry children in those good days, and if, indeed, as the people said, there were no more giants. So she thought and thought, as she went on with her work before the open window.

Presently she looked up from her work and gazed across the city. There she saw a terrible thing – something so terrible that she gave a low cry of fear and wonder, and leaned out of the window, shading her eyes with her hand to see more clearly.

In the sky beyond the city she saw a vast shadowy form with its arms raised. It was shrouded in a great misty robe that covered it, fading away into air so that she could only see the face and the grim, spectral hands.

The form was so mighty that the city below it seemed like a child's toy. It was still far off the city.

The little maid's heart seemed to stand still with fear as she thought to herself, The giants, then, are not dead. This is another of them.

Quickly she ran down the high stairs and out into the street. There she saw some people, and cried to them, 'Look! look! the giant, the giant!' and pointed towards the form which she still saw moving slowly onwards to the city.

The people looked up, but they could not see anything, and they laughed and said, 'The child is mad.'

Then poor little Zaya was more than ever frightened, and ran down the street crying out still, 'Look! look! the giant, the giant!' But no one heeded her, and all said, 'The child is mad,' and they went on their own ways.

Then the naughty boys came around her and cried out, 'Big Bird has lost her mates. She sees a bigger bird in the sky, and she wants it.' And they made rhymes about her, and sang them as they danced round.

Zaya ran away from them; and she hurried right through the city, and out into the country beyond it, for she still saw the great form before her in the air.

As she went on, and got nearer and nearer to the giant, it grew a little darker. She could see only the clouds; but still there was visible the form of a giant hanging dimly in the air.

A cold mist closed around her as the giant appeared to come onwards towards her. Then she thought of all the poor people in the city, and she hoped that the giant would spare them, and she knelt down before him and lifted up her hands appealingly, and cried aloud: 'Oh, great giant! spare them, spare them!'

But the giant moved onwards still as though he never heard. She cried aloud all the more, 'Oh, great giant! spare them, spare them!' And she bowed down her head and wept, and the giant still, though very slowly, moved onwards towards the city.

There was an old man not far off standing at the door of a small house built of great stones, but the little maid saw him not. His face wore a look of fear and wonder, and when he saw the child kneel and raise her hands, he drew nigh and listened to her voice. When he heard her say, 'Oh, great giant!' he murmured to himself, 'It is then even as I feared. There are more giants, and truly this is another.' He looked upwards, but he saw nothing, and he murmured again, 'I see not, yet this child can see; and yet I feared, for something told me that there was danger. Truly knowledge is blinder than innocence.'

The little maid, still not knowing there was any human being near her, cried out again, with a great cry of anguish: 'Oh, do not, do not, great giant, do them harm. If someone must suffer, let it be me. Take me. I am willing to die, but spare them. Spare them, great giant; and do with me even as thou wilt.' But the giant heeded not.

And Knoal – for he was the old man – felt his eyes fill with tears, and he said to himself, 'Oh, noble child, how brave she is, she would sacrifice herself!' And, coming closer to her, he put his hand upon her head.

Zaya, who was again bowing her head, started and looking round when she felt the touch. However, when she saw that it was Knoal, she was comforted, for she knew how wise and good he was, and felt that if any person could help her, he could. So she clung to him, and hid her face in his breast; and he stroked her hair and comforted her. But still he could see nothing.

The cold mist swept by, and when Zaya looked up, she saw that the giant had passed by, and was moving onwards to the city.

'Come with me, my child,' said the old man; and the two arose, and went into the dwelling built of great stones.

When Zaya entered, she started, for lo! the inside was as a tomb. The old man felt her shudder, for he still held her close to him, and he said: 'Weep not, little one, and fear not. This place reminds me and all who enter it, that to the tomb we must all come at the last. Fear it not, for it has grown to be a cheerful home to me.'

Then the little maid was comforted, and began to examine all around her more closely. She saw all sorts of curious instruments, and many strange and many common herbs and simples hung to dry in bunches on the walls. The old man watched her in silence till her fear was gone, and then he said: 'My child, saw you the features of the giant as he passed?'

She answered, 'Yes.'

'Can you describe his face and form to me?' he asked again.

Whereupon she began to tell him all that she had seen. How the giant was so great that all the sky seemed filled. How the great arms were outspread, veiled in his robe, till far away the shroud was lost in air. How the face was as that of a strong man, pitiless, yet without malice; and that the eyes were blind.

The old man shuddered as he heard, for he knew that the giant was a very terrible one; and his heart wept for the doomed city where so many would perish in the midst of their sin.

They determined to go forth and warn again the doomed people; and making no delay, the old man and the little maid hurried towards the city.

As they left the small house, Zaya saw the giant before them, moving still towards the city. They hurried on; and when they had passed through the cold mist, Zaya looked back, and saw the giant behind them.

Presently they came to the city.

It was a strange sight to see that old man and that little maid flying to tell the people of the terrible plague that was coming upon them. The old man's long white beard and hair and the child's golden locks were swept behind them in the wind, so quick they came. The faces of both were white as death. Behind them, seen only to the eyes of the pure-hearted little maid when she looked back, came ever onwards at slow pace the spectral giant that hung a dark shadow in the evening air.

But those in the city never saw the giant; and when the old man and the little maid warned them, still they heeded not, but scoffed and jeered at them, and said, 'Tush! there are no giants now;' and they went on their way, laughing and jeering.

Then the old man came and stood on a raised place amongst them, on the lowest step of the great fountain with the little maid by his side, and he spake thus: 'Oh, people, dwellers in this land, be warned in time. This pure-hearted child, round whose sweet innocence even the little birds that fear men and women gather in peace, has this night seen in the sky the form of a giant that advances ever onwards menacingly to our city. Believe, oh, believe; and be warned, whilst ye may. To myself even as to you the sky is a blank; and yet see that I believe. For listen to me: all unknowing that another giant had invaded our land, I sat pensive in my dwelling; and, without cause or motive, there came into my heart a sudden fear for the safety of our city. I arose and looked north and south and east and west, and on high and below, but never a sign of danger could I see. So I said to myself, "Mine eyes are dim with a hundred years of watching and waiting, and so I cannot see." And yet, oh people, dwellers in this land, though that century has dimmed mine outer eyes, still it has quickened mine inner eyes – the eyes of my soul. Again I went forth, and lo! this little maid knelt and implored a giant, unseen by me, to spare the city; but he heard her not, or, if he heard, answered her not, and she fell prone. So hither was come to warn you. Yonder, says the maid, he passes onwards to the city. Oh, be warned! be warned in time.'

Still the people heeded not; but they scoffed and jeered the more, and said, 'Lo, the maid and the old man both are mad;' and they passed onwards to their homes – to dancing and feasting as before.

Then the naughty boys came and mocked them, and said that Zaya had lost her birds, and had gone mad; and they made songs, and sang them as they danced round.

Zaya was so sorely grieved for the poor people that she heeded not the cruel boys. Seeing that she did not heed them, some of them got still more rude and wicked; they went a little way off, and threw things at her, and mocked her all the more.

Then, sad of heart, the old man arose, and took the little maid by the hand, and brought her away into the wilderness; and lodged her with him in the house built with great stones. That night Zaya slept with the sweet smell of the drying herbs all around her; and the old man held her hand that she might have no fear.

In the morning Zaya arose betimes, and awoke the old man, who had fallen asleep in his chair.

She went to the doorway and looked out, and then a thrill of gladness came upon her heart; for outside the door, as though waiting to see her, sat all her little birds, and many many more. When the birds saw the little maid they sang a few loud joyous notes, and flew about foolishly for very joy – some of them fluttering their wings and looking so funny that she could not help laughing a little.

When Knoal and Zaya had eaten their frugal breakfast and given some to their little feathered friends, they set out with sorrowful hearts to visit the city, and to try once more to warn the people. The birds flew around them as they went, and to cheer them sang as joyously as they could, although their little hearts were heavy.

As they walked they saw before them the great shadowy giant; and he had now advanced to the very confines of the city.

Once again they warned the people, and great crowds came around them, but only mocked them more than ever; and naughty boys threw stones and sticks at the little birds and killed some of them. Poor Zaya wept bitterly, and Knoal's heart was very sad. After a time, when they had moved from the fountain, Zaya looked up and started with joyous surprise, for the great shadowy giant was nowhere to be seen. She cried out in joy, and the people laughed, and said, 'Cunning child! she sees that we will not believe her, and she pretends that the giant has gone.'

They surrounded her, jeering, and some of them said, 'Let us put her under the fountain and duck her, as a lesson to liars who would frighten us.' Then they approached her with menaces. She clung close to Knoal, who had looked terribly grave when she had said she did not see the giant any longer, and who was now as if in a dream, thinking. But at her touch he seemed to wake up; and he spoke sternly to the people, and rebuked them. But they cried out on him also, and said that as he had aided Zaya in her lie he should be ducked also, and they advanced closer to lay hands on them both.

The hand of one who was a ringleader was already outstretched, when he gave a low cry, and pressed his hand to his side; and, whilst the others turned to look at him in wonder, he cried out in great pain, and screamed horribly. Even whilst the people looked, his face grew blacker and blacker, and he fell down before them, and writhed a while in pain, and then died.

All the people screamed out in terror, and ran away, crying aloud, 'The giant! the giant! he is indeed amongst us!'

They feared all the more that they could not see him.

But before they could leave the market-place, in the centre of which was the fountain, many fell dead, and there their corpses lay.

There in the centre knelt the old man and the little maid, praying; and the birds sat perched around the fountain, mute and still, and there was no sound heard save the cries of the people far off. Then their wailing sounded louder and louder, for the giant – Plague – was amongst and around them, and there was no escaping, for it was now too late to fly.

Alas! in the Country Under the Sunset there was much weeping that day; and when the night came there was little sleep, for there was fear in some hearts and pain in others. None were still except the dead, who lay stark about the city, so still and lifeless that even the cold light of the moon and the shadows of the drifting clouds moving over them could not make them seem as though they lived.

And for many a long day there was pain and grief and death in the Country Under the Sunset.

Knoal and Zaya did all they could to help the poor people, but it was hard indeed to aid them, for the unseen giant was amongst them, wandering through the city to and fro, so that none could tell where next he would lay his ice-cold hand.

Some people fled away out of the city; but it was little use, for go how they would and fly never so fast they were still within the grasp of the unseen giant. Ever and anon he turned their warm hearts to ice with his breath and his touch, and they fell dead.

Some, like those within the city, were spared, and of these some perished of hunger, and the rest crept sadly back to the city and lived or died amongst their friends. And it was all, oh! so sad, for there was nothing but grief and fear and weeping from morn till night.

Now, see how Zaya's little bird friends helped her in her need.

They seemed to see the coming of the giant when no one – not even the little maid herself – could see anything, and they managed to tell her when there was danger just as well as though they could talk.

At first Knoal and she went home every evening to the house built of great stones to sleep, and came again to the city in the morning, and stayed with the poor sick people, comforting them and feeding them, and giving them medicine which Knoal, from his great wisdom, knew would do them good. Thus they saved many precious human lives, and those who were rescued were very thankful, and henceforth ever after lived holier and more unselfish lives.

After a few days, however, they found that the poor sick people needed help even more at night than in the day, and so they came and lived in the city altogether, helping the stricken folk day and night.

At the earliest dawn Zaya would go forth to breathe the morning air; and there, just waked from sleep, would be her feathered friends waiting for her. They sang glad songs of joy, and came and perched on her shoulders and her head, and kissed her. Then, if she went to go towards any place where, during the night, the plague had laid his deadly hand, they would flutter before her, and try to impede her, and scream out in their own tongue, 'Go back! go back!'

They pecked of her bread and drank of her cup before she touched them; and when there was danger – for the cold hand of the giant was placed everywhere – they would cry, 'No, no!' and she would not touch the food, or let anyone else do so. Often it happened that, even whilst it pecked at the bread or drank of the cup, a poor little bird would fall down and flutter its wings and die; but all they that died, did so with a chirp of joy, looking at their little mistress, for whom they had gladly perished. Whenever the little birds found that the bread and the cup were pure and free from danger, they would look up at Zaya jauntily, and flap their wings and try to crow, and seemed so saucy that the poor sad little maiden would smile.

There was one old bird that always took a second, and often a great many pecks at the bread when it was good, so that he got quite a hearty meal; and sometimes he would go on feeding till Zaya would shake her finger at him and say, 'Greedy!' and he would hop away as if he had done nothing.

There was one other dear little bird – a robin, with a breast as red as the sunset – that loved Zaya more than one can think. When he tried the food and found that it was safe to eat, he would take a little tiny piece in his bill, and fly up and put it in her mouth.

Every little bird that drank from Zaya's cup and found it good raised its head to say grace; and ever since then the little birds do the same, and they never forget to say their grace – as some thankless children do.

Thus Knoal and Zaya lived, although many around them died, and the giant still remained in the city. So many people died that one began to wonder that so many were left; for it was only when the town began to get thinned that people thought of the vast numbers that had lived in it.

Poor little Zaya had got so pale and thin that she looked like a shadow, and Knoal's form was bent more with the sufferings of a few weeks than it had been by his century of age. But although the two were weary and worn, they still kept on their good work of aiding the sick.

Many of the little birds were dead.

One morning the old man was very weak – so weak that he could hardly stand. Zaya got frightened about him, and said, 'Are you ill, father?' for she always called him father now.

He answered her in a voice alas! hoarse and low, but very, very tender: 'My child, I fear the end is coming: take me home, that there I may die.'

At his words Zaya gave a low cry and fell on her knees beside him, and buried her head in his bosom and wept bitterly, whilst she hugged him close. But she had little time for weeping, for the old man struggled up to his feet, and, seeing that he wanted aid, she dried her tears and helped him.

The old man took his staff, and with Zaya helping to support him, got as far as the fountain in the midst of the market-place; and there, on the lowest step, he sank down as though exhausted. Zaya felt him grow cold as ice, and she knew that the chilly hand of the giant had been laid upon him.

Then, without knowing why, she looked up to where she had last seen the giant as Knoal and she had stood beside the fountain. And lo! as she looked, holding Knoal's hand, she saw the shadowy form of the terrible giant who had been so long invisible growing more and more clearly out of the clouds.

His face was stern as ever, and his eyes were still blind.

Zaya cried to the giant, still holding Knoal tightly by the hand: 'Not him, not him! Oh, mighty giant! not him! not him!' and she bowed down her head and wept.

There was such anguish in her heart that to the blind eyes of the shadowy giant came tears that fell like dew on the forehead of the old man. Knoal spake to Zaya: 'Grieve not, my child. I am glad that you see the giant again, for I have hope that he will leave our city free from woe. I am the last victim, and I gladly die.'

Then Zaya knelt to the giant, and said: 'Spare him! oh! spare him and take me! but spare him! spare him!'

The old man raised himself upon his elbow as he lay, and spake to her: 'Grieve not, little one, and repine not. Sooth I know that you would gladly give your life for mine. But we must give for the good of others that which is dearer to us than our lives. Bless you, my little one, and be good. Farewell! farewell!'

As he spake the last word he grew cold as death, and his spirit passed away.

Zaya knelt down and prayed; and when she looked up she saw the shadowy giant moving away.

The giant turned as he passed on, and Zaya saw that his blind eyes looked towards her as though he were trying to see. He raised the great shadowy arms, draped still in his shroud of mist, as though blessing her; and she thought that the wind that came by her moaning bore the echo of the words: 'Innocence and devotion save the land.'

Presently she saw far off the great shadowy giant Plague moving away to the border of the land, and passing between the guardian spirits out through the portal into the deserts beyond – for ever.

The Dualitists

Once Henry Irving had severed his partnership agreement and, aided by Bram Stoker as his manager, become independent, he proceeded to star in a lengthy run of Shakespearian plays at the Lyceum. These included *Hamlet*, *Macbeth*, *Henry VIII*, and *Richard III*. Flushed with the success and acclaim of these productions, Irving turned to more varied plays and in 1880 put on *The Corsican Brothers*, based on the famous novel by Alexandre Dumas *père*. This story of twin brothers who had been joined together physically at birth, were later separated surgically, yet retained a psychic bond, had long intrigued Irving because of his interest in the supernatural. Stoker, too, shared his enthusiasm for the book, writing later, 'The story is so weird that it obtains a new credibility from unfamiliar *entourage*. Corsica has always been accepted as a land of strange happenings and stormy passions. Things are accepted under such circumstances which would ordinarily be passed as bizarre.'

During the months of preparation before the opening of the production in September 1880, Irving and Stoker at their supper meetings frequently discussed the story of double identity, with its appearance of a ghost predicting the death of one of the twins in a duel. A major problem was how best to create supernatural phenomena on the stage and this was finally solved by clever use of lighting and make-up. Another headache was the 'double', as Stoker has also explained:

In a play where one actor plays two parts there is usually at least one time when the two have to be seen together. In *The Corsican Brothers*, where one of the two *sees the other seeing his brother*, more than one double is required. At the Lyceum, Irving's chief double was Arthur Morrison, who though a much smaller man than Irving, resembled him faintly in his facial aspect. He actually had a firm belief that he *was* Irving's double and that no one could tell them apart!

Bram Stoker himself also had a small part in the production. Unable to get enough actors to appear in a masked-ball scene, Irving coerced his manager into appearing as one of the revellers. *The Corsican Brothers* became an immediate sensation with London theatre-goers and ran uninterrupted for 190 performances. Bram's work on the play also gave him the idea for the following story, 'The Dualitists; or, the Death Doom of the Double Born', to give the tale its full title. Appropriately, he submitted the story for publication in *The Theatre Annual* of 1887 and it was published in the Christmas issue. There it has remained forgotten for the past one hundred years.

I   BIS DAT QUI NON CITO DAT

THERE WAS JOY in the house of Bubb.

For ten long years had Ephraim and Sophonisba Bubb mourned in vain the loneliness of their life. Unavailingly had they gazed into the emporia of baby-linen, and fixed their searching glances on the basket-makers' warehouses where the cradles hung in tempting rows. In vain had they prayed, and sighed, and groaned, and wished, and waited, and wept, but never had even a ray of hope been held out by the family physician.

But now at last the wished-for moment had arrived. Month after month had flown by on leaden wings, and the destined days had slowly measured their course. The months had become weeks; the weeks had dwindled down to days; the days had been attenuated to hours; the hours had lapsed into minutes, the minutes had slowly died away, and but seconds remained.

Ephraim Bubb sat cowering on the stairs, and tried with high-strung ears to catch the strain of blissful music from the lips of his first-born. There was silence in the house – silence as of the deadly calm before the cyclone. Ah! Ephraim Bubb, little thinkest thou that another moment may for ever destroy the peaceful, happy course of

thy life, and open to thy too-craving eyes the portals of that wondrous land where childhood reigns supreme, and where the tyrant infant with the wave of his tiny hand and the imperious treble of his tiny voice sentences his parent to the deadly vault beneath the castle moat. As the thought strikes thee thou becomest pale. How thou tremblest as thou findest thyself upon the brink of the abyss! Wouldst that thou could recall the past!

But hark! the die is cast for good or ill. The long years of praying and hoping have found an end at last. From the chamber within comes a sharp cry, which shortly after is repeated. Ah! Ephraim, that cry is the feeble effort of childish lips as yet unused to the rough, worldly form of speech to frame the word 'father'. In the glow of thy transport all doubts are forgotten; and when the doctor cometh forth as the harbinger of joy he findeth thee radiant with new-found delight.

'My dear sir, allow me to congratulate you – to offer twofold felicitations. Mr Bubb, sir, you are the father of twins!'

2 HALCYON DAYS

The twins were the finest children that ever were seen – so at least said the *cognoscenti*, and the parents were not slow to believe. The nurse's opinion was in itself a proof.

It was not, ma'am, that they was fine for twins, but they was fine for singles, and she had ought to know, for she had nussed a many in her time, both twins *and* singles. All they wanted was to have their dear little legs cut off and little wings on their dear little shoulders, for to be put one on each side of a white marble tombstone, cut beautiful, sacred to the relic of Ephraim Bubb, that they might, sir, if so be that missus was to survive the father of two such lovely twins – although she would make bold to say, and no offence intended, that a handsome gentleman, though a trifle or two older than his good lady, though for the matter of that she heerd that gentlemen was never too old at all, and for her own part she liked them the better for it: not like bits of boys that didn't know their own minds – that a gentleman what was the father of two such 'eavenly twins (God bless them!) couldn't be called anything but a boy; though for the matter of that she never knowed in her experience – which it was much – of a boy as had such twins, or any twins at all so much for the matter of that.

The twins were the idols of their parents, and at the same time their pleasure and their pain. Did Zerubbabel cough, Ephraim would start from his balmy slumbers with an agonized cry of consternation, for visions of innumerable twins black in the face from croup haunted his nightly pillow. Did Zacariah rail at ethereal expansion, Sophonisba with pallid hue and dishevelled locks would fly to the cradle of her offspring. Did pins torture or strings afflict, or flannel or flies tickle, or light dazzle, or darkness affright, or hunger or thirst assail the synchronous productions, the household of Bubb would be roused from quiet slumbers or the current of its manifold workings changed.

The twins grew apace; were weaned; teethed; and at length arrived at the stage of three years!

> They grew in beauty side by side,
> They filled one home, *etc*.

3 RUMOURS OF WARS

Harry Merford and Tommy Santon lived in the same range of villas as Ephraim Bubb. Harry's parents had taken up their abode in no. 25, no. 27 was happy in the perpetual sunshine of Tommy's smiles, and between these two residences Ephraim Bubb reared his blossoms, the number of his mansion being 26. Harry and Tommy had been accustomed from the earliest times to meet each other daily. Their primal method of communication had been by the housetops, till their respective sires had been obliged to pay compensation to Bubb for damages to his roof and dormer windows; and from that time they had been forbidden by the home authorities to meet, whilst their mutual neighbour had taken the precaution of having his garden walls pebble-dashed and topped with broken glass to prevent their incursions. Harry and Tommy, however, being gifted with daring souls, lofty, ambitious, impetuous natures, and strong seats to their trousers, defied the rugged walls of Bubb and continued to meet in secret.

Compared with these two youths, Castor and Pollux, Damon and Pythias, Eloisa and Abelard are but tame examples of duality or constancy and friendship. All the poets from Hyginus to Schiller might sing of noble deeds and desperate dangers held as naught for friendship's sake, but they would have been mute had they but known of the mutual affection of Harry and Tommy. Day by day, and often night by night, would these two brave the perils of nurse, and father, and mother, of whip and imprisonment, and hunger and thirst, and solitude and darkness to meet together. What they discussed in secret none other knew. What deeds of darkness were perpetrated in their symposia none could tell. Alone they met, alone they remained, and alone they departed to their several abodes. There was in the garden of Bubb a summer-house overgrown with trailing plants, and surrounded by young poplars which the fond father had planted on his children's natal day, and whose rapid growth he had proudly watched. These trees quite obscured the summer-house, and here Harry and Tommy, knowing after a careful observation that none ever entered the place, held their conclaves. Time after time they met in full security and followed their customary pursuit of pleasure. Let us raise the mysterious veil and see what was the great Unknown at whose shrine they bent the knee.

Harry and Tommy had each been given as a Christmas box a new knife; and for a long time – nearly a year – these knives, similar in size and pattern, were their chief delights. With them they cut and hacked in their respective homes all things which would not be likely to be noticed; for the young gentlemen were wary and had no wish that their moments of pleasure should be atoned for by moments of pain. The insides of drawers, and desks, and boxes, the underparts of tables and chairs, the backs of pictures frames, even the floors, where corners of the carpets could surreptitiously be turned up, all bore marks of their craftsmanship; and to compare notes on these artistic triumphs was a source of joy. At length, however, a critical time came, some new field of action should be opened up, for the old appetites were sated, and the old joys had begun to pall. It was absolutely necessary that the existing schemes of destruction should be enlarged; and yet this could hardly be done without a terrible risk of discovery, for the limits of safety had long since been reached and passed. But, be the risk great or small, some new ground should be broken – some new joy found, for the old earth was barren, and the craving for pleasure was growing fiercer with each successive day.

The crisis had come: who could tell the issue?

4 THE TUCKET SOUNDS

They met in the arbour, determined to discuss this grave question. The heart of each was big with revolution, the head of each was full of scheme and strategy, and the pocket of each was full of sweet-stuff, the sweeter for being stolen. After having dispatched the sweets, the conspirators proceeded to explain their respective views with regard to the enlargement of their artistic operations. Tommy unfolded with much pride a scheme which he had in contemplation of cutting a series of holes in the sounding board of the piano, so as to destroy its musical properties. Harry was in no wise behindhand in his ideas of reform. He had conceived the project of cutting the canvas at the back of his great-grandfather's portrait, which his father held in high regard among his lares and penates, so that in time when the picture should be moved the skin of paint would be broken, the head fall bodily out from the frame.

At this point of the council a brilliant thought occurred to Tommy. 'Why should not the enjoyment be doubled, and the musical instruments and family pictures of both establishments be sacrificed on the altar of pleasure?' This was agreed to *nem. con.*; and then the meeting adjourned for dinner. When they next met it was evident that there was a screw loose somewhere – that there was 'something rotten in the state of Denmark'. After a little fencing on both sides, it came out that all the schemes of domestic reform had been foiled by maternal vigilance, and that so sharp had been the reprimand consequent on a partial discovery of the schemes that they would have to be abandoned – till such time, at least, as increased physical strength would allow the reformers to laugh to scorn parental threats and injunctions.

Sadly the two forlorn youths took out their knives and regarded them; sadly, sadly they thought, as erst did Othello, of all the fair chances of honour and triumph and glory gone for ever. They compared knives with almost the fondness of doting parents. There they were – so equal in size and strength and beauty – dimmed by no corrosive rust, tarnished by no stain, and with unbroken edges of the keenness of Saladin's sword.

So like were the knives that but for the initials scratched in the handles neither boy could have been sure which was his own. After a little while they began mutually to brag of the superior excellence of their respective weapons. Tommy insisted that his was the sharper, Harry asserted that his was the stronger of the two. Hotter and hotter grew the war of words. The tempers of Harry and Tommy got inflamed, and their boyish bosoms glowed with manly thoughts of daring and hate. But there was abroad in that hour a spirit of a bygone age – one that penetrated even to that dim arbour in the grove of Bubb. The world-old scheme of ordeal was whispered by the spirit in the ear of each, and suddenly the tumult was allayed. With one impulse the boys suggested that they should test the quality of their knives by the ordeal of the Hack.

No sooner said than done. Harry held out his knife edge uppermost; and Tommy, grasping his firmly by the handle, brought down the edge of the blade crosswise on Harry's. The process was then reversed, and Harry became in turn the aggressor. Then they paused and eagerly looked for the result. It was not hard to see; in each knife were two great dents of equal depth; and so it was necessary to renew the contest, and seek a further proof.

What needs it to relate seriatim the details of that direful strife? The sun had long since gone down, and the moon with fair, smiling face had long risen over the roof of Bubb, when, wearied and jaded, Harry and Tommy sought their respective homes. Alas! the splendour of the knives was gone for ever. Ichabod! – Ichabod! the glory had departed and naught remained but two useless wrecks, with keen edges destroyed, and now like unto nothing save the serried hills of Spain.

But though they mourned for their fondly cherished weapons, the hearts of the boys were glad; for the bygone day had opened to their gaze a prospect of pleasure as boundless as the limits of the world.

5 THE FIRST CRUSADE

From that day a new era dawned in the lives of Harry and Tommy. So long as the resources of the parental establishments could hold out so long would their new amusement continue. Subtly they obtained surreptitious possession of articles of family cutlery not in general use, and brought them one by one to their rendezvous. These came fair and spotless from the sanctity of the butler's pantry. Alas! they returned not as they came.

But in course of time the stock of available cutlery became exhausted, and again the inventive faculties of the youths were called into requisition. They reasoned thus: 'The knife game, it is true, is played out, but the excitement of the hack is not to be dispensed with. Let us carry, then, this great idea into new worlds; let us still live in the sunshine of pleasure; let us continue to hack, but with objects other than knives.'

It was done. Not knives now engaged the attention of the ambitious youths. Spoons and forks were daily flattened and beaten out of shape; pepper castor met pepper castor in combat, and both were borne dying from the field; candlesticks met in fray to part no more on this side of the grave; even epergnes were used as weapons in the crusade of hack.

At last all the resources of the butler's pantry became exhausted, and then began a system of miscellaneous destruction that proved in a little time ruinous to the furniture of the respective homes of Harry and Tommy. Mrs Santon and Mrs Merford began to notice that the wear and tear in their households became excessive. Day after day some new domestic calamity seemed to have occurred. Today a valuable edition of some book whose luxurious binding made it an object for public display would appear to have suffered some dire misfortune, for the edges were frayed and broken and the back loose if not altogether displaced; tomorrow the same awful fate would seem to have followed some miniature frame; the day following the legs of some chair or spider-table would show signs of extraordinary hardship. Even in the nursery the sounds of lamentation were heard.

It was a thing of daily occurrence for the little girls to state that when going to bed at night they had laid their dear dollies in their beds with tender care, but that when again seeking them in the period of recess they had found them with all their beauty gone, with legs and arms amputated and faces beaten from all semblance of human form.

Then articles of crockery began to be missed. The thief could in no case be discovered, and the wages of the servants, from constant stoppages, began to be nominal rather than real. Mrs Merford and Mrs Santon mourned their losses, but Harry and Tommy gloated day after day over their spoils, which lay in an ever-increasing heap in the hidden grove of Bubb. To such an extent had the fondness of the hack now grown that with both youths it was an infatuation – a madness – a frenzy.

At length one awful day arrived. The butlers of the houses of Merford and Santon, harassed by constant losses and complaints, and finding that their breakage account was in excess of their wages, determined to seek some sphere of occupation where, if they did not meet with a suitable reward or recognition of their services, they would, at least, not lose whatever fortune and reputation they had already acquired. Accordingly, before rendering up their keys and the goods entrusted to their charge, they proceeded to take a preliminary stock of their own accounts, to make sure of their accredited accuracy. Dire indeed was their distress when they knew to the full the havoc which had been wrought; terrible their anguish of the present, bitter their thoughts of the future. Their hearts, bowed down with weight of woe, failed them quite; reeled the strong brains that had erst overcome foes of deadlier spirit than grief; and fell their stalwart forms prone on the floors of their respective sancta sanctorum.

Late in the day when their services were required they were sought for in bower and hall, and at length discovered where they lay.

But alas for justice! They were accused of being drunk and for having, whilst in that degraded condition, deliberately injured all the property on which they could lay hands. Were not the evidences of their guilt patent to all in the hecatombs of the destroyed? Then they were charged with all the evils wrought in the houses, and on their indignant denial Harry and Tommy, each in his own home, according to their concerted scheme of action, stepped forward and relieved their minds of the deadly weight that had for long in secret borne them down. The story of each ran that time after time he had seen the butler, when he thought that nobody was looking, knocking knives together in the pantry, chairs and books and pictures in the drawing-room and study, dolls in the nursery, and plates in the kitchen. Then, indeed, was the master of each household stern and uncompromising in his demands for justice. Each butler was committed to the charge of myrmidons of the law under the double charge of drunkenness and wilful destruction of property.

Softly and sweetly slept Harry and Tommy in their little beds that night. Angels seemed to whisper to them, for they smiled as though lost in pleasant dreams. The rewards given by proud and grate-ful parents lay in their pockets, and in their hearts the happy consciousness of having done their duty.

Truly sweet should be the slumbers of the just.

6 'LET THE DEAD PAST BURY ITS DEAD'

It might be supposed that now the operations of Harry and Tommy would be obliged to be abandoned.

Not so, however. The minds of these youths were of no common order, nor were their souls of such weak nature as to yield at the first summons of necessity. Like Nelson, they knew not fear; like Napoleon, they held 'impossible' to be the adjective of fools; and they revelled in the glorious truth that in the lexicon of youth is no such word as 'fail'. Therefore on the day following the *éclaircissement* of the butlers' misdeeds, they met in the arbour to plan a new campaign.

In the hour when all seemed blackest to them, and when the narrowing walls of possibility hedged them in on every side, thus ran the deliberations of these dauntless youths: 'We have played out the meaner things that are inanimate and inert; why not then trench on the domains of life? The dead have lapsed into the regions of the forgotten past – let the living look to themselves.'

That night they met when all households had retired to balmy sleep, and naught but the amorous wailings of nocturnal cats told of the existence of life and sentience. Each bore into the arbour in his arms a pet rabbit and a piece of sticking-plaster. Then, in the peaceful, quiet moonlight, commenced a work of mystery, blood, and gloom. The proceedings began by the fixing of a piece of sticking-plaster over the mouth of each rabbit to prevent it making a noise, if so inclined. Then Tommy held up his rabbit by its scutty tail, and it hung wriggling, a white mass in the moonlight. Slowly Harry raised his rabbit holding it in the same manner, and when level with his head brought it down on Tommy's client.

But the chances had been miscalculated. The boys held firmly to the tails, but the chief portions of the rabbits fell to earth. Ere the doomed beasts could escape, however, the operators had pounced upon them, and this time holding them by the hind legs renewed the trial.

Deep into the night the game was kept up, and the eastern sky began to show signs of approaching day as each boy bore triumphantly the dead corse of his favourite bunny and placed it within its sometime hutch.

Next night the same game was renewed with a new rabbit on each side, and for more than a week – so long as the hutches supplied the wherewithal – the battle was sustained. True that there were sad hearts and red eyes in the juveniles of Santon and Merford as one by one the beloved pets were found dead, but Harry and Tommy, with the hearts of heroes steeled to suffering and deaf to the pitiful cries of childhood, still fought the good fight on to the bitter end.

When the supply of rabbits was exhausted, other munition was not wanting, and for some days the war was continued with white mice, dormice, hedgehogs, guinea pigs, pigeons, lambs, canaries, para-keets, linnets, squirrels, parrots, marmots, poodles, ravens, tortoises, terriers, and cats. Of these, as might be expected, the most difficult to manipulate were the terriers and the cats, and of these two classes the proportion of the difficulties in the way of terrier-hacking was, when compared with those of cat-hacking, about that which the simple lac of the British pharmacopoeia bears to water in the compound which dairymen palm off upon a too-confiding public as milk. More than once when engaged in the rapturous delights of cat-hacking had Harry and Tommy wished that the silent tomb could ope its ponderous and massy jaws and engulf them, for the feline victims were not patient in their death agonies, and often broke the bonds in which the security of the artists rested, and turned fiercely on their executioners.

At last, however, all the animals available were sacrificed; but the passion for hacking still remained. How was it all to end?

7   A CLOUD WITH GOLDEN LINING

Tommy and Harry sat in the arbour dejected and disconsolate. They wept like two Alexanders because there were no more worlds to conquer. At last the conviction had been forced upon them that the resources available for hacking were exhausted. That very morning they had had a desperate battle, and their attire showed the ravages of direful war. Their hats were battered into shapeless masses, their shoes were soleless and heel-less and had the uppers broken, the ends of their braces, their sleeves, and their trousers were frayed, and had they indulged in the manly luxury of coat-tails these too would have gone.

Truly, hacking had become an absorbing passion with them. Long and fiercely had they been swept onwards on the wings of the demon of strife, and powerless at the best of times had been the promptings of good; but now, heated with combat, maddened by the equal success of arms, and with the lust for victory still unsated, they longed more fiercely than ever for some new pleasure: like tigers that have tasted blood they thirsted for a larger and more potent libation.

As they sat, with their souls in a tumult of desire and despair, some evil genius guided into the garden the twin blossoms of the tree of Bubb. Hand in hand Zacariah and Zerubbabel advanced from the back door; they had escaped from their nurses, and with the exploring instinct of humanity, advanced boldly into the great world – the *terra incognita*, the *ultima Thule* of the paternal domain.

In the course of time they approached the hedge of poplars, from behind which the anxious eyes of Harry and Tommy looked for their approach, for the boys knew that where the twins were the nurses were accustomed to be gathered together, and they feared discovery if their retreat should be cut off.

It was a touching sight, these lovely babes, alike in form, feature, size, expression, and dress; in fact, so like each other that one 'might not have told either from which'. When the startling similarity was recognized by Harry and Tommy, each suddenly turned, and, grasping the other by the shoulder, spoke in a keen whisper: 'Hack! They are exactly equal! This is the very apotheosis of our art!'

With excited faces and trembling hands they laid their plans to lure the unsuspecting babes within the precincts of their charnel house, and they were so successful in their efforts that in a little time the twins had toddled behind the hedge and were lost to the sight of the parental mansion.

Harry and Tommy were not famed for gentleness within the immediate precincts of their respective homes, but it would have delighted the heart of any philanthropist to see the kindly manner in which they arranged for the pleasures of the helpless babes. With smiling faces and playful words and gentle wiles they led them within the arbour, and then, under pretence of giving them some of those sudden jumps in which infants rejoice, they raised them from the ground. Tommy held Zacariah across his arm with his baby moon-face smiling up at the cobwebs on the arbour roof, and Harry, with a mighty effort, raised the cherubic Zerubbabel aloft.

Each nerved himself for a great endeavour, Harry to give, Tommy to endure a shock, and then the form of Zerubbabel was seen whirling through the air round Harry's glowing and determined face. There was a sickening crash and the arm of Tommy yielded visibly.

The pasty face of Zerubbabel had fallen fair on that of Zacariah, for Tommy and Harry were by this time artists of too great experience to miss so simple a mark. The putty-like noses collapsed, the putty-like cheeks became for a moment flattened, and when in an instant more they parted, the faces of both were dabbled in gore. Immediately the firmament was rent with a series of such yells as might have awakened the dead. Forthwith from the house of Bubb came the echoes in parental cries and footsteps. As the sounds of scurrying feet rang through the mansion, Harry cried to Tommy: 'They will be on us soon. Let us cut to the roof of the stable and draw up the ladder.'

Tommy answered by a nod, and the two boys, regardless of consequences, and bearing each a twin, ascended to the roof of the stable by means of a ladder which usually stood against the wall, and which they pulled up after them.

As Ephraim Bubb issued from his house in pursuit of his lost darlings, the sight which met his gaze froze his very soul. There, on the coping of the stable roof, stood Harry and Tommy renewing their game. They seemed like two young demons forging some diabolical implement, for each in turn the twins were lifted high in air and let fall with stunning force on the supine form of its fellow. How Ephraim felt none but a tender and imaginative father can conceive. It would be enough to wring the heart of even a callous parent to see his children, the darlings of his old age – his own beloved twins – being sacrificed to the brutal pleasure of unregenerate youths, without being made unconsciously and helplessly guilty of the crime of fratricide.

Loudly did Ephraim and also Sophonisba, who, with dishevelled locks, had now appeared upon the scene, bewail their unhappy lot and shriek in vain for aid; but by rare ill-chance no eyes save their own saw the work of butchery or heard the shrieks of anguish and despair. Wildly did Ephraim, mounting on the shoulders of his spouse, strive, but in vain, to scale the stable wall.

Baffled in every effort, he rushed into the house and appeared in a moment bearing in his hands a double-barrelled gun, into which he poured the contents of a shot pouch as he ran. He came anigh the stable and hailed the murderous youths: 'Drop them twins and come down here or I'll shoot you like a brace of dogs.'

'Never!' exclaimed the heroic two with one impulse, and continued their awful pastime with a zest tenfold as they knew that the agonized eyes of parents wept at the cause of their joy.

'Then die!' shrieked Ephraim, as he fired both barrels, right – left, at the hackers.

But, alas! love for his darlings shook the hand that never shook before. As the smoke cleared off and Ephraim recovered from the kick of his gun, he heard a loud twofold laugh of triumph and saw Harry and Tommy, all unhurt, waving in the air the trunks of the twins – the fond father had blown the heads completely off his own offspring.

Tommy and Harry shrieked aloud in glee, and after playing catch with the bodies for some time, seen only by the agonized eyes of the infanticide and his wife, flung them high in the air. Ephraim leaped forward to catch what had once been Zacariah, and Sophonisba grabbed wildly for the loved remains of her Zerubbabel.

But the weight of the bodies and the height from which they fell were not reckoned by either parent, and from being ignorant of a simple dynamical formula each tried to effect an object which calm, common sense, united with scientific knowledge, would have told them was impossible. The masses fell, and Ephraim and Sophonisba were stricken dead by the falling twins, who were thus posthumously guilty of the crime of parricide.

An intelligent coroner's jury found the parents guilty of the crimes of infanticide and suicide, on the evidence of Harry and Tommy, who swore, reluctantly, that the inhuman monsters, maddened by drink, had killed their offspring by shooting them into the air out of a cannon

– since stolen – whence like curses they had fallen on their own heads; and that then they had slain themselves *suis manibus* with their own hands.

Accordingly Ephraim and Sophonisba were denied the solace of Christian burial, and were committed to the earth with 'maimed rites', and had stakes driven through their middles to pin them down in their unhallowed graves till the crack of doom.

Harry and Tommy were each rewarded with national honours and were knighted, even at their tender years.

Fortune seemed to smile upon them all the long after-years, and they lived to a ripe old age, hale of body, and respected and beloved of all.

Often in the golden summer eves, when all nature seemed at rest, when the oldest cask was opened and the largest lamp was lit, when the chestnuts glowed in the embers and the kid turned on the spit, when their great-grandchildren pretended to mend fictional armour and to trim an imaginary helmet's plume, when the shuttles of the good wives of their grandchildren went flashing each through its proper loom, with shouting and with laughter they were accustomed to tell the tale of THE DUALITISTS; OR, THE DEATH DOOM OF THE DOUBLE BORN.

Death in the Wings

One of the first plays in which Henry Irving had been acclaimed as a young actor was *The Bells*. He appeared in it in 1871 and revived it frequently, and with great success, over the next thirty-four years. In fact, he played the famous French melodrama more than 600 times and made it almost a fixture during his years at the Lyceum. In 1883 when Irving decided to venture across the Atlantic for what was to prove the first of several tours of America, he included *The Bells* in his repertoire. The story of Mathias, the pillar of society with a murderous past, it was based on a classic French novel of terror written in 1850 by Emile Erckmann and Alexandre Chatrian. So impressive was Irving in the leading role that the occult scholar, Montague Summers, wrote later, 'Never have I seen, and certainly never can I hope to see again, such acting upon the English stage. Mathias as played by Henry Irving was a character as great as Hamlet or Lear, Othello or Macbeth.'

The tour of America was an eventful one, both for Irving on stage (where he was greeted enthusiastically by audiences from one coast to the other) and for Stoker, busy as ever behind the scenes. One night, while appearing at the Star Theatre in New York, an accident with some of the scenery for *The Bells* provided Stoker with the idea for this next story. Arriving at the theatre before an evening performance, Stoker was confronted by Arthur Arnott, the man in charge of the props and scenery, who pointed to a pile of debris on the stage. It had been a piece of machinery operating the set which enabled one of the 'ghosts' in *The Bells* to appear and disappear. The machinery was situated at the spot where Irving made a dramatic entrance, Arnott informed Stoker, and if it had fallen while the actor had been on stage it would surely have killed him. The machinery was safely repaired, though no cause for its sudden collapse could be found. After the performance Stoker was able to tell the Chief of his narrow escape, and both enjoyed a good

Death in the Wings

laugh about the incident. Indeed, their supper conversation that
night was almost entirely taken up with stories of accidents in the
theatre, and Irving recounted one tale he had heard of a property
master who had deliberately used a piece of scenery to exact
revenge of an actor who had wronged him. The story intrigued
Stoker, and shortly afterwards he used the idea as the basis for
'Death In The Wings'. The facts are much as Irving related them
during that New York supper – only the names were changed. The
tale was originally published in the American monthly journal
Collier's Magazine in November 1888.

I DARE SAY SOME of you will remember the case of a harlequin who
was killed in an accident in the pantomime a few years ago. We
needn't mention names; Mortimer will do for a name to call him by –
Henry Mortimer. The cause of it was never found out. But I knew it;
and I've kept silent for so long that I may speak now without hurting
anyone. They're all dead long ago that was interested in the death of
Henry Mortimer or of the man who wrought his death.

Any of you who know of the case will remember what a handsome,
dapper, well-built man Mortimer was. To my own mind he was the
handsomest man I ever saw. Mortimer was also the nimblest chap at
the traps I ever saw. He was so sure of himself that he would have extra
weight put on so that when the counter weights fell he'd shoot up five
or six feet higher than anyone else could even try to. Moreover, he
had a way of drawing up his legs when in the air – the way a frog
does when he is swimming – that made his jump look ever so much
higher.

I think the girls were all in love with him, the way they used to stand
in the wings when the time was comin' for his entrance. That wouldn't
have mattered much, for girls are always falling in love with some man
or other, but it made trouble, as it always does when the married ones
take the same start. There were several of these that were always after
him, more shame for them, with husbands of their own. That was
dangerous enough, and hard to stand for a man who might mean to be
decent in any way. But the real trial – and the real trouble, too – was
none other than the young wife of my own guvnor, Jack Haliday, the
Master Machinist, and she was more than flesh and blood could stand.

She had come into the panto, the season before as a high-kicker – and she could! She could kick higher than girls that was more than a foot taller than her; for she was a wee bit of a thing and as pretty as pie; a gold-haired, blue-eyed, slim thing with much the figure of a boy, except for . . . and they saved her from any mistaken idea of that kind. Jack Haliday went crazy over her, and when the notice was up, and there was no young spark with plenty of oof coming along to do the proper thing by her, she married him. It was, when they was joined, what you would call a marriage of convenience; but after a bit they two got on very well, and we all thought she was beginning to like the old man – for Jack was old enough to be her father, with a bit to spare. In the summer, when the house was closed, he took her to the Isle of Man; and when they came back he made no secret of it that he'd had the happiest time of his life. She looked quite happy, too, and treated him affectionate; and we all began to think that the marriage had not been a failure at any rate.

Things began to change, however, when the panto rehearsals began next year. Old Jack began to look unhappy, and didn't take no interest in his work. Loo – that was Mrs Haliday's name – didn't seem over fond of him now, and was generally impatient when he was by. Nobody said anything about this, however, to us men; but the married women smiled and nodded their heads and whispered that perhaps there were reasons. One day on the stage, when the harlequinade rehearsal was beginning, someone mentioned as how perhaps Mrs Haliday wouldn't be dancing that year, and they smiled as if they was all in the secret. Then Mrs Jack ups and gives them Johnny-up-the-orchard for not minding their own business and telling a pack of lies, and such like. The rest of us tried to soothe her all we could, and she went off home.

It wasn't long after that that she and Henry Mortimer left together after rehearsal was over, he saying he'd leave her at home. She didn't make no objections – I told you he was a very handsome man.

Well, from then on she never seemed to take her eyes from him during every rehearsal, right up to the night of the last rehearsal, which, of course, was full dress – 'Everybody and Everything'.

Jack Haliday never seemed to notice anything that was going on, like the rest of them did. True, his time was taken up with his own work, for I'm telling you that a master machinist hasn't got no loose time on his hands at the first dress rehearsal of a panto. And, of course, none of the company ever said a word or gave a look that would call his attention to it. Men and women are queer beings. They will be blind and deaf whilst danger is being run; and it's only after the scandal is beyond repair that they begin to talk – just the very time when most of all they should be silent.

I saw all that went on, but I didn't understand it. I liked Mortimer myself and admired him – like I did Mrs Haliday, too – and I thought he was a very fine fellow. I was only a boy, you know, and Haliday's apprentice, so naturally I wasn't looking for any trouble I could help, even if I'd seen it coming. It was when I looked back afterwards at the whole thing that I began to comprehend; so you will all understand now, I hope, that what I tell you is the result of much knowledge of what I saw and heard and was told of afterwards – all morticed and clamped up by thinking.

The panto had been on about three weeks when one Saturday, between the shows, I heard two of our company talking. Both of them was among the extra girls that both sang and danced and had to make themselves useful. I don't think either of them was better than she should be; they went out to too many champagne suppers with young men that had money to burn. That part doesn't matter in this affair – except that they was naturally enough jealous of women who was married – which was what they was aiming at – and what lived straighter than they did. Women of that kind like to see a good woman tumble down; it seems to make them all more even. Now real bad girls that have gone under altogether will try to save a decent one from following their road. That is, so long as they're young; for a bad one what is long in the tooth is the limit. They'll help anyone downhill – so long as they get something out of it.

Well these two girls was enjoyin' themselves over Mrs Haliday and the mash she had set up on Mortimer. They didn't see that I was sitting on a stage box behind a built-out piece of the prologue of the panto, which was set ready for the night. They were both in love with Mortimer, who wouldn't look at either of them, so they was miaw 'n cruel, like cats on the tiles. Says one: 'The Old Man seems worse than blind; he *won't* see.'

'Don't you be too sure of that,' says the other. 'He don't mean to take no chances. I think you must be blind, too, Kissie.' That was her name – on the bills anyhow, Kissie Mountpelier. 'Don't he make a point of taking her home hisself every night after the play. You should know, for you're in the hall yourself waiting for your young man till he comes from his club.'

'Wot-ho, you bally geeser,' says the other – her language was mostly coarse – 'don't you know there's two ends to everything? The Old Man looks to one end only!'

Then they began to snigger and whisper; and presently the other one says: 'Then he thinks harm can be only done when work is over!'

'Jest so,' she answers. 'Her and him knows that the old man has to be down long before the risin' of the rag; but she doesn't come in till the Vision of Venus dance after half-time; and he not till the harlequinade!'

Then I quit. I didn't want to hear any more of that sort.

All that week things went on as usual. Poor old Haliday wasn't well. He looked worried and had a devil of a temper. I had reason to know that, for what worried him was his work. He was always a hard worker, and the panto season was a terror with him. He didn't ever seem to mind anything else outside his work. I thought at the time that that was how those two chattering girls made up their slanderous story; for, after all, a slander, no matter how false it may be, must have some sort of beginning. Something that seems, if there isn't something that is! But no matter how busy he might be, old Jack always made time to leave the wife at home.

As the week went on he got more and more pale; and I began to think he was in for some sickness. He generally remained in the theatre between the shows on Saturday; that is, he didn't go home, but took a high tea in the coffee shop close to the theatre, so as to be handy in case there might be a hitch anywhere in the preparation for the night. On that Saturday he went out as usual when the first scene was set, and the men were getting ready the packs for the rest of the scenes. By-and-by there was some trouble – the usual Saturday kind – and I went off to tell him. When I went into the coffee shop I couldn't see him. I thought it best not to ask or to seem to take any notice, so I came back to the theatre, and heard that the trouble had settled itself as usual, by the men who had been quarrelling going off to have another drink. I hustled up those who remained, and we got things smoothed out in time for them all to have their tea. Then I had my own. I was just then beginning to feel the responsibility of my business, so I wasn't long over my food, but came back to look things over and see that all was right, especially the trap, for that was a thing Jack Haliday was most particular about. He would overlook a fault for anything else; but if it was along of a trap, the man had to go. He always told the men that that wasn't ordinary work; it was life or death.

I had just got through my inspection when I saw old Jack coming in from the hall. There was no one about at that hour, and the stage was dark. But dark as it was I could see that the old man was ghastly pale. I didn't speak, for I wasn't near enough, and as he was moving very silently behind the scenes I thought that perhaps he wouldn't like anyone to notice that he had been away. I thought the best thing I could do would be to clear out of the way, so I went back and had another cup of tea.

I came away a little before the men, who had nothing to think of except to be in their places when Haliday's whistle sounded. I went to report myself to my master, who was in his own little glass-partitioned den at the back of the carpenter's shop. He was there bent over his own bench, and was filing away at something so intently that he did not seem to hear me; so I cleared out. From an apprentice point of view it is not wise to be too obtrusive when your master is attending to some private matter of his own!

When the 'get-ready' time came and the lights went up, there was Haliday as usual at his post. He looked very white and ill – so ill that the stage manager, when he came in, said to him that if he liked to go home and rest he would see that all his work would be attended to. He thanked him, and said that he thought he would be able to stay. 'I do feel a little weak and ill, sir,' he said. 'I felt just now for a few moments as if I was going to faint. But that's gone by already, and I'm sure I shall be able to get through the work before us all right.'

Then the doors was opened, and the Saturday night audience came rushing and tumbling in. The Victoria was a great Saturday night house. No matter what other nights might be, *that* was sure to be good. They used to say in the profession that the Victoria lived on it, and that the management was on holiday for the rest of the week. The actors knew it, and no matter how slack they might be from Monday to Friday they was all taut and trim then. There was no walking through and no fluffing on Saturday nights – or else they'd have had the bird.

Mortimer was one of the most particular of the lot in this way. He never was slack at any time – indeed, slackness is not a harlequin's fault, for if there's slackness there's no harlequin, that's all. But

Mortimer always put on an extra bit on the Saturday night. When he jumped up through the star trap he always went a couple of feet higher. To do this we had always to put on a lot more weight. This he always saw to himself; for, mind you, it's no joke being driven up through the trap as if you was shot out of a gun. The points of the star had to be kept free, and the hinges at their bases must be well oiled, or else there can be a disaster at any time. Moreover, 'tis the duty of someone appointed for the purpose to see that all is clear upon the stage. I remember hearing that once at New York, many years ago now, a harlequin was killed by a 'grip' – as the Yankees call a carpenter – what outsiders here call a scene-shifter – walking over the trap just as the stroke had been given to let go the counter-weights. It wasn't much satisfaction to the widow to know that the 'grip' was killed, too.

That night Mrs Haliday looked prettier than ever, and kicked even higher than I had ever seen her do. Then, when she got dressed for home, she came as usual and stood in the wings for the beginning of the harlequinade. Old Jack came across the stage and stood beside her; I saw him from the back follow up the sliding ground-row that closed in on the Realms of Delight. I couldn't help noticing that he still looked ghastly pale. He kept turning his eyes on the star trap. Seeing this, I naturally looked at it too, for I feared lest something might have gone wrong. I had seen that it was in good order, and that the joints were properly oiled when the stage was set for the evening show, and as it wasn't used all night for anything else I was reassured. Indeed, I thought I could see it shine a bit as the limelight caught the brass hinges. There was a spot light just above it on the bridge, which was intended to make a good show of harlequin and his big jump. The people used to howl with delight as he came rushing up through the trap and when in the air drew up his legs and spread them wide for an instant and then straightened them again as he came down – only bending his knees just as he touched the stage.

When the signal was given the counterweight worked properly. I knew, for the sound of it at that part was all right.

But something was wrong. The trap didn't work smooth, and open at once as the harlequin's head touched it. There was a shock and a tearing sound, and the pieces of the star seemed torn about, and some of them were thrown about the stage. And in the middle of them came the coloured and spangled figure that we knew.

But somehow it didn't come up in the usual way. It was erect enough, but there was not the usual elasticity. The legs never moved; and when it went up a fair height – though nothing like usual – it seemed to topple over and fall on the stage on its side. The audience shrieked, and the people in the wings – actors and staff all the same – closed in, some of them in their stage clothes, others dressed for going home. But the man in the spangles lay quite still.

The loudest shriek of all was from Mrs Haliday; and she was the first to reach the spot where he – it – lay. Old Jack was close behind her, and caught her as she fell. I had just time to see that, for I made it my business to look after the pieces of the trap; there was plenty of people to look after the corpse. And the pit was by now crossing the orchestra and climbing up on the stage.

I managed to get the bits together before the rush came. I noticed that there were deep scratches on some of them, but I didn't have time for more than a glance. I put a stage box over the hole lest anyone should put a foot through it. Such would mean a broken leg at least; and if one fell through, it might mean worse. Amongst other things I found a queer-looking piece of flat steel with some bent points on it. I knew it didn't belong to the trap; but it came from *somewhere*, so I put it in my pocket.

By this time there was a crowd where Mortimer's body lay. That he was stone dead nobody could doubt. The very attitude was enough. He was all straggled about in queer positions; one of the legs was doubled under him with the toes sticking out in the wrong way. But let that suffice! It doesn't do to go into details of a dead body. . . .

There was another crowd round Mrs Haliday, who was lying a little on one side nearer the wings where her husband had carried her and laid her down. She, too, looked like a corpse; for she was as white as one and as still, and looked as cold. Old Jack was kneeling beside her, chafing her hands. He was evidently frightened about her, for he, too, was deathly white. However, he kept his head, and called his men round him. He left his wife in care of Mrs Homcroft, the Wardrobe Mistress, who had by this time hurried down. She was a capable woman, and knew how to act promptly. She got one of the men to lift Mrs Haliday and carry her up to the wardrobe. I heard afterwards that when she got her there she turned out all the rest of them that followed up – the women as well as the men – and looked after her herself.

I put the pieces of the broken trap on the top of the stage box, and told one of our chaps to mind them, and see that no one touched them, as they might be wanted. By this time the police who had been on duty in front had come round, and as they had at once telephoned to headquarters, more police kept coming in all the time. One of them took charge of the place where the broken trap was; and when he heard who put the box and the broken pieces there, sent for me. More of them took the body away to the property room, which was a large room with benches in it, and which could be locked up. Two of them stood at the door, and wouldn't let anyone go in without permission.

The man who was in charge of the trap asked me if I had seen the accident. When I said I had, he asked me to describe it. I don't think he had much opinion of my powers of description, for he soon dropped that part of his questioning. Then he asked me to point out where I found the bits of the broken trap. I simply said: 'Lord bless you, sir, I couldn't tell. They was scattered all over the place. I had to pick them up between people's feet as they were rushing in from all sides.'

'All right, my boy,' he said, in quite a kindly way, for a policeman, 'I don't think they'll want to worry you. There are lots of men and women, I am told, who were standing by and saw the whole thing. They will be all subpoenaed.' I was a small-made lad in those days – I ain't a giant now! – and I suppose he thought it was no use having children for witnesses when they had plenty of grown-ups. Then he said something about me and an idiot asylum that was not kind – no, nor wise either, for I dried up and did not say another word.

Gradually the public was got rid of. Some strolled off by degrees, going off to have a glass before the pubs closed, and talk it all over. The rest of us and the police ballooned out. Then, when the police had taken charge of everything and put in men to stay all night, the coroner's officer came and took off the body to the city mortuary, where the police doctor made a post-mortem. I was allowed to go home. I did so – and gladly – when I had seen the place settling down. Mr Haliday took his wife home in a four-wheeler. It was perhaps just as well, for Mrs Homcroft and some other kindly souls had poured so much whisky and brandy and rum and gin and beer and peppermint into her that I don't believe she could have walked if she had tried.

When I was undressing myself something scratched my leg as I was taking off my trousers. I found it was the piece of flat steel which I had picked up on the stage. It was in the shape of a star fish, but the spikes of it were short. Some of the points were turned down, the rest were pulled out straight again. I stood with it in my hand wondering where it had come from and what it was for, but I couldn't remember anything in the whole theatre that it could have belonged to. I looked at it closely again, and saw that the edges were all filed and quite bright. But that did not help me, so I put it on the table and thought I would take it with me in the morning; perhaps one of the chaps might know. I turned out the gas and went to bed – and to sleep.

I must have begun to dream at once, and it was, naturally enough, all about the terrible thing that had occurred. But, like all dreams, it was a bit mixed. They were all mixed. Mortimer with his spangles flying up the trap, it breaking, and the pieces scattering round. Old Jack Haliday looking on at one side of the stage with his wife beside him – he as pale as death, and she looking prettier than ever. And then Mortimer coming down all crooked and falling on the stage, Mrs Haliday shrieking, and her and Jack running forward, and me picking up the pieces of the broken trap from between people's legs, and finding the steel star with the bent points.

I woke in a cold sweat, saying to myself as I sat up in bed in the dark: 'That's it!'

And then my head began to reel about so that I lay down again and began to think it all over. And it all seemed clear enough then. It was Mr Haliday who made that star and put it over the star trap where the points joined! That was what Jack Haliday was filing at when I saw him at his bench; and he had done it because Mortimer and his wife had been making love to each other. Those girls were right, after all. Of course, the steel points had prevented the trap opening, and when Mortimer was driven up against it his neck was broken.

But then came the horrible thought that if Jack did it, it was murder, and he would be hung. And, after all, it was his wife that the harlequin had made love to – and old Jack loved her very much indeed himself and had been good to her – and she was his wife. And that bit of steel would hang him if it should be known. But no one but me – and whoever made it, and put it on the trap – even knew of its existence – and Mr Haliday was my master – and the man was dead – and he was a villain!

I was living then at Quarry Place; and in the old quarry was a pond so deep that the boys used to say that far down the water was boiling hot, it was so near hell.

I softly opened the window, and, there in the dark, threw the bit of steel as far as I could into the quarry.

No one ever knew, for I have never spoken a word of it till this very minute. I was not called at the inquest. Everyone was in a hurry; the coroner and the jury and the police. Our governor was in a hurry too, because we wanted to go on as usual at night; and too much talk of the tragedy would hurt business. So nothing was known; and all went on as usual. Except that after that Mrs Haliday didn't stand in the wings during the harlequinade, and she was as loving to her old husband as a woman can be. It was him she used to watch now; and always with a sort of respectful adoration. She knew, though no one else did, except her husband – and me.

The Gombeen Man

One of Henry Irving's great admirers and regular patrons at the Lyceum was the several-times Prime Minister, William Ewart Gladstone. First visiting the theatre to see *The Bells* in 1881, he thereafter turned up for virtually every new production during the next fourteen years until his health began to fail in 1895. In time, the box he occupied became known as 'Mr Gladstone's Seat', though he always took care to enter and leave by a private door in Burleigh Street to avoid the crowds anxious to see him. On many occasions he and Irving dined together in the Beefsteak Room and Bram Stoker was a guest at all of these meetings, during which Gladstone revealed a passionate interest in, and knowledge of, the theatre.

Perhaps the greatest of Gladstone's parliamentary interests was Ireland and the centuries-old troubles which existed there, and this was a topic which Bram Stoker, as an Irishman in exile, was happy to discuss with him whenever the opportunity arose around the supper table. Stoker confessed himself 'a philosophical Home-Ruler', but was much impressed by what the Prime Minister had been trying to do for the Irish people. After one of their talks, Stoker noted in his diary, 'Mr. Gladstone was full of Irish matters. He was especially interested in a case of oppression by a gombeen man over a loan secured on some land. He spoke to me of it very kindly and very searchingly.' Stoker knew all about gombeen men, grasping usurers familiar throughout Ireland, and the talk with Gladstone inspired him to write a story about one of them. To give added authenticity to the tale he chose to write the dialogue in the Irish dialect.

'The Gombeen Man' appeared in a London newspaper, *The People*, in November 1890 and Stoker sent a copy to Gladstone with his thanks for the part he had played in its creation. By return of

post, the Prime Minister penned a personal note, 'Dear Mr. Bram Stoker – My social memory is indeed a bad one, yet not so bad as to prevent my recollection of our various meetings. I thank you for your work and your sympathy. The scene at Mrs. Kelligan's is fine – very fine indeed!' Now follows that story which so impressed the great man, and which Stoker later incorporated into a novel, *The Snake's Pass* (1891).

'GOD SAVE ALL HERE,' said the man as he entered.

Room was made for him at the fire. He no sooner came near it and tasted the heat than a cloud of steam arose from him.

'Man! but ye're wet,' said Mrs Kelligan. 'One'd think ye'd been in the lake beyant!'

'So I have,' he answered, 'worse luck! I rid all the way from Galway this blessed day to be here in time, but the mare slipped coming down Curragh Hill and threw me over the bank into the lake. I wor in the wather nigh three hours before I could get out, for I was foreninst the Curragh Rock an' only got a foothold in a chink, an' had to hold on wid me one arm for I fear the other is broke.'

'Dear! dear! dear!' interrupted the woman. 'Sthrip yer coat off, acushla, an' let us see if we can do anythin'.'

He shook his head, as he answered: 'Not now, there's not a minute to spare. I must get up the Hill at once. I should have been there be six o'clock. But I mayn't be too late yit. The mare has broke down entirely. Can any one here lend me a horse?'

There was no answer till Andy spoke: 'Me mare is in the shtable, but this gintleman has me an' her for the day, an' I have to lave him at Carnaclif tonight.'

Here I struck in: 'Never mind me, Andy! If you can help this gentleman, do so: I'm better off here than driving through the storm. He wouldn't want to go on, with a broken arm, if he hadn't good reason!'

The man looked at me with grateful eagerness: 'Thank yer honour, kindly. It's a rale gintleman ye are! An' I hope ye'll never be sorry for helpin' a poor fellow in sore throuble.'

'What's wrong, Phelim?' asked the priest. 'Is there anything troubling you that any one here can get rid of?'

'Nothin', Father Pether, thank ye kindly. The throuble is me own intirely, an' no wan here could help me. But I must see Murdock tonight.'

There was a general sigh of commiseration; all understood the situation.

'Musha!' said old Dan Moriarty, *sotto voce*. 'An' is that the way of it! An' is he too in the clutches iv that wolf? Him that we all thought was so warrum. Glory be to God! but it's a quare wurrld it is; an' it's few there is in it that is what they seems. Me poor frind! is there any way I can help ye? I have a bit iv money by me that yer welkim to the lend iv av ye want it.'

The other shook his head gratefully: 'Thank ye kindly, Dan, but I have the money all right; it's only the time I'm in trouble about!'

'Only the time! me poor chap! It's be time that the Divil helps Black Murdock an' the likes iv him, the most iv all! God be good to ye if he has got his clutch on yer back, an' has time on his side, for ye'll want it!'

'Well! anyhow, I must be goin' now. Thank ye kindly, neighbours all. When a man's in throuble, sure the goodwill of his frinds is the greatest comfort he can have.'

'All but one, remember that! all but one!' said the priest.

'Thank ye kindly, Father, I shan't forget. Thank ye Andy: an' you, too, young sir, I'm much beholden to ye. I hope, some day, I may have it to do a good turn for ye in return. Thank ye kindly again, and good night.'

He shook my hand warmly, and was going to the door, when old Dan said: 'An' as for that black-jawed ruffian, Murdock –'

He paused, for the door suddenly opened, and a harsh voice said: 'Murtagh Murdock is here to answer for himself!' – It was my man at the window.

There was a sort of paralysed silence in the room, through which came the whisper of one of the old women: 'Musha! talk iv the Divil!'

Joyce's face grew very white; one hand instinctively grasped his riding switch, the other hung uselessly by his side. Murdock spoke: 'I kem here expectin' to meet Phelim Joyce. I thought I'd save him the throuble of comin' wid the money.'

Joyce said in a husky voice: 'What do ye mane? I have the money right enough here. I'm sorry I'm a bit late, but I had a bad accident – bruk me arrum, an' was nigh dhrownded in the Curragh Lake. But I was goin' up to ye at once, bad as I am, to pay ye yer money, Murdock.'

The Gombeen Man interrupted him: 'But it isn't to me ye'd have to come, me good man. Sure, it's the Sheriff, himself, that was waitin' for ye', an' whin ye didn't come' – here Joyce winced; the speaker smiled – 'he done his work.'

'What wurrk, acushla?' asked one of the women.

Murdock answered slowly: 'He sould the lease iv the farrum known as the Shleenanaher in open sale, in accordance wid the terrums of his notice, duly posted, and wid warnin' given to the houldher iv the lease.'

There was a long pause. Joyce was the first to speak: 'Ye're jokin', Murdock. For God's sake say ye're jokin! Ye tould me yerself that I might have time to git the money. An' ye tould me that the puttin' me farrum up for sale was only a matther iv forrum to let me pay ye back in me own way. Nay! more, ye asked me not to tell any iv the neighbours, for fear some iv them might want to buy some iv me land. An' it's niver so, that whin ye got me aff to Galway to rise the money, ye went on wid the sale, behind me back – wid not a soul by to spake for me or mine – an' sould up all I have! No! Murtagh Murdock, ye're a hard man I know, but ye wouldn't do that! Ye wouldn't do that!'

Murdock made no direct reply to him, but said seemingly to the company generally: 'I ixpected to see Phelim Joyce at the sale today, but as I had some business in which he was consarned, I kem here where I knew there'd be neighbours – an' sure so there is.'

He took out his pocket-book and wrote names, 'Father Pether Ryan, Daniel Moriarty, Bartholomew Moynahan, Andhrew McGlown, Mrs Katty Kelligan – that's enough! I want ye all to see what I done. There's nothin' undherhand about me! Phelim Joyce, I give ye formial notice that yer land was sould an' bought be me, for ye broke yer word to repay me the money lint ye before the time fixed. Here's the Sheriff's assignmint, an' I tell ye before all these witnessses that I'll proceed with ejectment on title at wanst.'

All in the room were as still as statues. Joyce was fearfully still and pale, but when Murdock spoke the word 'ejectment' he seemed to wake in a moment to frenzied life. The blood flushed up in his face and he seemed about to do something rash; but with a great effort he controlled himself and said: 'Mr Murdock, ye won't be too hard. I got the money today – it's here – but I had an accident that delayed me. I was thrown into the Curragh Lake and nigh drownded an' me arrum is bruk. Don't be so close as an hour or two – ye'll never be sorry for it. I'll pay ye all, and more, and thank ye into the bargain all me life; ye'll take back the paper, won't ye, for me childhren's sake – for Norah's sake?'

He faltered; the other answered with an evil smile: 'Phelim Joyce, I've waited years for this moment – don't ye know me betther nor to think I would go back on meself whin I have shtarted on a road? I wouldn't take yer money, not if ivery pound note was spread into an acre and cut up in tin-pound notes. I want yer land – I have waited for it, an' I mane to have it! – Now don't beg me any more, for I won't go back – an' tho' it's many a grudge I owe ye, I square them all before the neighbours be refusin' yer prayer. The land is mine, bought be open sale; an' all the judges an' coorts in Ireland can't take it from me! An' what do ye say to that now, Phelim Joyce?'

The tortured man had been clutching the ash sapling which he had used as a riding whip, and from the nervous twitching of his fingers I knew that something was coming. And it came; for, without a word, he struck the evil face before him – struck as quick as a flash of lightning – such a blow that the blood seemed to leap out round the stick, and a vivid welt rose in an instant. With a wild, savage cry the Gombeen Man jumped at him; but there were others in the room as quick, and before another blow could be struck on either side both men were grasped by strong hands and held back.

Murdock's rage was tragic. He yelled, like a wild beast, to be let get at his opponent. He cursed and blasphemed so outrageously that all were silent, and only the stern voice of the priest was heard: 'Be silent Murtagh Murdock! Aren't you afraid that the God overhead will strike you dead? With such a storm as is raging as a sign of His power, you are a foolish man to tempt Him.'

The man stopped suddenly, and a stern dogged sullenness took the place of his passion. The priest went on: 'As for you, Phelim Joyce, you ought to be ashamed of yourself; ye're not one of my people, but I speak as your own clergyman would if he were here. Only this day has the Lord seen fit to spare you from a terrible death; and yet you dare to go back of His mercy with your angry passion. You had cause for anger – or temptation to it, I know – but you must learn to kiss the chastening rod, not spurn it. The Lord knows what He is doing for you as for others, and it may be that you will look back on this day in gratitude for His doing, and in shame for your own anger. Men, hold off your hands – let those two men go; they'll quarrel no more – before me at any rate, I hope.'

The men drew back. Joyce held his head down, and a more despairing figure or a sadder one I never saw. He turned slowly away, and leaning against the wall put his face between his hands and sobbed. Murdock scowled, and the scowl gave place to an evil smile as looking all around he said: 'Well, now that me work is done, I must be gettin' home.'

'An' get some wan to iron that mark out iv yer face,' said Dan.

Murdock turned again and glared around him savagely as he hissed out: 'There'll be iron for someone before I'm done. Mark me well! I've never gone back or wakened yit whin I promised to have me own turn.

There's thim here what'll rue this day yit! If I am the shnake on the hill – thin beware the shnake. An' for him what shtruck me, he'll be in bitther sorra for it yit – him an' his!' He turned his back and went to the door.

'Stop!' said the priest. 'Murtagh Murdock, I have a word to say to you – a solemn word of warning. Ye have today acted the part of Ahab towards Naboth the Jezreelite; beware of his fate! You have coveted your neighbour's goods – you have used your power without mercy; you have made the law an engine of oppression. Mark me! It was said of old that what measure men meted should be meted out to them again. God is very just. "Be not deceived, God is not mocked. For what things a man shall sow, those also shall he reap." Ye have sowed the wind this day – beware lest you reap the whirlwind! Even as God visited his sin upon Ahab the Samarian, and as He has visited similar sins on others in His own way – so shall He visit yours on you. You are worse than the land-grabber – worse than the man who only covets. Saintough is a virtue compared with your act! Remember the story of Naboth's vineyard, and the dreadful end of it. Don't answer me! Go and repent if you can, and leave sorrow and misery to be comforted by others – unless you wish to undo your wrong yourself. If you don't – then remember the curse that may come upon you yet!'

Without a word Murdock opened the door and went out, and a little later we heard the clattering of his horse's feet on the rocky road to Shleenanaher.

When it was apparent to all that he was really gone a torrent of commiseration, sympathy and pity broke over Joyce. The Irish nature is essentially emotional, and a more genuine and stronger feeling I never saw. Not a few had tears in their eyes, and one and all were manifestly deeply touched. The least moved was, to all appearance, poor Joyce himself. He seemed to have pulled himself together, and his sterling manhood and courage and pride stood by him. He seemed, however, to yield to the kindly wishes of his friends; and when we suggested that his hurt should be looked to, he acquiesced: 'Yes, if you will. Betther not go home to poor Norah and distress her with it. Poor child! she'll have enough to bear without that.'

His coat was taken off, and between us we managed to bandage the wound. The priest, who had some surgical knowledge, came to the conclusion that there was only a simple fracture. He splinted and bandaged the arm, and we all agreed that it would be better for Joyce to wait until the storm was over before starting for home. Andy said he could take him on the car, as he knew the road well, and that, as it was partly on the road to Carnaclif, we should only have to make a short detour and would pass the house of the doctor, by whom the arm could be properly attended to.

So we sat around the fire again, whilst, without, the storm howled and the fierce gusts which swept the valley seemed at times as if they would break in the door, lift off the roof, or in some way annihilate the time-worn cabin which gave us shelter.

There could, of course, be only one subject of conversation now, and old Dan simply interpreted the public wish, when he said: 'Tell us, Phelim, sure we're all friends here! how Black Murdock got ye in his clutches? Sure any wan of us would get you out of thim if he could.'

There was a general acquiescence. Joyce yielded himself, and said: 'Let me thank ye, neighbours all, for yer kindness to me and mine this sorraful night. Well! I'll say no more about that; but I'll tell ye how it was that Murdock got me into his power. Ye know that boy of mine, Eugene?'

'Oh! and he's the fine lad, God bless him! an' the good lad too!' – this from the women.

'Well! ye know too that he got on so well whin I sint him to school that Dr Walsh recommended me to make an ingineer of him. He said he had such promise that it was a pity not to see him get the right start in life, and he gave me, himself, a letther to Sir George Henshaw, the great ingineer. I wint and seen him, and he said he would take the boy. He tould me that there was a big fee to be paid, but I was not to throuble about that – at any rate, that he himself didn't want any fee, and he would ask his partner if he would give up his share too. But the latther was hard up for money. He said he couldn't give up all fee, but that he would take half the fee, provided it was paid down in dhry money. Well! the regular fee to the firm was five hundhred pounds, and as Sir George had giv up half an' only half th' other half was to be paid, that was possible. I hadn't got more'n a few pounds by me – for what wid dhrainin' and plantin' and fencin' and the payin' the boy's schoolin', and the girl's at the Nuns' in Galway, it had put me to the pin iv me collar to find the money up to now. But I didn't like to let the boy lose his chance in life for want of an effort, an' I put me pride in me pocket an' kem an' asked Murdock for the money. He was very smooth an' nice wid me – I know why now – an' promised he would give it at wanst if I would give him security on me land. Sure he joked an' laughed wid me, an' was that cheerful that I didn't misthrust him. He tould me it was only forrums I was signin' that'd never be used.'

Here Dan Moriarty interrupted him: 'What did ye sign, Phelim?'

'There wor two papers. Wan was a writin' iv some kind, that in considheration iv the money lent an' his own land – which I was to take over if the money wasn't paid at the time appointed – he was to get me lease from me: an' the other was a power of attorney to enther judgment for the amount if the money wasn't paid at the right time. I thought I was all safe as I could repay him in the time named, an' if the worst kem to the worst I might borry the money from somewan else – for the lease is worth the sum tin times over – an' repay him. Well! what's the use of lookin' back, anyhow! I signed the papers – that was a year ago, an' one week. An' a week ago the time was up!' He gulped down a sob, and went on: 'Well! ye all know the year gone has been a terrible bad wan, an' as for me it was all I could do to hould on – to make up the money was impossible. Thrue the lad cost me next to nothin', for he arned his keep be exthra work, an' the girl, Norah, kem home from school and laboured wid me, an' we saved every penny we could, But it was all no use! – we couldn't get the money together anyhow. Thin we had the misfortin wid the cattle that ye all know of; an' three horses, that I sould in Dublin, up an' died before the time I guaranteed them free from sickness.'

Here Andy struck in: 'Thrue for ye! Sure there was some dhreadful disordher in Dublin among the horse cattle, intirely; an' even Misther Docther Perfesshinal Ferguson himself couldn't git undher it!'

Joyce went on: 'An' as the time grew nigh I began to fear, but Murdock came down to see me whin I was alone, an' tould me not to throuble about the money an' not to mind about the Sheriff, for he had to give him notice. "An'," says he, "I wouldn't, if I was you, tell Norah anythin' about it, for it might frighten the girl – for weemin is apt to take to heart things like that that's only small things to min like us." An' so, God forgive me, I believed him; an' I niver tould me child anything about it – even whin I got the notice from the Sheriff. An' whin the notice tellin' of the sale was posted up on me, I tuk it down meself so that the poor child wouldn't be frightened – God help me!' He broke down for a bit, but then went on: 'But somehow I wasn't asy in me mind, an' whin the time iv the sale dhrew nigh I couldn't keep it to meself any longer, an' I tould Norah. That was only yisterday, and look at me today! Norah agreed wid me that we shouldn't trust the Gombeen, an' she sent me off to the Galway Bank to borry the money. She said I was an honest man an' farmed me own land, and that the bank might lind the money on it. An' sure enough whin I wint there this mornin' be appointment, wid the Coadjuthor himself to introduce me, though he didn't know why I wanted the money – that was Norah's idea, and the Mother Superior settled it for her – the manager, who is a nice gintleman, tould me at wanst that I might have the money on me own note iv hand. I only gave him a formal writin', an' I took away the money. Here it is in me pocket in good notes; they're wet wid the lake, but I'm thankful to say all safe. But it's too late, God help me!' Here he broke down for a minute, but recovered himself with an effort: 'Anyhow the bank that thrusted me mustn't be wronged. Back the money goes to Galway as soon as iver I can get it there. If I am a ruined man I needn't be a dishonest wan! But poor Norah! God help her! it will break her poor heart.'

There was a spell of silence only broken by sympathetic moans. The first to speak was the priest.

'Phelim Joyce, I told you a while ago, in the midst of your passion, that God knows what He is doin', and works in His own way. You're an honest man, Phelim, and God knows it, and, mark me, He won't let you nor yours suffer. "I have been young", said the Psalmist, "and now am old; and I have not seen the just forsaken, nor his seed seeking bread." Think of that, Phelim! – may it comfort you and poor Norah. God bless her! but she's the good girl. You have much to be thankful for, with a daughter like her to comfort you at home and take the place of her poor mother, who was the best of women; and with such a boy as Eugene, winnin' name and credit, and perhaps fame to come, even in England itself. Thank God for His many mercies, Phelim, and trust Him.'

There was a dead silence in the room. The stern man rose, and coming over took the priest's hand.

'God bless ye, Father!' he said, 'it's the true comforter ye are.'

The scene was a most touching one; I shall never forget it. The worst of the poor man's trouble seemed now past. He had faced the darkest hour; he had told his trouble, and was now prepared to make the best of everything – for the time at least – for I could not reconcile to my mind the idea that that proud, stern man, would not take the blow to heart for many a long day, that it might even embitter his life.

Old Dan tried comfort in a practical way by thinking of what was to be done. Said he: 'Iv course, Phelim, it's a mighty trouble to give up yer own foine land an' take Murdock's bleak shpot instead, but I daresay ye will be able to work it well enough. Tell me, have ye signed away all the land, or only the lower farm? I mane, is the Cliff Fields yours or his?'

Here was a gleam of comfort evidently to the poor man. His face lightened as he replied: 'Only the lower farm, thank God! Indeed, I couldn't part wid the Cliff Fields, for they don't belong to me – they are Norah's, that her poor mother left her – they wor settled on her, whin we married, be her father, and whin he died we got them. But, indeed, I fear they're but small use be themselves; shure there's no wather in them at all, savin' what runs off me ould land; an' if we have to carry wather all the way down the hill from – from me new land' – this was said with a smile, which was a sturdy effort at cheerfulness – 'it will be but poor work to raise anythin' there – ayther shtock or craps. No doubt but Murdock will take away the sthrame iv wather that runs there now. He'll want to get the cliff lands, too, I suppose.'

I ventured to ask a question: 'How do your lands lie compared with Mr Murdock's?'

There was bitterness in his tone as he answered, in true Irish fashion: 'Do you mane me ould land, or me new?'

'The lands that were – that ought still to be yours,' I answered.

He was pleased at the reply, and his face softened as he replied: 'Well, the way of it is this. We two owns the west side of the hill between us. Murdock's land – I'm spakin' iv them as they are, till he gets possession iv mine – lies at the top iv the hill; mine lies below. My land is the best bit on the mountain, while the Gombeen's is poor soil, with only a few good patches here and there. Moreover, there is another thing. There is a bog which is high up the hill, mostly on his houldin', but my land is free from bog, except one end of the big bog, an' a stretch of dry turf, the best in the counthry, an' wid' enough turf to last for a hundhred years, it's that deep.'

Old Dan joined in: 'Thrue enough! that bog of the Gombeen's isn't much use anyhow. It's rank and rotten wid wather. Whin it made up its mind to sthay, it might have done better!'

'The bog? Made up its mind to stay! What on earth do you mean?' I asked. I was fairly puzzled.

'Didn't ye hear talk already,' said Dan, 'of the shiftin' bog on the mountain?'

'I did.'

'Well, that's it! It moved an' moved an' moved longer than anywan can remimber. Me grandfather wanst tould me that whin he was a gossoon it wasn't nigh so big as it was when he tould me. It hasn't shifted in my time, and I make bould to say that it has made up its mind to settle down where it is. Ye must only make the best of it, Phelim. I daresay ye will turn it to some account.'

'I'll try what I can do, anyhow. I don't mane to fould me arms an' sit down op-pawsit me property an' ate it!' was the brave answer.

For myself, the whole idea was most interesting. I had never before even heard of a shifting bog, and I determined to visit it before I left this part of the country.

By this time the storm was beginning to abate. The rain had ceased, and Andy said we might proceed on our journey. So after a while we were on our way; the wounded man and I sitting on one side of the car, and Andy on the other. The whole company came out to wish us God-speed, and with such comfort as good counsel and good wishes could give we ventured into the inky darkness of the night.

Andy was certainly a born car-driver. Not even the darkness, the comparative strangeness of the road, or the amount of whiskey-punch which he had on board could disturb his driving in the least; he went steadily on. The car rocked and swayed and bumped, for the road was a by one, and in but poor condition – but Andy and the mare went on alike unmoved. Once or twice only, in a journey of some three miles of winding by-lanes, crossed and crossed again by lanes or watercourses, did he ask the way. I could not tell which was roadway and which waterway, for they were all watercourses at present, and the darkness was profound. Still, both Andy and Joyce seemed to have a sense lacking in myself, for now and again they spoke of things which I could not see at all. As, for instance, when Andy asked: 'Do we go up or down where the road branches beyant?' Or again: 'I disremimber, but is that Micky Dolan's ould apple three, or didn't he cut it down? an' is it Tim's fornent us on the lift?'

Presently we turned to the right, and drove up a short avenue towards a house. I knew it to be a house by the light in the windows, for shape it had none. Andy jumped down and knocked, and after a short colloquy, Joyce got down and went into the Doctor's house. I was asked to go too, but thought it better not to, as it would only have disturbed the Doctor in his work; and so Andy and I possessed our souls in patience until Joyce came out again, with his arm in a proper splint. And then we resumed our journey through the inky darkness.

However, after a while either there came more light into the sky, or my eyes became accustomed to the darkness, for I thought that now and again I beheld 'men as trees walking'.

Presently something dark and massive seemed outlined in the sky before us – a blackness projected on a darkness – and, said Andy, turning to me: 'That's Knockcalltecrore; we're nigh the foot iv it now, and pretty shortly we'll be at the enthrance iv the boreen, where Misther Joyce'll git aff.'

We plodded on for a while, and the hill before us seemed to overshadow whatever glimmer of light there was, for the darkness grew more profound than ever; then Andy turned to my companion: 'Sure, isn't that Miss Norah I see sittin' on the sthyle beyant?' I looked eagerly in the direction in which he evidently pointed, but for the life of me I could see nothing.

'No! I hope not,' said the father, hastily. 'She's never come out in the shtorm. Yes! It is her, she sees us.'

Just then there came a sweet sound down the lane: 'Is that you, father?'

'Yes! my child; but I hope you've not been out in the shtorm.'

'Only a bit, father; I was anxious about you. Is it all right, father; did you get what you wanted?' She had jumped off the stile and had drawn nearer to us, and she evidently saw me, and went on in a changed and shyer voice: 'Oh! I beg your pardon, I did not see you had a stranger with you.'

This was all bewildering to me; I could hear it all – and a sweeter voice I never heard – but yet I felt like a blind man, for not a child could I see, whilst each of the three others was seemingly as much at ease as in the daylight.

'This gentleman has been very kind to me, Norah. He has given me a seat on his car, and indeed he's come out of his way to lave me here.'

'I am sure we're all grateful to you, sir; but, father, where is your horse? Why are you on a car at all? Father, I hope you haven't met with any accident – I have been so fearful for you all the day.' This was spoken in a fainter voice; had my eyes been of service, I was sure I would have seen her grow pale.

'Yes, my darlin', I got a fall on the Curragh Hill, but I'm all right. Norah dear! Quick, quick! catch her, she's faintin'! – my God! I can't stir!'

I jumped off the car in the direction of the voice, but my arms sought the empty air. However, I heard Andy's voice beside me: 'All right! I have her. Hould up, Miss Norah; yer dada's all right, don't ye see him there, sittin' on me car. All right, sir, she's a brave girrul! she hasn't fainted.'

'I am all right,' she murmured, faintly; 'but, father, I hope you are not hurt?'

'Only a little, my darlin', just enough for ye to nurse me a while; I daresay a few days will make me all right again. Thank ye, Andy; steady now, till I get down; I'm feelin' a wee bit stiff.' Andy evidently helped him to the ground.

'Good night, Andy, and good night you too, sir, and thank you kindly for your goodness to me all this night. I hope I'll see you again.' He took my hand in his uninjured one, and shook it warmly.

'Good night,' I said, and 'good-bye: I am sure I hope we shall meet again.'

Another hand took mine as he relinquished it – a warm, strong one – and a sweet voice said, shyly: 'Good night, sir, and thank you for your kindness to father.'

I faltered 'Good night,' as I raised my hat; the aggravation of the darkness at such a moment was more than I could equably bear. We heard them pass up the boreen, and I climbed on the car again.

The night seemed darker than ever as we turned our steps towards Carnaclif, and the journey was the dreariest one I had ever taken. I had only one thought which gave me any pleasure, but that was a pretty constant one through the long miles of damp, sodden road – the warm hand and the sweet voice coming out of the darkness, and all in the shadow of that mysterious mountain, which seemed to have become a part of my life. The words of the old story-teller came back to me again and again: 'The Hill can hould tight enough! A man has raysons – sometimes wan thing and sometimes another – but the Hill houlds him all the same!'

And a vague wonder grew upon me as to whether it could ever hold me, and how!

The Squaw

Another of Henry Irving's long-running successes during his years at the Lyceum was Goethe's *Faust*, completed in 1832. This tale of the disillusioned scholar Faust, his deal with Satan in return for supernatural powers, his seduction of a beautiful village maiden and decline into degradation, was perfect material for the stage and Irving played the part of Mephistopheles with enormous bravado for almost 800 performances from 1885 to 1902. The actor's striking appearance in a flowing cloak has already been mentioned as providing inspiration for the figure of Dracula. And Irving may also have suggested another scene for his manager's later book when he described to him how he and his co-star would appear in the play: 'My appearance in flaming scarlet will be intensified by the storm on the mountain – and you shall see how Ellen Terry's white dress and even the red scar across her throat will stand out in the midst of that turmoil of lightning!'

Not surprisingly, with such pyrotechnics to devise (requiring the use of electrical flashes and a great deal of steam), *Faust* proved a difficult production for Irving and Stoker to mount, and many nights they sat over dinner deep in discussion. The cost of staging the extravaganza was obviously enormous, and Irving also insisted on visiting the Brocken Mountains in Germany where the climactic scenes were set to ensure authenticity. After viewing these famous mountains, which according to tradition are one of the great meeting places of witches, Stoker and Irving took a trip to Nuremberg. With their love of the macabre, the two men could not miss the opportunity to visit the town's torture tower which housed the infamous 'Nuremberg Virgin'. Neither man forgot the sight of that terrible instrument of torture with its iron spikes, and it became a subject of dinner-table discussion as well as the central figure in what some believe to be Bram Stoker's most gruesome short story, 'The Squaw'. The tale was not published until a few years later in the special Christmas 1893 number of *The Illustrated Sporting and Dramatic News*, where it no doubt induced a good many shivers around even the warmest firesides in Britain! The story has lost none of its power in the intervening years.

As for Irving's production of *Faust*, it was received with critical and public acclaim, despite an early stage fire and an accident with some machinery which was designed to lift Irving to the ceiling but which almost dropped him fifteen feet into a cellar. When the play crossed the Atlantic in 1887 there were some curious reactions among audiences as Stoker later noted in his biography:

> In Boston, where the old puritanical belief of a real devil still holds, we took in one evening $4,582, the largest dramatic house up to then known in America. But in Chicago, which as a city neither fears the devil nor troubles its head about him or all his works, the receipts were not much more than half the other places!

NUREMBERG AT THE TIME was not so much exploited as it has been since then. Irving had not been playing *Faust*, and the very name of the old town was hardly known to the great bulk of the travelling public. My wife and I being in the second week of our honeymoon, naturally wanted someone else to join our party, so that when the cheery stranger, Elias P. Hutcheson, hailing from Isthmian City, Bleeding Gulch, Maple Tree County, Neb., turned up at the station at Frankfurt, and casually remarked that he was going on to see the most all-fired old Methuselah of a town in Yurrup, and that he guessed that so much travelling alone was enough to send an intelligent, active citizen into the melancholy ward of a daft house, we took the pretty broad hint and suggested that we should join forces. We found, on comparing notes afterwards, that we had each intended to speak with some diffidence or hesitation so as not to appear too eager, such not being a good compliment to the success of our married life; but the effect was entirely marred by our both beginning to speak at the same instant – stopping simultaneously and then going on together again. Anyhow, no matter how, it was done; and Elias P. Hutcheson became one of our party. Straightway Amelia and I found the pleasant benefit;

instead of quarrelling, as we had been doing, we found that the restraining influence of a third party was such that we now took every opportunity of spooning in odd corners. Amelia declares that ever since she has, as the result of that experience, advised all her friends to take a friend on the honeymoon. Well, we 'did' Nuremberg together, and much enjoyed the racy remarks of our transatlantic friend, who, from his quaint speech and his wonderful stock of adventures, might have stepped out of a novel. We kept for the last object of interest in the city to be visited the Burg, and on the day appointed for the visit strolled round the outer wall of the city by the eastern side.

The Burg is seated on a rock dominating the town, and an immensely deep fosse guards it on the northern side. Nuremberg has been happy in that it was never sacked; had it been it would certainly not be so spick and span perfect as it is at present. The ditch has not been used for centuries, and now its base is spread with tea-gardens and orchards, of which some of the trees are of quite respectable growth. As we wandered round the wall, dawdling in the hot July sunshine, we often paused to admire the views spread before us, and in especial the great plain covered with towns and village and bounded with a blue line of hills, like a landscape of Claude Lorrain. From this we always turned with new delight to the city itself, with its myriad of quaint old gables and acre-wide red roofs dotted with dormer windows, tier upon tier. A little to our right rose the towers of the Burg, and nearer still, standing grim, the torture tower, which was, and is, perhaps, the most interesting place in the city. For centuries the tradition of the Iron Virgin of Nuremberg has been handed down as an instance of the horrors of cruelty of which man is capable; we had long looked forward to seeing it; and here at last was its home.

In one of our pauses we leaned over the wall of the moat and looked down. The garden seemed quite fifty or sixty feet below us, and the sun pouring into it with an intense, moveless heat like that of an oven. Beyond rose the grey grim wall seemingly of endless height, and losing itself right and left in the angles of bastion and counterscarp. Trees and bushes crowned the wall, and above again towered the lofty houses on whose massive beauty time has only set the hand of approval. The sun was hot and we were lazy; time was our own, and we lingered, leaning on the wall. Just below us was a pretty sight – a great black cat lying stretched in the sun, whilst round her gambolled prettily a tiny black kitten. The mother would wave her tail for the kitten to play with, or would raise her feet and push away the little one as an encouragement to further play. They were just at the foot of the wall, and Elias P. Hutcheson, in order to help the play, stooped and took from the walk a moderate sized pebble.

'See!' he said, 'I will drop it near the kitten, and they will both wonder where it came from.'

'Oh, be careful,' said my wife; 'you might hit the dear little thing!'

'Not me, ma'am,' said Elias P. 'Why, I'm as tender as a Maine cherry tree. Lor, bless ye, I wouldn't hurt the poor pooty little critter more'n I'd scalp a baby. An' you may bet your variegated socks on that! See, I'll drop it fur away on the outside so's not to go near her!' Thus saying, he leaned over and held his arm out at full length and dropped the stone. It may be that there is some attractive force which draws lesser matters to greater; or more probably that the wall was not plumb but sloped to its base – we not noticing the inclination from above; but the stone fell with a sickening thud that came up to us through the hot air, right on the kitten's head, and shattered out its little brains then and there. The black cat cast a swift upward glance, and we saw her eyes like green fire fixed an instant on Elias P. Hutcheson; and then her attention was given to the kitten, which lay still with just a quiver of her tiny limbs, whilst a thin red stream trickled from a gaping wound. With a muffled cry, such as a human being might give, she bent over the kitten, licking its wound and moaning. Suddenly she seemed to realize that it was dead, and again threw her eyes up at us. I shall never forget the sight, for she looked the perfect incarnation of hate. Her green eyes blazed with lurid fire, and the white, sharp teeth seemed to almost shine through the blood which dabbled her mouth and whiskers. She gnashed her teeth, and her claws stood out stark and at full length on every paw. Then she made a wild rush up the wall as if to reach us, but when the momentum ended fell back, and further added to her horrible appearance for she fell on the kitten, and rose with her black fur smeared with its brains and blood. Amelia turned quite faint, and I had to lift her back from the wall. There was a seat close by in shade of a spreading plane tree, and here I placed her whilst she composed herself. Then I went back to Hutcheson, who stood without moving, looking down on the angry cat below.

As I joined him, he said: 'Wall, I guess that air the savagest beast I ever see – 'cept once when an Apache squaw had an edge on a half-breed what they nicknamed "Splinters" 'cos of the way he fixed up her papoose which he stole on a raid just to show that he appreciated the way they had given his mother the fire torture. She got that kinder look so set on her face that it jest seemed to grow there. She followed Splinters more'n three year till at last the braves got him and handed him over to her. They did say that no man, white or Injun, had ever been so long a-dying under the tortures of the Apaches. The only time I ever see her smile was when I wiped her out. I kem on the camp just in time to see Splinters pass in his checks, and he wasn't sorry to go either. He was a hard citizen, and though I never could shake with him after that papoose business – for it was bitter bad, and he should have been a white man, for he looked like one – I see he had got paid out in full. Durn me, but I took a piece of his hide from one of his skinnin' posts an' had it made into a pocket-book. It's here now!' and he slapped the breast pocket of his coat.

Whilst he was speaking the cat was continuing her frantic efforts to get up the wall. She would take a run back and then charge up, sometimes reaching an incredible height. She did not seem to mind the heavy fall which she got each time but started with renewed vigour; and at every tumble her appearance became more horrible. Hutcheson was a kind-hearted man – my wife and I had both noticed little acts of kindness to animals as well as to persons – and he seemed concerned at the state of fury to which the cat had wrought herself.

'Wall, now!' he said, 'I du declare that that poor critter seems quite desperate. There! there! poor thing, it was all an accident – though that won't bring back your little one to you. Say! I wouldn't have had such a thing happen for a thousand! Just shows what a clumsy fool of a man can do when he tries to play! Seems I'm too darned slipperhanded to even play with a cat. Say Colonel!' it was a pleasant way he had to bestow titles freely – 'I hope your wife don't hold no grudge against me on account of this unpleasantness? Why, I wouldn't have had it occur on no account.'

He came over to Amelia and apologized profusely, and she with her usual kindness of heart hastened to assure him that she quite under-stood that it was an accident. Then we all went again to the wall and looked over.

The cat missing Hutcheson's face had drawn back across the moat, and was sitting on her haunches as though ready to spring. Indeed, the very instant she saw him she did spring, and with a blind unreasoning fury, which would have been grotesque, only that it was so frightfully real. She did not try to run up the wall, but simply launched herself at him as though hate and fury could lend her wings to pass straight through the great distance between them. Amelia, womanlike, got quite concerned, and said to Elias P. in a warning voice: 'Oh! you must be very careful. That animal would try to kill you if she were here; her eyes look like positive murder.'

He laughed out jovially. 'Excuse me, ma'am,' he said, 'but I can't help laughin'. Fancy a man that has fought grizzlies an' Injuns bein' careful of bein' murdered by a cat!'

When the cat heard him laugh, her whole demeanour seemed to change. She no longer tried to jump or run up the wall, but went quietly over, and sitting again beside the dead kitten began to lick and fondle it as though it were alive.

'See!' said I, 'the effect of a really strong man. Even that animal in the midst of her fury recognizes the voice of a master, and bows to him!'

'Like a squaw!' was the only comment of Elias P. Hutcheson, as we moved on our way round the city fosse. Every now and then we looked over the wall and each time saw the cat following us. At first she had kept going back to the dead kitten, and then as the distance grew greater took it in her mouth and so followed. After a while, however, she abandoned this, for we saw her following all alone; she had evidently hidden the body somewhere. Amelia's alarm grew at the cat's persistence, and more than once she repeated her warning; but the American always laughed with amusement, till finally, seeing that she was beginning to be worried, he said: 'I say, ma'am, you needn't be skeered over that cat. I go heeled, I du!' Here he slapped his pistol pocket at the back of his lumbar region. 'Why sooner'n have you worried, I'll shoot the critter, right here, an' risk the police interferin' with a citizen of the United States for carryin' arms contrary to reg'lations!' As he spoke he looked over the wall, but the cat, on seeing him, retreated, with a growl, into a bed of tall flowers, and was hidden. He went on: 'Blest if that ar critter ain't got more sense of what's good for her than most Christians. I guess we've seen the last of her! You bet, she'll go back now to that busted kitten and have a private funeral of it, all to herself!'

Amelia did not like to say more, lest he might, in mistaken kindness to her, fulfil his threat of shooting the cat: and so we went on and crossed the little wooden bridge leading to the gateway whence ran the steep paved roadway between the Burg and the pentagonal torture tower. As we crossed the bridge we saw the cat again down below us. When she saw us her fury seemed to return, and she made frantic efforts to get up the steep wall. Hutcheson laughed as he looked down at her, and said: 'Good-bye, old girl. Sorry I in-jured your feelin's, but you'll get over it in time! So long!' And then we passed through the long, dim archway and came to the gate of the Burg.

When we came out again after our survey of this most beautiful old place which not even the well-intentioned efforts of the Gothic restorers of forty years ago have been able to spoil – though their restoration was then glaring white – we seemed to have quite forgotten the unpleasant episode of the morning. The old lime tree and its great trunk gnarled with the passing of nearly nine centuries, the deep well cut through the heart of the rock by those captives of old, and the lovely view from the city wall whence we heard, spread over almost a full quarter of an hour, the multitudinous chimes of the city, had all helped to wipe out from our minds the incident of the slain kitten.

We were the only visitors who had entered the torture tower that morning – so at least said the old custodian – and as we had the place all to ourselves were able to make a minute and more satisfactory survey than would have otherwise been possible. The custodian, looking to us as the sole source of his gains for the day, was willing to meet our wishes in any way. The torture tower is truly a grim place, even now when many thousands of visitors have sent a stream of life, and the joy that follows life, into the place; but at the time I mention it wore its grimmest and most gruesome aspect. The dust of ages seemed to have settled on it, and the darkness and the horror of its memories to have become sentient in a way that would have satisfied the pantheistic souls of Philo or Spinoza. The lower chamber where we entered was seemingly, in its normal state, filled with incarnate darkness; even the hot sunlight streaming in through the door seemed to be lost in the vast thickness of the walls, and only showed the masonry rough as when the builder's scaffolding had come down, but coated with dust and marked here and there with patches of dark stain which, if walls could speak, could have given their own dread memories of fear and pain. We were glad to pass up the dusty wooden staircase, the custodian leaving the outer door open to light us somewhat on our way; for to our eyes the one long-wick'd, evil-smelling candle stuck in a sconce on the wall gave an inadequate light. When we came up through the open trap in the corner of the chamber overhead, Amelia held on to me so tightly that I could actually feel her heart beat. I must say for my own part that I was not surprised at her fear, for this room was even more gruesome than that below. Here there was certainly more light, but only just sufficient to realize the horrible surroundings of the place. The builders of the tower had evidently intended that only they who should gain the top should have any of the joys of light and prospect. There, as we had noticed from below, were ranges of windows, albeit of medieval smallness, but elsewhere in the tower were only a very few narrow slits such as were habitual in places of medieval defence. A few of these only lit the chamber, and these so high up in the wall that from no part could the sky be seen through the thickness of the walls. In racks, and leaning in disorder against the walls, were a number of headsmen's swords, great double-handed weapons with broad blade and keen edge. Hard by were several blocks whereon the necks of the victims had lain, with here and there deep notches where the steel had bitten through the guard of flesh and shored into the wood. Round the chamber, placed in all sorts of irregular ways, were many implements of torture which made one's heart ache to see – chairs full of spikes which gave instant and excruciating pain; chairs and couches with dull knobs whose torture was seemingly less, but which, though slower, were equally efficacious; racks, belts, boots, gloves, collars, all made for compressing at will; steel baskets in which the head could be slowly crushed into a pulp if necessary; watchmen's hooks with long handle and knife that cut at resistance – this a speciality of the old Nuremberg police system; and many, many other devices for man's injury to man. Amelia grew quite pale with the horror of the things, but fortunately did not faint, for being a little overcome she sat down on a torture chair, but jumped up again with a shriek, all tendency to faint gone. We both pretended that it was the injury done to her dress by the dust of the chair, and the rusty spikes which had upset her, and Mr Hutcheson acquiesced in accepting the explanation with a kind-hearted laugh.

But the central object in the whole of this chamber of horrors was the engine known as the Iron Virgin, which stood near the centre of the room. It was a rudely shaped figure of a woman, something of the bell order, or, to make a closer comparison, of the figure of Mrs Noah in the children's Ark, but without that slimness of waist and perfect *rondeur* of hip which marks the aesthetic type of the Noah family. One would hardly have recognized it as intended for a human figure at all had not the founder shaped on the forehead a rude semblance of a woman's face. The machine was coated with rust without, and covered with dust; a rope was fastened to a ring in the front of the figure, about where the waist should have been, and was drawn through a pulley, fastened on the wooden pillar which sustained the flooring above. The custodian pulling this rope showed that a section of the front was hinged like a door at one side; we then saw that the engine was of considerable thickness, leaving just room enough inside for a man to be placed. The door was of equal thickness and of great weight, for it took the custodian all his strength, aided though he was by the contrivance of the pulley, to open it. This weight was partly due to the fact that the door was of manifest purpose hung so as to throw its weight downwards, so that it might shut of its own accord when the strain was released. The inside was honeycombed with rust – nay more, the rust alone that comes through time would hardly have eaten so deep into the iron walls; the rust of the cruel stains was deep indeed! It was only, however, when we came to look at the inside of the door that the diabolical intention was manifest to the full. Here were several long spikes, square and massive, broad at the base and sharp at the points, placed in such a position that when the door should close the upper ones would pierce the eyes of the victim, and the lower ones his heart and vitals. The sight was too much for poor Amelia, and this time she fainted dead off, and I had to carry her down the stairs, and place her on a bench outside till she recovered. That she felt it to the quick was afterwards shown by the fact that my eldest son bears to this day a rude birthmark on his breast, which has, by family consent, been accepted as representing the Nuremberg Virgin.

When we got back to the chamber we found Hutcheson still opposite the Iron Virgin; he had been evidently philosophizing, and now gave us the benefit of his thought in the shape of a sort of exordium.

'Wall, I guess I've been learnin' somethin' here while madam has been gettin' over her faint. 'Pears to me that we're a long way behind the times on our side of the big drink. We uster think out on the plains that the Injun could give us points in tryin' to make a man oncomfort-able; but I guess your old medieval law-and-order party could raise him every time. Splinters was pretty good in his bluff on the squaw, but this here young miss held a straight flush all high on him. The points of them spikes air sharp enough still, though even the edges air eaten out by what uster be on them. It'd be a good thing for our Indian section to get some specimens of this here play-toy to send round to the reservations jest to knock the stuffin' out of the bucks, and the squaws too, by showing them as how old civilization lays over them at their best. Guess but I'll get in that box a minute jest to see how it feels!'

'Oh no! no!' said Amelia. 'It is too terrible!'

'Guess, ma'am, nothin's too terrible to the explorin' mind. I've been in some queer places in my time. Spent a night inside a dead horse while a prairie fire swept over me in Montana territory – an' another time slept inside a dead buffler when the Comanches was on the war-path an' I didn't keer to leave my kyard on them. I've been two days in a caved-in tunnel in the Billy Broncho gold mine in New Mexico, an' was one of the four shut up for three parts of a day in the caisson what slid over on her side when we was settin' the foundations of the Buffalo Bridge. I've not funked an odd experience yet, an' I don't propose to begin now!'

We saw that he was set on the experiment, so I said: 'Well, hurry up, old man, and get through it quick.'

'All right, General,' said he, 'but I calculate we ain't quite ready yet. The gentlemen, my predecessors, what stood in that thar canister, didn't volunteer for the office – not much! And I guess there was some ornamental tyin' up before the big stroke was made. I want to go into this thing fair and square, so I must get fixed up proper first. I dare say this old galoot can rise some string and tie me up accordin' to sample?'

This was said interrogatively to the old custodian, but the latter, who understood the drift of his speech, though perhaps not appreciating to the full the niceties of dialect and imagery, shook his head. His protest was, however, only formal and made to be overcome. The American thrust a gold piece into his hand, saying, 'Take it, pard! it's your pot; and don't be skeer'd. This ain't no necktie party that you're asked to assist in!' He produced some thin frayed rope and proceeded to bind our companion with sufficient strictness for the purpose. When the upper part of his body was bound, Hutcheson said: 'Hold on a moment, Judge. Guess I'm too heavy for you to tote into the

94

canister. You jest let me walk in, and then you can wash up regardin' my legs!'

Whilst speaking he had backed himself into the opening which was just enough to hold him. It was a close fit and no mistake. Amelia looked on with fear in her eyes, but she evidently did not like to say anything. Then the custodian completed his task by tying the American's feet together so that he was now absolutely helpless and fixed in his voluntary prison. He seemed to really enjoy it, and the incipient smile which was habitual to his face blossomed into actuality as he said: 'Guess this here Eve was made out of the rib of a dwarf! There ain't much room for a full-grown citizen of the United States to hustle. We uster make our coffins more roomier in Idaho territory. Now, Judge, you jest begin to let this door down, slow, on to me. I want to feel the same pleasure as the other jays had when those spikes began to move toward their eyes!'

'Oh no! no! no!' broke in Amelia hysterically. 'It is too terrible! I can't bear to see it! – I can't! I can't!'

But the American was obdurate. 'Say, Colonel,' said he, 'Why not take Madame for a little promenade? I wouldn't hurt her feelin's for the world; but now that I am here, havin' kem eight thousand miles, wouldn't it be too hard to give up the very experience I've been pinin' an' pantin' fur? A man can't get to feel like canned goods every time! Me and the Judge here'll fix up this thing in no time, an' then you'll come back, an' we'll all laugh together!'

Once more the resolution that is born of curiosity triumphed, and Amelia stayed holding tight to my arm and shivering whilst the custodian began to slacken slowly inch by inch the rope that held back the iron door. Hutcheson's face was positively radiant as his eyes followed the first movement of the spikes.

'Wall!' he said, 'I guess I've not had enjoyment like this since I left Noo York. Bar a scrap with a French sailor at Wapping – an' that warn't much of a picnic neither – I've not had a show fur real pleasure in this dod-rotted continent, where there ain't no b'ars nor no Injuns, an' wheer nary man goes heeled. Slow there, Judge! Don't you rush this business! I want a show for my money this game – I du!'

The custodian must have had in him some of the blood of his predecessors in that ghastly tower, for he worked the engine with a deliberate and excruciating slowness which after five minutes, in which the outer edge of the door had not moved half as many inches, began to overcome Amelia. I saw her lips whiten, and felt her hold upon my arm relax. I looked around an instant for a place whereon to lay her, and when I looked at her again found that her eye had become fixed on the side of the Virgin. Following its direction I saw the black cat crouching out of sight. Her green eyes shone like danger lamps in the gloom of the place, and their colour was heightened by the blood which still smeared her coat and reddened her mouth. I cried out: 'The cat! look out for the cat!' for even then she sprang out before the engine. At this moment she looked like a triumphant demon. Her eyes blazed with ferocity, her hair bristled out till she seemed twice her normal size, and her tail lashed about as does a tiger's when the quarry is before it.

Elias P. Hutcheson when he saw her was amused, and his eyes positively sparkled with fun as he said: 'Darned if the squaw hain't got on all her war-paint! Jest give her a shove off if she comes any of her tricks on me, for I'm so fixed everlastingly by the boss, that durn my skin if I can keep my eyes from her if she wants them! Easy there, Judge! don't you slack that ar rope or I'm euchred!'

At this moment Amelia completed her faint, and I had to clutch hold of her round the waist or she would have fallen to the floor. Whilst attending to her I saw the black cat crouching for a spring, and jumped up to turn the creature out.

But at that instant, with a sort of hellish scream, she hurled herself, not as we expected at Hutcheson, but straight at the face of the custodian. Her claws seemed to be tearing wildly as one sees in the Chinese drawings of the dragon rampant, and as I looked I saw one of them light on the poor man's eye, and actually tear through it and down his cheek, leaving a wide band of red where the blood seemed to spurt from every vein.

With a yell of sheer terror which came quicker than even his sense of pain, the man leaped back, dropping as he did so the rope which held back the iron door. I jumped for it, but was too late, for the cord ran like lightning through the pulley-block, and the heavy mass fell forward from its own weight.

As the door closed I caught a glimpse of our poor companion's face. He seemed frozen with terror. His eyes stared with a horrible anguish as if dazed, and no sound came from his lips.

And then the spikes did their work. Happily the end was quick, for when I wrenched open the door they had pierced so deep that they had locked in the bones of the skull through which they had crushed, and actually tore him – it – out of his iron prison till, bound as he was, he fell at full length with a sickly thud upon the floor, the face turning upwards as he fell.

I rushed to my wife, lifted her up and carried her out, for I feared for her very reason if she should wake from her faint to such a scene. I laid her on the bench outside and ran back. Leaning against the wooden column was the custodian moaning in pain whilst he held his reddening handkerchief to his eyes. And sitting on the head of the poor American was the cat, purring loudly as she licked the blood which trickled through the gashed sockets of his eyes.

I think no one will call me cruel because I seized one of the old executioners' swords and shore her in two as she sat.

A Deed of Vengeance?

One of the many duties that Bram Stoker performed for Henry Irving was to read and pass judgement on the ever-increasing number of scripts sent in by playwrights for the great actor's consideration. One such submission was to introduce Stoker to the creator of another famous literary character – Arthur Conan Doyle, the author of the Sherlock Holmes stories. This episode began on a day in 1891 when Irving bustled into Stoker's office in the Lyceum, dumped a packet of typewritten folio sheets on to his desk, asked for his manager's views on the manuscript, and then swept out of the room once again. Stoker later wrote, 'I read the manuscript with profound interest and was touched by its humour and pathos to my very heart's core. It was very short, and before Irving came in again from the stage I had read it a second time.' Stoker was in no doubt as to his verdict. 'I told Irving that the play must never leave the Lyceum. He must own it at any price. It was made for him.' To Bram's surprise, his Chief told him that he *had* already read the manuscript and totally agreed with his decision. Stoker also noted in his biography, 'The author's name was Conan Doyle and the play was his first attempt at drama. It was then named *A Straggler of '15*, but this was later simplified to *Waterloo*.'

Irving's masterly playing of the central character, an old military veteran, made the play an enormous success and also helped establish Conan Doyle's reputation as a dramatist, a fact of which he remained inordinately proud. *Waterloo* was played over 340 times by Irving in Britain and America between 1894 and 1905, and Stoker rated it as one of the company's finest productions: 'To my mind, as an acting play it is perfect, and Irving's playing in it was the high-water mark of histronic art.'

As a result of this success, Conan Doyle became a guest at Irving's Beefsteak Room, and he and Bram Stoker found they had much in common where writing and literature were concerned.

And indeed the two men were later approached independently by *The Gentlewoman*, a leading weekly journal for ladies and invited to take part in an unusual literary experiment. Both were happy to accept the challenge. The journal was proposing a serial novel entitled *The Fate of Fenella* in which twenty-four well-known male and female authors of fiction were invited to write a chapter taking the story on from his or her predecessor and further compounding the mystery of the tale. Among those who took part in this literary curiosity – described by the publishers as 'the most extraordinary novel of modern times' – were Florence Marryat, Helen Mathers, F. Anstey, Conan Doyle and Bram Stoker. Bram's chapter was the tenth in the serial and appeared in the issue of 30 January 1892. In this episode Lord Francis Onslow, who believes his wife Fenella to be implicated in a murder, has an unexpected meeting both with her and with a friend who can throw some light on the mystery. . . .

LORD FRANCIS ONSLOW lifted his cap. The action was an instinctive one, for he was face to face with a lady; but he was half dazed with the unexpected meeting, and could not collect his thoughts. He only remembered that when he had last seen his wife she was opening the door of her chamber to De Mürger. For weeks he had been schooling himself for such a meeting, for he knew that on his return such might at any time occur; but now, when the moment had come, and unexpectedly, the old pain of his shame overwhelmed him anew. His face grew white – white till it seemed to Fenella that it was of the pallor of death. She knew that she had been so far guilty of what had happened that the murder had been the outcome of her previous acts. She knew also that her husband was ignorant of his part in the deed – and her horror of the man, blood-guilty in such a way, was fined down by the sense of her own partial guilt. The trial, with all its consequent pain to a proud and sensitive woman, had softened her, and she grasped at any hope. The sight of Frank, his gaunt cheeks, which told their tale of suffering, and now the deadly pallor, awoke all the protective feeling which is a part of a woman's love. It was with her whole soul in her voice that she said again: 'Frank!'

His voice was stern as well as sad as he answered her: 'What is it?'

Her heart went cold, but she persevered. 'Frank, I must have a word with you – I must. For God's sake, for Ronny's sake, do not deny me.'

She did not know that as yet Frank Onslow was in ignorance of De Mürger's death; and when his answer came it seemed more hard than even he intended: 'Do you wish to speak of that night?'

In a faint voice she answered: 'I do.' Then looking in his eyes and seeing the hard look becoming harder still – for a man is seldom generous with a woman where his honour is concerned, she added: 'O Heaven! Frank! You do not think me guilty! No, no, not you! not you! That would be too cruel!'

Frank Onslow paused and said: 'Fenella, God help me! but I do,' and he turned away his head. His wife, of course, thought that he alluded to the murder, and not to her sin against him as he saw it, and with a low moan she turned away and hid her face in her hands. Then with an effort she drew herself up, and without a word or a single movement to show that she even recognized his presence, she passed on up the street.

Frank Onslow stood for a few moments watching her retreating figure, and then went across the street and turned the next corner on his way to the post office, for which he had been enquiring when he met his wife. At the door he was stopped by a cheery voice and an outstretched hand: 'Onslow!'

'Castleton!' The two men shook hands warmly.

'I see you did not get my telegram,' said Lord Castleton. 'It is waiting for you at the post office.'

'What telegram?'

'To tell you that I was on my way here from London. I went in your interest, old fellow. I thought you would like full particulars – the newspapers are so vague.'

'What papers? My interest? Tell me all. I am ignorant of all that has passed for the last six weeks.' A vague, shadowy fear began to creep over his spirits.

Castleton's voice was full of sympathy as he answered: 'Then you have not heard of – but stay. It is a long story. Come back to the yacht. I was just going to join you there. We shall be all alone, and I can tell you all. I have the newspapers here for you.' He motioned to a roll under his arm.

The two went down to the harbour, and finding the sailor waiting with the boat at the steps, were rowed to the yacht and got on board.

Here the two men were all alone. Then, with a preliminary clearing of his voice, Castleton began his story: 'Frank Onslow – better get the worst over at once – just after you went away from Harrogate your wife was tried for murder and acquitted.'

'My God! Fenella tried for murder? Whose murder?'

'That scoundrel De Mürger. It seems he went into her room in the night and attempted violence, so she stabbed him –'

Castleton stopped in amazement, for a look of radiance came over Frank Onslow's face, as he murmured 'Thank God!' Recalled to himself by Castleton's silence, for he was too amazed to go on, Frank said. 'I have a reason, old fellow; I shall tell it to you later, but go on. Tell me all the facts, or let me read the papers. Remember I am as yet quite ignorant of it all and I am full of anxiety!'

Without a word Castleton handed him the papers, and, lighting a fresh cigar, sat down with his back to him, and presently yielded to the sun and fresh air and fell into a doze.

Frank Onslow took the papers, and read carefully from end to end the account of the trial of his wife for the murder of De Mürger. When he had finished he sat with the folded paper in his hand, and his eyes had the same far-away look in them which they had had on that fatal night. The hypnotic trance was on him again.

Presently he rose, and with stealthy steps approached his sleeping friend. Murmuring 'Why did I not kill him?' he struck with the folded paper, as though with a dagger, the form before him. Castleton, who had sunk into a pleasant sleep and whose fat face was wreathed with a smile, was annoyed at the rude awakening. 'What the devil!' he began angrily, and then stopped as his eyes met the face of his friend and he realized that he was in some sort of trance. He grew very pale as he saw Frank Onslow stab, and stab, and stab again. There was a certain grotesqueness in the affair – the man in such terrible earnest, in his mind committing murder, while his real weapon was but a folded paper. As he stabbed he hissed, 'Why did I not kill him? Why did I not kill him?' Then he went through a series of movements as though he were softly pulling an imaginary door shut behind him, and so back to his own chair, where he sat down hiding his face in his hands.

Castleton sat looking at him in amazement, and then murmured to himself: 'They thought it was someone stronger than Fenella whose grasp made those marks on the dead man's throat.' He suddenly looked round to see that no one but himself had observed what had happened, and then, being satisfied on this point, murmured again: 'A noble woman, by Jove! A noble woman!' He called out: 'Frank – Frank Onslow! Wake up, man.'

Onslow raised his head as a man does when suddenly awakened, and smiled as he said: 'What is it, old man? Have I been asleep?' It was quite evident that he had no recollection of what had just passed.

Castleton came and sat down beside him, and his kindly face was grave as he asked: 'You have read the papers?'

'I have.'

'Now tell me – you offered to do so – why you said "Thank God!" when I told you that your wife had killed De Mürger?'

Frank Onslow paused. Although the memory of what he had thought to be his shame had been with him daily and nightly until he had become familiarized with it, it was another thing to speak of it, even to such a friend as Castleton. Even now, when it was apparent from the issue of the trial that his wife had avenged so dreadfully the attempt upon her honour, he felt it hard to speak on the subject. Castleton saw the doubt and struggle in his mind which was reflected in his face, and said earnestly, as he laid his hand upon his shoulder: 'Do not hesitate to tell me, Frank. I do not ask out of mere curiosity. I am perhaps a better friend than you think in helping to clear up a certain doubt which I see before me. I think you know I am a friend.'

'One of the best a man ever had!' said Frank impulsively, as he took the other's hand. Then turning away his head, he said slowly: 'You were surprised because I was glad Fenella killed that scoundrel. I can tell you, Castleton, but I would not tell anyone else. It was because I saw him enter her room, and, God forgive me! I thought at the time that it was by her wish. That is why I came away from Harrogate that night. That is what kept me away. How could I go back and face my friends with such a shame fresh upon me? It was your lending me your yacht, old man, that made life possible. When I was by myself through the wildness of the Bay of Biscay and among the great billows of the Atlantic I began to be able to bear. I had steeled myself, I thought, and when I heard that so far from my wife being guilty of such a shame, she actually killed the man that attempted her honour, is it any wonder that I felt joyful?'

After a pause Castleton asked: 'How did you come to see – to see it. Why did you take no step to prevent it? Forgive me, old fellow, but I want to understand.'

Frank Onslow went to the rail, and leaned over. When he came back Castleton saw that his eyes were wet. With what cheerfulness he could assume, he answered: 'On that very night I had made up my mind to try to win back my wife's love. I wrote a letter to her, a letter in which I poured out my whole soul, and I left my room to put it under her door, so that she would get it in the morning. But' – here he paused, and then said, slowly, 'but when in the corridor, I saw her door open, and at the same moment De Mürger appeared.'

'Did she seem surprised?'

'Not at first. But a moment after a look of amazement crossed her face, and she stepped back into the room, he following her.' As he said this he put his head between his hands and groaned.

'And then?' added his friend.

'And then I hardly know what happened. My mind seems full of a dim memory of a blank existence, and then a series of wild whirling thoughts, something like that last moment after death in Wiertz's picture. I think I must have slept, for it was two o'clock when I saw Fenella, and the clock was striking five when I crossed the bridge after I had left the hotel.'

'And the letter? What became of it?'

Frank started. 'The letter? I never thought of it. Stay! I must have left it on the table in my room. I remember seeing it there a little while before I came away.'

'How was it addressed? Do not think me inquisitive, but I cannot help thinking that that letter may yet be of some great importance.'

Frank smiled, a sad smile enough, as he answered: 'By the pet name I had for Fenella – Mrs Right. I used to chaff her because she always defended her position when we argued, and so, when I wanted to tease her, I called her Mrs Right.'

'Was it written on hotel paper?'

'No. I was going to write on some, but I thought it would be better to use the sort we had when – when we were first married. There were a few sheets in my writing case, so I took one.'

'That was headed somewhere in Surrey, was it not?'

'Yes; Chiddingford, near Haslemere. It was a pretty place, too, called The Grange. Fenella fell in love with it, and made me buy it right away.'

'Is anyone living there now?'

'It is let to someone. I don't think that I heard the name. The agent knows. When the trouble came I told him to do what he could with it, and not to bother me with it any more. After a while he wrote and asked if I would mind it being let to a foreigner? I told him he might let it to a devil so long as he did not worry me.'

Lord Castleton paused awhile, and asked the next question in a hesitating way. He felt embarrassed, and showed it: 'Tell me one thing more, old fellow – if – if you don't mind.'

'My dear Castleton, I'll tell you anything you like.'

'How did you sign the letter?'

Onslow's face looked sad as he answered. 'I signed it by another old pet name we both understood. We had pet names – people always have when they are first married,' he added with embarrassment.

'Of course,' murmured the sympathetic Castleton.

'One such name lasted a long time. An old friend of my father's came to see us, and in a playful moment he said I was a "sad dog". Fenella took it up and used to call me "Doggie", and I often signed myself "Frank Doggie" – as men usually do.'

'Of course,' again murmured Castleton, as if such a signature was a customary thing. Then he added, 'And on this occasion?'

'On this occasion I used the name that seemed full of happiest memories. "Frank Doggie" may seem idiotic to an outsider, but to Fenella and myself it might mean much.'

The two men sat silent awhile, and then Castleton asked softly: 'I suppose it may be taken for granted that Lady Francis never got the letter?'

'I take it, it is so; but it is no matter now, I refused to speak with her just before I met you. I did not know then what I know now – and she will never speak to me again.' He sighed as he spoke, and turned away. Then he went to the rail of the yacht and leaned over with his head down, looking into the still blue water beneath him.

'Poor old Frank!' said Castleton to himself. 'I can't but think that this matter may come right yet. I must find out what became of that letter, in case Lady Francis never got it. It would prove to her that Frank –'

His train of thought suddenly stopped. A new idea seemed to strike him so forcibly that it quite upset him. Onslow, who had come over from the rail, noticed it. 'I say, Castleton, what is wrong with you? You have got quite white about the gills.'

'Nothing – nothing,' he answered hastily. 'I am subject to it. They call it heart. Pardon me for a bit, I'll go to my bunk and lie down,' and he went below.

In truth, he was overwhelmed by the thought which had just struck him. If his surmise were true, that Onslow, in a hypnotic trance, as he had almost proved by its recurrence, had killed De Mürger, where, then, was Fenella's heroism after all? True that she had taken the blame on herself; but might it not have been that she was morally guilty all the same? Why, then, had she taken the blame? Was it not because she feared that her husband might have refused to screen her shame; or because she feared that if any less heroic aspect of the tragedy was presented to the public, her own fair fame might suffer in greater degree? Could it indeed be that Fenella Onslow was not a heroine, but only a calculating woman of exceeding smartness? Then, again, if Frank Onslow believed that his wife had avenged her honour, was it wise to disturb such belief? He might think, if once the suggestion were made to him, that his honour was preserved only by his own unconscious act.

Was it then wise to disturb existing relations between the husband and wife, sad though they were? Did they come together again, they might in mutual confidence arrive at a real knowledge of the facts, and then – and then, what would be the result? And besides, might there not be some danger in any suggestion made as to his suspicion of who struck the blow? It was true that Lady Francis had been acquitted of the crime, although she confessed to the killing; but her husband might still be tried – and if tried? What then would be the result of the discovery of the missing letter on which he had been building such hopes?

The problem was too much for Lord Castleton. His life had been too sunny and easy-going to allow of familiarity with great emotions, and such a problem as this was to him overwhelming. The issue was too big for him; and revolving in his own mind all that belonged to it, he glided into sleep.

The Man from Shorrox'

It was always a great pleasure for Bram Stoker when Henry Irving's tours took him back to Ireland and especially to his home town of Dublin. Ever since 1876, Irving and Dublin had shared a mutual admiration, and whenever the actor played in the city he was sure of full houses and many invitations to dinner. Stoker, too, took the opportunity to see his relatives and old friends, and whenever possible invited them to join him and his Chief at supper.

A visit to Dublin in the autumn of 1893 provided Bram with the idea for another story when he and Irving dined with Thornley Stoker, Bram's elder brother, whom the actor had first met on an earlier visit to the city. Thornley was a bluff and exuberant man, and Bram described him as 'something like a schoolboy about to go off on a long-expected holiday'. During his life he had travelled a great deal all over Ireland and he was a fund of entertaining stories about the remoter areas of the country and some of the strange people and even stranger customs to be found there. While they dined one night, Thornley enraptured Bram and Henry Irving with a story about a grisly joke, involving a corpse, that had been played on a commercial traveller at an old inn. Bram at once saw the germ of a short story.

'The Man From Shorrox'' was written back home in London during the following winter and was published in the February 1894 issue of the prestigious *Pall Mall Magazine*. Bram told the story in a rich Irish dialect and in an over-the-bar fashion, creating eccentric and lively characters. Henry Irving particularly enjoyed it. Once again, however, the story was not included in any collected edition of Stoker's works and its appearance here marks its first return to print in close on one hundred years. I find this a particularly surprising fact in the light of a comment by Harry Ludlam in his book *A Biography of Dracula: The Life Story of Bram Stoker* (1962) that 'The Man From Shorrox'' is undeniably 'a stepping stone to Dracula'. For it was less than two years after Stoker had finished this story that he began to write the vampire novel that would make him world famous.

THROTH, YER 'ANN'RS, I'll tell ye wid pleasure; though, trooth to tell, it's only poor wurrk telling the same shtory over an' over agin. But I niver object to tell it to rale gintlemin, like yer 'ann'rs, what don't forget that a poor man has a mouth on to him as much as Creeshus himself has.

The place was a market town in Kilkenny – or maybe King's County or Queen's County. At all evints, it was wan of them counties what Cromwell – bad cess to him! – gev his name to. An' the house was called after him that was the Lord Liftinint an' invinted the polis – God forgive him! It was kep' be a man iv the name iv Misther Mickey Byrne an' his good lady – at laste it was till wan dark night whin the bhoys mistuk him for another gintleman, an unknown man, what had bought a contagious property – mind ye the impidence iv him. Mickey was comin' back from the Curragh Races wid his skin that tight wid the full of the whiskey inside of him that he couldn't open his eyes to see what was goin' on, or his mouth to set the bhoys right afther he had got the first tap on the head wid wan of the blackthorns what they done such jobs wid. The poor bhoys was that full of sorra for their mishap whin they brung him home to his widdy that the crather hadn't the hearrt to be too sevare on thim. At the first iv course she was wroth, bein' only a woman afther all, an' weemin not bein' gave to rayson like min is. Millia murdher! but for a bit she was like a madwoman, and was nigh to have cut the heads from aff av thim wid the mate chopper, till, seein' thim so white and quite, she all at wance flung down the chopper an' knelt down be the corp.

'Lave me to me dead,' she sez. 'Oh min! it's no use more people nor is needful bein' made unhappy over this night's terrible wurrk. Mick Byrne would have no man worse for him whin he was living, and he'll have harm to none for his death! Now go; an', oh bhoys, be dacent and quite, an' don't thry a poor widdied sowl too hard!'

Well, afther that she made no change in things ginerally, but kep' on the hotel jist the same; an' whin some iv her friends wanted her to get help, she only sez: 'Mick an' me run this house well enough; an' whin I'm thinkin' of takin' help I'll tell yez. I'll go on be meself, as I mane to, till Mick an' me comes together agin.'

An', sure enough, the ould place wint on jist the same, though, more betoken, there wasn't Mick wid his shillelagh to kape the pace whin things got pretty hot on fair nights, an' in the gran' ould election times, when heads was bruk like eggs – glory be to God!

My! but she was the fine woman, was the Widdy Byrne! A gran' crathur intirely: a fine upshtandin' woman, nigh as tall as a modherate-sized man, wid a forrm on her that'd warrm yer hearrt to look at, it sthood out that way in the right places. She had shkin like satin, wid a warrm flush in it, like the sun shinin' on a crock iv yesterday's crame; an' her cheeks an' her neck was that firrm that ye couldn't take a pinch iv thim – though sorra wan iver dar'd to thry, the worse luck! But her hair! Begor, that was the finishing touch that set all the min crazy. It was jist wan mass iv red, like the heart iv a burnin' furze-bush whin the smoke goes from aff iv it. Musha! but it'd make the blood come up in yer eyes to see the glint iv that hair wid the light shinin' on it. There was niver a man, what was a man at all at all, iver kem in be the door that he didn't want to put his two arrms round the widdy an' giv' her a hug immadiate. They was fine min too, some iv thim – and warrm men – big graziers from Kildare, and the like, that counted their cattle be scores, an' used to come ridin' in to market on huntin' horses what they'd refuse hundhreds iv pounds for from officers in the Curragh an' the quality. Begor, but some iv thim an' the dhrovers was rare min in a fight. More nor wance I seen them, forty, maybe half a hundred, strong, clear the market-place at Banagher or Athy. Well do I remimber the way the big, red, hairy wrists iv thim'd go up in the air, an' down'd come the springy ground-ash saplins what they carried for switches. The whole lot iv thim wanted to come coortin' the widdy; but sorra wan iv her'd look at thim. She'd flirt an' be coy an' taze thim and make thim mad for love iv her, as weemin likes to do. Thank God for the same! for mayhap we min wouldn't love thim as we do only for their thricky ways; an' thin what'd become iv the counthry wid nothin' in it at all except single min an' ould maids jist dyin', and growin' crabbed for want iv childher to kiss an' tache an' shpank an' make love to? Shure, yer 'ann'rs, 'tis childher as makes the hearrt iv man green, jist as it is fresh wather that makes the grass grow. Divil a shtep nearer would the widdy iver let mortial man come. 'No,' she'd say; 'whin I see a man fit to fill Mick's place, I'll let yez know iv it;

thank ye kindly'; an' wid that she'd shake her head till the beautiful red hair iv it'd be like shparks iv fire – an' the min more mad for her nor iver.

But, mind ye, she wasn't no shpoil-shport; Mick's wife knew more nor that, an' his widdy didn't forgit the thrick iv it. She'd lade the laugh herself if 'twas anything a dacent woman could shmile at; an' if it wasn't, she'd send the girrls aff to their beds, an' tell the min they might go on talkin' that way, for there was only herself to be insulted; an' that'd shut thim up pretty quick I'm tellin' yez. But av any iv thim'd thry to git affectionate, as min do whin they've had all they can carry, well, thin she had a playful way iv dalin' wid thim what'd always turn the laugh agin' thim. She used to say that she larned the beginnin' iv it at the school an' the rest iv it from Mick. She always kep by her on the counther iv the bar wan iv thim rattan canes wid the curly ends, what the soldiers carries whin they can't borry a whip, an' are goin' out wid their cap on three hairs, an' thim new oiled, to scorch the girrls. An' thin whin any iv the shuitors'd get too affectionate she'd lift the cane an' swish them wid it, her laughin' out iv her like mad all the time. At first wan or two iv the min'd say that a kiss at the widdy was worth a clip iv a cane; an' wan iv thim, a warrm horse-farmer from Poul-a-Phoka, said he'd complate the job av she was to cut him into ribbons. But she was a handy woman wid the cane – which was shtrange enough, for she had no childer to be practisin' on – an' whin she threw what was left iv him back over the bar, wid his face like a gridiron, the other min what was laughin' along wid her tuk the lesson to hearrt. Whiniver afther that she laid her hand on the cane, no matther how quietly, there'd be no more talk iv thryin' for kissin' in that quarther.

Well, at the time I'm comin' to there was great divarshuns intirely goin' on in the town. The fair was on the morra, an' there was a power iv people in the town; an' cattle, an' geese, an' turkeys, an' butther, an' pigs, an' vegetables, an' all kinds iv divilment, includin' a berryin' – the same bein' an ould attorney-man, savin' yer prisince; a lone man widout friends, lyin' out there in the gran' room iv the hotel what they call the 'Queen's Room'. Well, I needn't tell yer 'ann'rs that the place was pretty full that night. Musha, but it's the fleas thimselves what had the bad time iv it, wid thim crowded out on the outside, an' shakin', an' thrimblin' wid the cowld. The widdy, av coorse, was in the bar passin' the time iv the day wid all that kem in, an' keepin' her eyes afore an' ahint her to hould the girrls up to their wurrk an' not to be thriflin' wid the min. My! but there was a power iv min at the bar that night; warrm farmers from four counties, an' graziers wid their ground-ash plants an' big frieze coats, an' plinty iv commercials, too. In the middle iv it all, up the shtreet at a hand gallop comes an Athy carriage wid two horses, an' pulls up at the door wid the horses shmokin'. An' begor', the man in it was smokin' too, a big cygar nigh as long as yer arrm. He jumps out an' walks up as bould as brass to the bar, jist as if there was niver a livin' sowl but himself in the place. He chucks the widdy undher the chin at wanst, an', taking aff his hat, sez: 'I want the best room in the house. I travel for Shorrox', the greatest long-cotton firrm in the whole worrld, an' I want to open up a new line here! The best is what I want, an' that's not good enough for me!'

Well, gintlemin, ivery wan in the place was spacheless at his impidence; an', begor! that was the only time in her life I'm tould whin the widdy was tuk back. But, glory be, it didn't take long for her to recover herself, an' sez she quitely: 'I don't doubt ye, sur! The best can't be too good for a gintleman what makes himself so aisy at home!' an' she shmiled at him till her teeth shone like jools.

God knows, gintlemin, what does be in weemin's minds whin they're dalin' wid a man! Maybe it was that Widdy Byrne only wanted to kape the pace wid all thim min crowdin' roun' her, an' thim clutchin' on tight to their shticks an' aiger for a fight wid any man on her account. Or maybe it was that she forgive him his impidence; for well I know that it's not the most modest man, nor him what kapes his distance, that the girrls, much less the widdies, like the best. But anyhow she spake out iv her to the man from Manchesther: 'I'm sorry, sur, that I can't give ye the best room – what we call the best – for it is engaged already.'

'Then turn him out!' sez he.

'I can't,' she says – 'at laste not till tomorra; an' ye can have the room thin iv ye like.'

There was a kind iv a sort iv a shnicker among some iv the min, thim knowin' iv the corp, an' the Manchesther man tuk it that they was laughin' at him; so he sez: 'I'll shleep in that room tonight; the other gintleman can put up wid me iv I can wid him. Unless,' sez he, oglin' the widdy, 'I can have the place iv the masther iv the house, if there's a priest or a parson handy in this town – an' sober,' sez he.

Well, tho' the widdy got as red as a Claddagh cloak, she jist laughed an' turned aside, sayin': 'Throth, sur, but it's poor Mick's place ye might have, an' welkim, this night.'

'An' where might that be now, ma'am?' sez he, lanin' over the bar; an' him would have chucked her under the chin agin, only that she moved her head away that quick.

'In the churchyard!' she sez. 'Ye might take Mick's place there, av ye like, an' I'll not be wan to say ye no.'

At that the min round all laughed, an' the man from Manchesther got mad, an' shpoke out, rough enough too it seemed: 'Oh, he's all right where he is. I daresay he's quiter times where he is than whin he had my luk out. Him an' the Devil can toss for choice in bein' lonely or bein' quite.'

Wid that the widdy blazes up all iv a suddint, like a live sod shtuck in the thatch, an' sez she: 'Who are ye that dares to shpake ill iv the dead, an' to couple his name wid the Divil, an' to his widdy's very face? It's aisy seen that poor Mick is gone!' an' wid that she threw her apron over her head an' sot down an' rocked herself to and fro, as widdies do whin the fit is on thim iv missin' the dead.

There was more nor wan man there what'd like to have shtud opposite the Manchesther man wid a bit iv a blackthorn in his hand; but they knew the widdy too well to dar to intherfere till they were let. At length wan iv thim – Mr Hogan, from nigh Portarlington, a warrm man, that'd put down a thousand pounds iv dhry money any day in the week – kem over to the bar an' tuk aff his hat, an' sez he: 'Mrs Byrne, ma'am, as a friend of poor dear ould Mick, I'd be glad to take his quarrel on meself on his account, an' more than proud to take it on his widdy's, if, ma'am, ye'll only honour me be saying the wurrd.'

Wid that she tuk down the apron from aff iv her head an' wiped away the tears in her jools iv eyes wid the corner iv it.

'Thank ye kindly,' sez she; 'but, gintlemin, Mick an' me run this hotel long together, an' I've run it alone since thin, an' I mane to go on running' it be meself, even if new min from Manchesther itself does be bringin' us new ways. As to you, sur,' sez she, turnin' to him, 'it's powerful afraid I am that there isn't accommodation here for a gintlemin what's so requireful. An' so I think I'll be askin' ye to find convanience in some other hotel in the town.'

Wid that he turned on her an' sez, 'I'm here now, an' I offer to pay me charges. Be the law ye can't refuse to resave me or refuse me lodgmint, especially whin I'm on the primises.'

So the Widdy Byrne drewed herself up, an' sez she, 'Sur, ye ask yer legal rights; ye shall have them. Tell me what it is ye require.'

Sez he sthraight out: 'I want the best room.'

'I've tould you already,' sez she, 'there's a gintleman in it.'

'Well,' sez he, 'what other room have ye vacant?'

'Sorra wan at all,' sez she. 'Every room in the house is tuk. Perhaps, sur, ye don't think or remember that there's a fair on tomorra.'

She shpoke so polite that ivery man in the place knew there was somethin' comin' – later on. The Manchesther man felt that the laugh was on him; but he didn't want for impidence, so he up, an' sez he: 'Thin, if I have to share wid another, I'll share wid the best! It's the Queen's Room I'll be shleepin' in this night.'

Well, the min shtandin' by wasn't too well plazed wid what was going on; for the man from Manchesther he was plumin' himself for all the worrld like a cock on a dunghill. He laned agin over the bar an' began makin' love to the widdy hot an' fast. He was a fine, shtout-made man, wid a bull neck on to him an' short hair, like wan iv thim 'two-to-wan-bar-wans' what I've seen at Punchestown an' Fairy House an' the Galway races. But he seemed to have no manners at all in his coortin', but done it as quick an' business-like as takin' his commercial ordhers. It was like this: 'I want to make love; you want to be made love to, bein' a woman. Hould up yer head!'

We all could see the widdy was boilin' mad; but, to do him fair, the man from Manchesther didn't seem to care what any wan thought. But we all seen what he didn't see at first, that the widdy began widout thinkin' to handle the rattan cane on the bar. Well, prisintly he began agin to ask about his room, an' what kind iv a man it was that was to share it wid him.

So sez the widdy, 'A man wid less wickedness in him nor you have, an' less impidence.'

'I hope he's a quite man,' sez he.

So the widdy began to laugh, an' sez she: 'I'll warrant he's quite enough.'

'Does he shnore? I hate a man – or a woman ayther – what shnores.'

'Throth,' sez she, 'there's no shnore in him'; an' she laughed agin.

Some iv the min round what knew iv the ould attorney-man – saving yer prisince – began to laugh too; and this made the Manchesther man suspicious. When the likes iv him gets suspicious he gets rale nasty; so he sez, wid a shneer: 'You seem to be pretty well up in his habits, ma'am!'

The widdy looked round at the graziers, what was clutchin' their ash plants hard, an' there was a laughin' divil in her eye that kep' thim quite; an' thin she turned round to the man, and sez she: 'Oh, I know that much, anyhow, wid wan thing an' another, begor!'

But she looked more enticin' nor iver at that moment. For sure the man from Manchesther thought so, for he laned nigh his whole body over the counther, an' whispered somethin' at her, puttin' out his hand as he did so, an' layin' it on her neck to dhraw her to him. The widdy seemed to know what was comin', an' had her hand on the rattan; so whin he was draggin' her to him an' puttin' out his lips to kiss her – an' her first as red as a turkey-cock an' thin as pale as a sheet – she ups wid the cane and gev him wan skelp across the face wid it, shpringin' back as she done so. Oh jool! but that was a skelp! A big wale iv blood riz up as quick as the blow was shtruck, jist as I've seen on the pigs' backs whin they do be prayin' aloud not to be tuk where they're wanted.

'Hands off, Misther Impidence!' sez she. The man from Manchesther was that mad that he ups wid the tumbler forninst him an' was goin' to throw it at her, whin there kem an odd sound from the graziers – a sort of 'Ach!' as whin a man is workin' a sledge, an' I seen the ground-ash plants an' the big fists what held thim, and the big hairy wrists go up in the air. Begor, but polis thimselves wid bayonets wouldn't care to face thim like that! In the half of two twos the man from Manchesther would have been cut in ribbons, but there came a cry from the widdy what made the glasses ring: 'Shtop! I'm not goin' to have any fightin' here; an' besides, there's bounds to the bad manners iv even a man from Shorrox'. He wouldn't dar to shtrike me – though I have no head! Maybe I hit a thought too hard; but I had rayson to remimber that somethin' was due on Mick's account too. I'm sorry, sir,' sez she to the man, quite polite, 'that I had to defind meself; but whin a gintleman claims the law to come into a house, an' thin assaults th' owner iv it, though she has no head, it's more restrainful he should be intirely!'

'Hear, hear!' cried some iv the min, an' wan iv thim sez 'Amen', sez he, an' they all begin to laugh. The Manchesther man he didn't know what to do; for begor he didn't like the look of thim ash plants up in the air, an' yit he was not wan to like the laugh agin' him or to take it aisy. So he turns to the widdy an' he lifts his hat an' sez he wid mock politeness: 'I must complimint ye, ma'am, upon the shtrength iv yer arrm, as upon the mildness iv yer disposition. Throth, an' I'm thinkin' that it's misther Mick that has the best iv it, wid his body lyin' paceful in the churchyard, anyhow; though the poor sowl doesn't seem to have much good in changin' wan devil for another!' An' he looked at her rale spiteful.

Well, for a minit her eyes blazed, but thin she shmiled at him, an' made a low curtsey, an' sez she – oh! mind ye, she was a gran' woman at givin' back as good as she got – 'Thank ye kindly, sur, for yer polite remarks about me arrm. Sure me poor dear Mick often said the same; only he said more an' wid shuparior knowledge! "Molly", sez he – "I'd mislike the shtrength iv yer arrm whin ye shtrike, only that I forgive ye for it whin it comes to the huggin'!" But as to poor Mick's prisint condition I'm not goin' to argue wid ye, though I can't say that I forgive ye for the way you've shpoke iv him that's gone. Bedad, it's fond iv the dead y'are, for ye seem onable to kape thim out iv yer mouth. Maybe ye'll be more respectful to thim before ye die!'

'I don't want no sarmons!' sez he, wery savage. 'Am I to have me room tonight, or am I not?'

'Did I undherstand ye to say,' sez she, 'that ye wanted a share iv the Queen's Room?'

'I did! an' I demand it.'

'Very well, sur,' sez she very quitely, 'ye shall have it!' Jist thin the supper war ready, and most iv the min at the bar thronged into the coffee-room, an' among thim the man from Manchesther, what wint bang up to the top iv the table an sot down as though he owned the place, an' him niver in the house before.

A few iv the bhoys shtayed a minit to say another word to the widdy, an' as soon as they was alone Misther Hogan up, an' sez he: 'Oh, darlint! but it's a jool iv a woman y' are! Do ye raly mane to put him in the room wid the corp?'

'He said he insisted on being in that room!' she says, quite sarious; an' thin givin' a look undher her lashes at the bhoys as made thim lep, sez she: 'Oh! min, an ye love me give him his shkin that full that he'll tumble into his bed this night wid his sinses obscurified. Dhrink toasts till he misremimbers where he is! Whist! Go, quick, so that he won't suspect nothin'!'

That was a warrm night, I'm telling ye! The man from Shorrox' had wine galore wid his mate; an' afther, whin the plates an' dishes was tuk away an' the nuts was brought in, Hogan got up an' proposed his health, an' wished him prosperity in his new line. Iv coorse he had to dhrink that; an' thin others got up, an' there was more toasts dhrunk than there was min in the room, till the man, him not bein' used to whiskey-punch, began to git onsartin in his shpache. So they gev him more toasts – 'Ireland as a nation', an' 'Home Rule', an' 'The mimory iv Dan O'Connell', an' 'Bad luck to Boney', an' 'God save the Queen', an' 'More power to Manchesther', an' other things what they thought would plaze him, him bein' English. Long hours before it was time for the house to shut, he was as dhrunk as a whole row of fiddlers, an' kep shakin' hands wid ivery man an' promisin' thim to open a new line in Home Rule, an' sich nonsinse. So they tuk him up to the door iv the Queen's Room an' left him there.

He managed to undhress himself all except his hat, and got into bed wid the corp iv th' ould attorney-man, an' thin an' there fell asleep widout noticin' him.

Well, prisintly he woke wid a cowld feelin' all over him. He had lit no candle, an' there was only the light from the passage comin' in through the glass over the door. He felt himself nigh fallin' out iv the bed wid him almost on the edge, an' the cowld shtrange gintleman lyin' shlap on the broad iv his back in the middle. He had enough iv the dhrink in him to be quarrelsome.

'I'll throuble ye,' sez he, 'to kape over yer own side iv the bed – or I'll soon let ye know the rayson why.' An' wid that he give him a shove. But iv coorse the ould attorney-man tuk no notice whatsumiver.

'Y'are not that warrm that one'd like to lie contagious to ye,' sez he. 'Move over, I say, to yer own side!' But divil a shtir iv the corp.

Well, thin he began to get fightin' angry, an' to kick an' shove the corp; but not gittin' any answer at all, he turned round an' hit him a clip on the side iv the head.

'Git up,' he sez, 'iv ye're a man at all, an' put up yer dooks.'

Then he got more madder shtill, for the dhrink was shtirrin' in him, an' he kicked an' shoved an' grabbed him be the leg an' the arrm to move him.

'Begor!' sez he, 'but ye're the cowldest chap I iver kem anigh iv. Musha! but yer hairs is like icicles.'

Thin he tuk him be the head, an' shuk him an' brung him to the bedside, an' kicked him clane out on to the flure on the far side iv the bed.

'Lie there,' he sez, 'ye ould blast furnace! Ye can warrm yerself up on the flure till tomorra.'

Be this time the power iv the dhrink he had tuk got ahoult iv him agin, an' he fell back in the middle iv the bed, wid his head on the pilla an' his toes up, an' wint aff ashleep, like a cat in the frost.

By-an'-by, whin the house was about shuttin' up, the watcher from th' undhertaker's kem to sit be the corp till the mornin', an' th' attorney him bein' a Protestan' there was no candles. Whin the house was quite, wan iv the girrls, what was coortin' wid the watcher, shtole into the room.

'Are ye there, Michael?' sez she.

'Yis, me darlint!' he sez, comin' to her; an' there they shtood be the door, wid the lamp in the passage shinin' on the red heads iv the two iv thim.

'I've come,' sez Katty, 'to kape ye company for a bit, Michael; for it's crool lonesome worrk sittin' there alone all night. But I mustn't shtay long, for they're all goin' to bed soon, when the dishes is washed up.'

'Give us a kiss,' sez Michael.

'Oh, Michael!' sez she: 'kissin' in the prisince iv a corp! It's ashamed iv ye I am.'

'Sorra cause, Katty. Sure, it's more respectful than any other way. Isn't it next to kissin' in the chapel? – an' ye do that whin ye're bein' married. If ye kiss me now, begor but I don't know as it's mortial nigh a weddin' it is! Anyhow, give us a kiss, an' we'll talk iv the rights an' wrongs iv it afterwards.'

Well, somehow, yer 'ann'rs, that kiss was bein' gave – an' a kiss in the prisince iv a corp is a sarious thing an' takes a long time. Thim two was payin' such attintion to what was going on betune thim that they didn't heed nothin', whin suddint Katty stops, and sez: 'Whist! what is that?'

Michael felt creepy too, for there was a quare sound comin' from the bed. So they grabbed one another as they shtud in the doorway an' looked at the bed almost afraid to breathe till the hair on both iv thim began to shtand up in horror; for the corp rose up in the bed, an' they seen it pointin' at thim, an' heard a hoarse voice say, 'It's in hell I am – Divils around me! Don't I see thim burnin' wid their heads like flames? an' it's burnin' I am too – burnin', burnin', burnin'! Me throat is on fire, an' me face is burnin'! Wather! wather! Give me wather, if only a dhrop on me tongue's tip!'

Well, thin Katty let one screetch out iv her, like to wake the dead, an' tore down the passage till she kem to the shtairs, and tuk a flyin' lep down an' fell in a dead faint on the mat below; and Michael yelled 'murdher' wid all his might.

It wasn't long till there was a crowd in that room, I tell ye; an' a mighty shtrange thing it was that sorra wan iv the graziers had even tuk his coat from aff iv him to go to bed, or laid by his shtick. An' the widdy too, she was as nate an' tidy as iver, though seemin' surprised out iv a sound shleep, an' her clothes onto her, all savin' a white bedgown, an' a candle in her hand. There was some others what had been in bed, min an' wimin wid their bare feet an' slippers on to some iv thim, wid their bracers down their backs, an' their petticoats flung on anyhow. An' some iv thim in big nightcaps, an' some wid their hair all screwed up in knots wid little wisps iv paper, like farden screws iv Limerick twist or Lundy Foot snuff. Musha! but it was the ould weemin what was afraid iv things what didn't alarrm the young wans at all. Divil resave me! but the sole thing they seemed to dhread was the min – dead or alive it was all wan to thim – an' 'twas ghosts an' corpses an' mayhap divils that the rest was afeard iv.

Well, whin the Manchesther man seen thim all come tumblin' into the room he began to git his wits about him; for the dhrink was wearin' aff, an' he was thryin' to remimber where he was. So whin he seen the widdy he put his hand up to his face where the red welt was, an' at wance seemed to undhershtand, for he got mad agin an' roared out: 'What does this mane? Why this invasion iv me chamber? Clear out the whole kit, or I'll let yez know!'

Wid that he was goin' to jump out of bed, but the moment they seen his toes the ould weemin let a screech out iv thim, an' clung to the min an' implored thim to save thim from murdher – an' worse. An' there was the Widdy Byrne laughin' like mad; an' Misther Hogan shtepped out, an' sez he: 'Do jump out, Misther Shorrox! The boys has their switches, an' it's a mighty handy costume ye're in for a leatherin'!'

So wid that he jumped back into bed an' covered the clothes over him.

'In the name of God,' sez he, 'what does it all mane?'

'It manes this,' sez Hogan, goin' round the bed an' draggin' up the corp an' layin' it on the bed beside him. 'Begorra! but it's cantanker-ous kind iv a scut y'are. First nothin' will do ye but sharin' a room wid a corp; an' thin ye want the whole place to yerself.'

'Take it away! Take it away,' he yells out.

'Begorra,' sez Mister Hogan, 'I'll do no such thing. The gintleman ordhered the room first, an' it's he has the right to ordher you to be brung out!'

'Did he shnore much, sur?' says the widdy; an' wid that she burst out laughin' an' cryin' all at wanst. 'That'll tache ye to shpake ill iv the dead agin!' An' she flung her petticoat over her head an' run out iv the room.

Well, we turned the min all back to their own rooms; for the most part iv thim had plenty iv dhrink on board, an' we feared for a row. Now that the fun was over, we didn't want any unplisintness to follow. So two iv the graziers wint into wan bed, an' we put the man from Manchesther in th' other room, an' gev him a screechin' tumbler iv punch to put the hearrt in him agin.

I thought the widdy had gone to her bed; but whin I wint to put out the lights I seen one in the little room behind the bar, an' I shtepped quite, not to dishturb her, and peeped in. There she was on a low shtool rockin' herself to an' fro, an' goin' on wid her laughin' an' cryin' both together, while she tapped wid her fut on the flure. She was talkin' to herself in a kind iv a whisper, an' I heerd her say: 'Oh, but it's the crool woman I am to have such a thing done in me house – an' that poor sowl, wid none to weep for him, knocked about that a way for shport iv dhrunken min – while me poor dear darlin' himself is in the cowld clay! – But oh! Mick, Mick, if ye were only here! Wouldn't it be you – you wid the fun iv ye an' yer merry hearrt – that'd be plazed wid the doin's iv this night!'

The Red Stockade

The sea was another subject that held a strong interest for Henry Irving, particularly after his success in 1878 in *Vanderdecken* by W. G. Wills. Irving played the role of the captain of the legendary ghost ship the *Flying Dutchman* and repeated this stage triumph several times during the remainder of his career. Stoker, who was present at the first performance of the play, thought that Irving gave 'a wonderful impression of a dead man fictitiously alive' and particularly noticed, 'his eyes like cinders of glowing red from out of his marble face'. Bram had actually done some re-writing of the script for Irving, and its success gave him a similar interest in the lore and legends of the sea. Both men also enjoyed travelling by ship and always found their crossings of the Atlantic relaxing and invigorating.

When, in May 1894, the famous United States cruiser *Chicago* docked in London on a courtesy call, Irving and Stoker played a part in welcoming the American officers and crew. In command were Admiral Erben who had coined the famous phrase 'Blood is thicker than water' while engaged in the China Seas, and Captain Alfred Mahan, a serving officer already famed for his nautical history books *The Influence of Sea Power on History* (1890) and *The Sea Power of England* (1892). The two seamen were invited to the Lyceum, and during their stay in London twice dined in the Beefsteak Room. The supper-table conversation was mostly about the sea, Stoker recalled later, and the genial Admiral Erben's colourful stories of his service in dangerous waters were well offset by Captain Mahan's encyclopedic knowledge of naval actions throughout history.

When Bram left for home after the second of these suppers, his mind was again buzzing with ideas for short stories. Pressure of work seems to have prevented him from writing more than one tale which he called 'The Red Stockade' and subtitled 'A Story Told by

the Old Coastguard'. There is strong evidence to suggest that this dramatic story of action against Malay pirates in the China Seas was based on one of Admiral Erben's yarns, for in his biography of Irving, Stoker has written of their guest:

It will be remembered that whilst a flotilla of British boats were attacking a fort in Chinese waters and had met a reverse they were aided by the crew of Admiral Erben's ship of war. They were on a mud flat at the mercy of the Chinese who were wiping them out. But the crew of the neutral vessel – unaided by their officers, who had of course to show an appearance of neutrality in accord with the wisdom of international law – put off their boats and took them off. On protest being made, the answer was given by Admiral Erben, 'Blood is thicker than water!'

But to whatever extent Stoker drew on Admiral Erben's reminiscences, there can be no denying that the tale which follows is another example of his skill as a storyteller. It too has never been reprinted since its original magazine publication. This may, though, be partly explained by the fact that it appeared only in America, in the famous *Cosmopolitan Magazine* of September 1894, and has remained virtually unknown in Britain ever since.

WE WAS ON THE southern part of the China station, when the *George Ranger* was ordered to the Straits of Malacca, to put down the pirates that had been showing themselves of late. It was in the forties, when ships was ships, not iron-kettles full of wheels, and other devilments, and there was a chance of hand-to-hand fighting – not being blown up in an iron cellar by you don't know who. Ships was ships in them days!

There had been a lot of throat-cutting and scuttling, for them devils stopped at nothing. Some of us had been through the straits before, when we was in the *Polly Phemus*, seventy-four, going to the China station, and although we had never come to quarters with the Malays, we had seen some of their work, and knew what kind they was. So, when we had left Singapore in the *George Ranger*, for that was our saucy, little thirty-eight-gun frigate – the place wasn't in them days what it is now – many and many's the yarn was told in the fo'c'sle, and on the watches, of what the yellow devils could do, and had done. Some of us took it one way, and some another, but all, save a few, wanted to get into hand-grips with the pirates, for all their kreeses, and their stinkpots, and the devil's engines what they used. There was some that didn't mind cold steel of an ordinary kind, and would have faced cutlasses and boarding-pikes, any day, for a holiday, but that didn't like the idea of those knives like crooked flames, and that sliced a man in two, and hacked through the bowels of him. Naturally, we didn't take much stock of this kind; and many's the joke we had on them, and some of them cruel enough jokes, too.

You may be sure there was good stories, with plenty of cutting, and blood, and tortures in them, told in their watches, and nigh the whole ship's crew was busy, day and night, remembering and inventing things that'd make them gasp and grow white. I think that, somehow, the Captain and the officers must have known what was goin' on, for there came tales from the ward-room that was worse nor any of ours. The midshipmen used to delight in them, like the ship's boys did, and one of them, that had a kreese, used to bring it out when he could, and show how the pirates used it when they cut the hearts out of men and women, and ripped them up to the chins. It was a bit cruel, at times, on them poor, white-livered chaps – a man can't help his liver, I suppose – but, anyhow, there's no place for them in a warship, for they're apt to do more harm by living where there's men of all sorts, than they can do by dying. So there wasn't any mercy for them, and the Captain was worse on them than any. Captain Wynyard was him that commanded the corvette *Sentinel* on the China station, and was promoted to the *George Ranger* for cutting up a fleet of junks that was hammering at the *Rajah*, from Canton, racing for Southampton with the first of the season's tea. He was a man, if you like, a bulldog full of hell-fire, when he was on for fighting; he wouldn't have a white liver at any price. 'God hates a coward,' he said once, 'and under Her Britannic Majesty I'm here to carry out God's will. Trice him up, and give him a dozen!' At least, that's the story they tell of him when he was round Shanghai, and one of his men had held back when the time came for boarding a fire-junk that was coming down the tide. And with that he went in, and steered her off with his own hands.

Well, the Captain knew what work there was before us, and that it weren't no time for kid gloves and hair-oil, much less a bokey in your buttonhole and a top-hat, and he didn't mean that there should be any funk on his ship. So you take your davy that it wasn't his fault if things was made too pleasant aboard for men what feared fallin' into the clutches of the Malays.

Now and then he went out of his way to be nasty over such folk, and, boy or man, he never checked his tongue on a hard word when anyone's face was pale before him. There was one old chap on board that we called 'Old Land's End', for he came from that part, and that had a boy of his on the *Billy Ruffian*, when he sailed on her, and after got lost, one night, in cutting out a Greek sloop at Navarino in 1827. We used to chaff him when there was trouble with any of the boys, for he used to say that his boy might have been in that trouble, too. And now, when the chaff was on about bein' afeered of the Malays, we used to rub it into the old man; but he would flame up, and answer us that his boy died in his duty, and that he couldn't be afeered of nought.

One night there was a row on among the midshipmen, for they said that one of them, Tempest by name, owned up to being afraid of being kreesed. He was a rare bright little chap of about thirteen, that was always in fun and trouble of some kind; but he was soft hearted, and sometimes the other lads would tease him. He would own up truthfully to anything he thought, or felt, and now they had drawn him to own something that none of them would – no matter how true it might be. Well, they had a rare fight, for the boy was never backwards with his fists, and by accident it came to the notice of the Captain. He insisted on being told what it was all about, and when young Tempest spoke out, and told him, he stamped on the deck, and called out: 'I'll have no cowards in this ship,' and was going on, when the boy cut in: 'I'm no coward, sir; I'm a gentleman!'

'Did you say you were afraid? Answer me – yes, or no?'

'Yes, sir, I did, and it was true! I said I feared the Malay kreeses; but I did not mean to shirk them, for all that. Henry of Navarre was afraid, but, all the same, he –'

'Henry of Navarre be damned,' shouted the Captain, 'and you, too! You said you were afraid, and that, let me tell you, is what we call a coward in the Queen's navy. And if you are one, you can, at least, have the grace to keep it to yourself! No answer to me! To the masthead for the remainder of the day! I want my crew to know what to avoid, and to know it when they see it!' and he walked away, while the lad, without a word, ran up the maintop.

Some way, the men didn't say much about this. The only one that said anything to the point was Old Land's End, and says he: 'That may be a coward, but I'd chance it that he was a boy of mine.'

As we went up the straits and got the sun on us, and the damp heat of that kettle of a place – Lor' bless ye! ye steam there, all day and all night like a copper at the galley – we began to look around for the pirates, and there wasn't a man that got drowsy on the watch. We coasted along as we went up north, and took a look into the creeks and rivers as we went. It was up these that the Malays hid themselves; for the fevers and such that swept off their betters like flies, didn't seem to have any effect on them. There was pretty bad bits, I tell you, up some of them rivers through the mango groves, where the marshes spread away, mile after mile, as far as you could see, and where everything that is noxious, both beast, and bird, and fish, and crawling thing, and insect, and tree, and bush, and flower, and creeper, is most at home.

But the pirate ships kept ahead of us; or, if they came south again, passed us by in the night, and so we ran up till about the middle of the peninsula, where the worst of the piracies had happened. There we got up as well as we could to look like a ship in distress; and, sure enough, we deceived the beggars, for two of them came out one early dawn and began to attack us. They was ugly-looking craft, too – long, low hull and lateen-sails, and a double crew twice told in every one of them.

But if the crafts was ugly the men was worse, for uglier devils I never saw. Swarthy, yellow chaps, some of them, and some with shaven crowns and white eyeballs, and others as black as your shoe, with one or two white men, more shame, among them, but all carrying kreeses as long as your arm, and pistols in their belts.

They didn't get much change from us, I tell you. We let them get close, and then gave them a broadside that swept their decks like a hailstorm; but we was unlucky that we didn't grapple them, for they managed to shift off and ran for it. Our boats was out quick, but we daren't follow them where they ran into a wide creek, with mango swamps on each side as far as the eye could reach. The boat came back after a bit and reported that they had run up the river which was deep enough but with a winding channel between great mud-banks, where alligators lay in hundreds. There seemed some sort of fort where the river narrowed, and the pirates ran in behind it and disappeared up the bend of the river.

Then the preparations began. We knew that we had got two craft, at any rate, caged in the river, and there was every chance that we had found their lair. Our Captain wasn't one that let things go asleep, and by daylight the next morning we was ready for an attack. The pinnace and four other boats started out under the first lieutenant to prospect, and the rest that was left on board waited, as well as they could, till we came back.

That was an awful day. I was in the second boat, and we all kept well together when we began to get into the narrows of the mouth of the river. When we started, we went in a couple of hours after the flood-tide, and so all we saw when the light came seemed fresh and watery. But as the tide ran out, and the big black mud-banks began to show their heads above everywhere, it wasn't nice, I can tell you. It was hardly possible for us to tell the channels, for everywhere the tide raced quick, and it was only when the boat began to touch the black slime that you knew that you was on a bank. Twice our boat was almost caught this way, but by good luck we pulled and pushed off in time into the ebbing tide; and hardly a boat but touched somewhere. One that was a bit out from the rest of us got stuck at last in a nasty cut between two mud-banks, and as the water ran away the boat turned over on the slope, despite all her crew could do, and we saw the poor fellows thrown out into the slime. More than one of them began to swim toward us, but behind each came a rush of something dark, and though we shouted and made what noise we could, and fired many shots, the alligators was too close, and with shriek after shriek they went down to the bottom of the filth and slime. Oh, man! it was a dreadful sight, and none the better that it was new to nigh all of us. How it would have taken us if we had time to think about it, I hardly know, but I doubt that more than a few would have grown cold over it; but just then there flew amongst us a hail of small shot from a fleet of boats that had stolen down on us. They drove out from behind a big mud-bank that rose steeper than the others and that seemed solider, too, for the gravel of it showed, as the scour of the tide washed the mud away. We was not sorry, I tell you, to have men to fight with, instead of alligators and mud-banks, in an ebbing tide, in a strange tropical river.

We gave chase at once, and the pinnace fired the twelve-pounder which she carried in the bows, in among the huddle of the boats, and the yells arose as the rush of the alligators turned to where the Malay heads bobbed up and down in the drift of the tide. Then the pirates turned and ran, and we after them as hard as we could pull, till round a sharp bend of the river we came to a narrow place, where one side was steep for a bit and then tailed away to a wilderness of marsh, worse than we had seen. The other side was crowned by a sort of fort, built on the top of a high bank, but guarded by a stockade and a mud-bank which lay at its base. From this there came a rain of bullets, and we saw some guns turned towards us. We was hardly strong enough to attack such a position without reconnoitring, and so we drew away; but not quite quick enough, for before we could get out of range of their guns a round shot carried away the whole of the starboard oars of one of our boats.

It was a dreary pull to the ship, and the tide was agin us, for we all got thinking of what we had to tell – one boat and crew lost entirely, and a set of oars shot away – and no work done.

The Captain was furious; and, in the ward-room, and in the fo'c'sle that night, there was nothing that wasn't flavoured with anger and curses. Even the boys, of all sorts, from the cabin-boys to the midshipmen, was wanting to get at the Malays. However, sharp was the order; and by daylight three boats was up at the stockaded fort, making an accurate survey. I was again in one of the boats; and, in spite of what the Captain had said to make us all so angry – and he had a tongue like vitriol, I tell you – we all felt pretty down and cold when we got again amongst those terrible mud-banks and saw the slime that shone on them bubble up, when the grey of the morning let us see anything.

We found that the fort was one that we would have to take if we wanted to follow the pirates up the river, for it barred the way without a chance. There was a gut of the river between the two great ridges of gravel, and this was the only channel where there was a chance of passing. But it had been staked on both sides, so that only the centre was left free. Why, from the fort they could have stoned anyone in the boats passing there, only that there wasn't any stone, that we could see, in their whole blasted country!

When we got back, with two cases of sunstroke among us, and reported, the Captain ordered preparations for an attack on the fort, and the next morning the ball began. It was ugly work. We got close up to the fort, but, as the tide ran out, we had to sheer away somewhat so as not to get stranded. The whole place swarmed with those grinning devils. They evidently had some way of getting to and from their boats behind the stockade. They did not fire a shot at us – not at first – and that was the most aggravating thing that you can imagine. They seemed to know something that we did not, and they only just waited. As the tide sank lower and lower, and the mud-banks grew steeper, and the sun on them began to fizzle, a steam arose that nigh turned our stomachs. Why, the sight of them alone would make your heart sink!

The slime shimmered in all kinds of colours, like the water when there's tarring work on hand, and the whole place seemed alive with all that was horrible. The alligators kept off the boats and the banks close to us, but the thick water was full of eels and water-snakes, and the mud was alive with water-worms and leeches, and horrible, gaudy-coloured crabs. The very air was filled with pests – flies of all kinds, and a sort of big-striped insect that they call the 'tiger mos-quito', which comes out in the daytime and bites you like red-hot pincers. It was bad enough, I tell you, for us men with hair on our faces, but some of the boys got very white and pale, and they was all pretty silent for a while. All at once the crowd of Malays behind the stockade began to roll their eyes and wave their kreeses and to shout. We knew that there was some cause for it, but couldn't make it out, and this exasperated us more than ever. Then the Captain sings out to us to attack the stockade; so out we all jumped into the mud. We knew it couldn't be very deep just there, on account of the gravel beneath. We was knee-deep in a moment, but we struggled, and slipped, and fell over each other; and, when we got to the top of that bank, we was the queerest, filthiest-looking crowd you ever see. But the mud hadn't took the heart out of us, and the Malays, with their necks craned over the stockade, and with the nearest thing to a laugh or a smile that the Devil lets them have, drew back and fell, one on another, when they heard our cheer.

Between them and us there was a bit of a dip where the water had been running in the ebb-tide, but which seemed now as dry as the rest, and the foremost of our men charged down the slope, and then we knew why they had kept silent and waited! We was in a regular trap. The first ranks disappeared at once in the mud and ooze in the hollow, and those next were up to their armpits before they could stop. Then those Malay devils opened on us, and while we tried to pull our chaps out, they mowed us down with every kind of small arm they had – and they had a queer assortment, I tell you.

It was all we could do to get back over the slope and to the boats again – what was left of us – and, as we hadn't hands enough left even to row with full strength, we had to make for the ship as far as we could, for their boats began to pass out in a cloud through the narrow by the stockade. But before we went we saw them dragging the live and dead out of the mud with hooks on the end of long bamboos; and there was terrible shrieks from some poor fellows when the kreeses gashed through them. We daren't wait; but we saw enough to make us swear revenge. When we saw them devils stick the bleeding heads of our comrades on the spikes of the stockade, there was nigh a mutiny because the Captain wouldn't let us go back and have another try for it. He was cool enough now; and those of us that knew him and understood what was in his mind, when the smile on him showed the white teeth in the corners of his mouth, felt that it was no good day's work that the pirates had done for themselves.

When we got back to the ship and told our tale, it wasn't long till the men was all on fire; and nigh every man took a turn with the grindstone at his cutlass, till they was all like razors. The Captain mustered everyone on board, and detailed every man to his work in the boats, ready for the next time; and we knew that, by daylight, we were to have another slap at the pirates. We got six-pounders and twelve-pounders in most of the boats, for we was to give them a dose of big shot before we came to close quarters.

When we got up near the stockade, the tide had turned, and we thought it better to wait till dawn, for it was bad work among the mud-banks at the ebb in the dark. So we hung on a while, and then when the sky began to lighten, we made for the fort. When we got nigh enough to see it, there wasn't a man of us who didn't want to have some bloody revenge, for there, on the spikes of the stockade, were the heads of all the poor fellows that we had lost the day before, with a cloud of mosquitoes and flies already beginning to buzz around them in the dawn. But beyond that again, they had painted the outside of the stockade with blood, so that the whole place was a crimson mass. You could smell it as the sun came up!

Well, that day was a hard one. We opened fire with our guns, and the Malays returned it, with all they had got. A fleet of boats came out from beyond the fort, and for a while we had to turn our attention to these. The small guns served us well, and we made a rare havoc among the boats, for our shot went crashing through them, and quite a half of them were sunk. The water was full of bobbing heads; but the tide carried them away from us, and their cries and shrieks came from beyond the fort and then died away. The other boats recognized their danger, and turned and ran in through the narrow, and let us alone for hours after. Then we went at the fort again. We turned our guns at the piles of the stockade, and, of course, every shot told – but their fire was at too close quarters, and with their rifles and matchlocks, and the rest, they picked us off too fast, and we had to sheer off where our heavy metal could tell without our being within their range. Before we sheered off, we could see that the hole we had knocked in the stockade was only in the outer work, and that the real fort was within. We had to go down the river, as we couldn't go far enough across without danger from the banks, and this only gave us a side view, and, do what we would, we couldn't make an impression – at least any that we could see.

That was a long and awful day! The sun was blazing on us like a furnace, and we was nigh mad with heat, and flies, and drouth, and anger. It was that hot that if you touched metal it fairly burned you. When the tide was near the flood, the Captain ordered up the boats in the wide water now opposite the fort: and there, for a while, we got a fair chance, till, when the ebb began, we should have to sheer off again. By this time our shot was nearly run out, and we thought that we should have to give over; but all at once came order to prepare for attack, and in a few minutes we was working for dear life across the river, straight for the stockade. The men set up a cheer, and the pirates showed over the top of the stockade and waved their kreeses, and more than one of them sliced off pieces of the heads on the spikes, and jeered at us, as much as to say that they would do the same for us in our turn! When we got close up, every one of them had disappeared, and there was a silence of the grave. We knew that there was something up, but what the move was we could not tell, till from behind the fort came rushing again a fleet of boats. We turned on them, and, like we did before, we made mincemeat of them. This time the tide made for us, and the bobbing heads went by us in dozens. Now and then there was a wild yell, as an alligator pulled some one down into the mud. This went on for a little, and we had beaten them off enough to be able to get our grappling-irons ready for climbing the stockade, when the second lieutenant, who was in the outer boat, called out: 'Back with the boats! Back, quick, the tide is falling!' and with one impulse we began to shove off. Then, in an instant, the place became alive again with the Malays, and they began firing on us so quickly that before we could get out into the whirl of tide there was many a dead man in our boats.

There was no use trying to do any more that day, and after we had done what could be done for the wounded, and patched up our boats, for there was plenty of shot-holes to plug, we pulled back to the ship. The alligators had had a good day, and as we went along, and the mud-banks grew higher and higher with the falling of the tide, we could see them lie out lazily, as if they had been gorged. Aye! And there was enough left for the ground-sharks out in the offing; for the men on board told us that every while on the ebb something would go along, bobbing up and down in the swell, till presently there would be a swift ripple of a fin, and then there was no more pirate.

Well! when we got aboard, the rest was mighty anxious to know what had been done; and when we began, with the heads on spikes of the red stockade, the men ground their teeth, and Old Land's End up, and says he: 'The Red Stockade! We'll not forget the name! It'll be our turn next, and then we'll paint it inside this time.'

And so it was that we came to know the place by that name. That night the Captain was like a man that would do murder. His face was like steel, and his eyes was as red as flames. He didn't seem to have a thought for any one; and everything he did was as hard as though his heart were brass. He ordered all that was needful to be done for the wounded, but he added to the doctor: 'And, mind you, get them well as soon as you can. We're too short-handed already!'

Up to now, we all had known him treat men as men, but now he only thought of us as machines for fighting! True enough, he thought the same of himself. Twice that very night he cut up rough in a new way. Of course, the men was talking of the attack, and there was lots of brag and chaff, for all they was so grim earnest, and some of the old fooling went on about blood and tortures. The Captain came on deck, and as he walked along, he saw one of the men that didn't like the kreeses, and he didn't evidently like the looks of him, for he turned on his heel and said savagely: 'Send the doctor here!'

So the doctor came, and the Captain he says to him, cold as ice, and as polite as you please: 'Dr Fairbrother, there is a sick man here! Look at his pale face. Something wrong with his liver, I suppose. It's the only thing that makes a seaman's face white when there's fighting ahead. Take him down to sick bay, and do something for him. I'd like to cut the accursed white liver out of him altogether!' and with that he went down to his cabin.

Well if we was hot for fighting before, we was boiling after that, and we all came to know that the next attack on the Red Stockade would be the last, one way or the other! We had to wait two more days before that could come off, for the boats and tackle had to be made ready, and there wasn't going to be any mistakes made this time.

It was just after midnight when we began to get ready. Every man was to his post. The moon was up, and it was lighter nor a London day, and the Captain stood by and saw every man to his place, and nothing escaped him. By-and-by, as no. 6 boat was filling, and before the officer in charge of it got in, came the midshipman, young Tempest, and when the Captain saw him he called him up and hissed out before all the crew:'Why are you so white? What's wrong with you, anyway? Is your liver out of order, too?'

True enough, the boy was white, but at the flaming insult the blood rushed to his face and we could see it red in the starlight. Then in another moment it passed away and left him paler than ever, and he said with a gentle voice, though standing as straight as a ramrod: 'I can't help the blood in my face, sir. If I'm a coward because I'm pale, perhaps you are right. But I shall do my duty all the same!' and with that he pulled himself up, touched his cap, and went down into the boat.

Old Land's End was behind me in the boat with him, number five to my six, and he whispered to me through his shut teeth: 'Too rough that! He might have thought a bit that he's only a child. And he came all the same, even if he was afeer'd!'

We stole away with muffled oars, and dropped silently into the river on the flood-tide. If any man had had any doubts as to whether we was in earnest at other times, he had none then, anyhow. It was a pretty grim time, I tell you, for the most of us felt that whether we won or not this time, there would be many empty hammocks that night in the *George Ranger*; but we meant to win even if we went into the maws of the sharks and crocodiles for it. When we came up close on the flood we lost no time but went slap at the fort. At first, of course, we had crawled up the river in silence, and I think that we took the beggars by surprise, for we was there before the time they expected us. Howsomever, they turned out quick enough and there was soon music on both sides of the stockade. We didn't want to take any chance on the mud-banks this time, so we ran in close under the stockade at once and hooked on. We found that they had repaired the breach we had made the last time. They fought like devils, for they knew that we could beat them hand to hand, if we could once get in, and they sent round the boats to take us on the flank, as they had done each time before. But this time we wasn't to be drawn away from our attack, and we let our boats outside tackle them, while we minded our own business closer home.

It was a long fight and a bloody one. They was sheltered inside, and they knew that time was with them, for when the tide should have fallen, if we hadn't got in we should have our old trouble with the mud-banks all over again. But we knew it, too, and we didn't lose no time. Still, men is only men, after all, and we couldn't fly up over a stockade out of a boat, and them as did get up was sliced about dreadful – they are handy workmen with their kreeses, and no doubt! We was so hot on the job we had on hand that we never took no note of time at all, and all at once we found the boat fixed tight under us.

The tide had fallen and left us on the bank under the Red Stockade, and the best half of the boats was cut off from us. We had some thirty men left, and we knew we had to fight whether we liked it or not. It didn't much matter, anyhow, for we was game to go through with it. The Captain, when he seen the state of things, gave his orders to take the boats out into mid-stream, and shell and shot the fort, whilst we was to do what we could to get in. It was no use trying to bridge over the slobs, for the masts of an old seventy-four wouldn't have done it. We was in a tight place, then, I can tell you, between two fires, for the guns in the boats couldn't fire high enough to clear us every time, without going over the fort altogether, and more than one of our own shots did some of us a harm. The cutter came into the game, and began sending the war-rockets from the tubes. The pirates didn't like that, I tell you, and more betoken, no more did we, for we got as much of them as they did, till the Captain saw the harm to us, and bade them cease. But he knew his business, and he kept all the fire of the guns on the one side of the stockade, till he knocked a hole that we could get in by. When this was done, the Malays left the outer wall and went within the fort proper. This gave us some protection, since they couldn't fire right down on us, and our guns kept the boats away that would have taken us from the riverside. But it was hot work, and we began dropping away with stray shots, and with the stinkpots and hand-grenades that they kept hurling over the stockade on to us.

So the time came when we found that we must make a dash for the fort, or get picked out, one by one, where we stood. By this time some of our boats was making for the opening, and there seemed less life behind the stockade; some of them was up to some move, and was sheering off to make up some other devilment. Still, they had their guns in the fort, and there was danger to our boats if they tried to cross the opening between the piles. One did, and went down with a hole in her within a minute. So we made a burst inside the stockade, and found ourselves in a narrow place between the two walls of piles. Anyhow, the place was drier, and we felt a relief in getting out of up to our knees in steaming mud. There was no time to lose, and the second lieutenant, Webster by name, told us to try to scale the stockade in front.

It wasn't high, but it was slimy below and greasy above, and do what we would, we couldn't get no nigher. A shot from a pistol wiped out the lieutenant, and for a moment we thought we was without a leader. Young Tempest was with us, silent all the time, with his face as white as a ghost, though he done his best, like the rest of us. Suddenly he called out: 'Here, lads! take and throw me in. I'm light enough to do it, and I know that when I'm in you'll all follow.'

N'er a man stirred. Then the lad stamped his foot and called again, and I remember his young, high voice now: 'Seamen to your duty! I command here!'

At the word we all stood at attention, just as if we was at quarters. Then Jack Pring, that we called the Giant, for he was six feet four and as strong as a bullock, spoke out: 'It's no duty, sir, to fling an officer into hell!' The lad looked at him and nodded.

'Volunteers for dangerous duty!' he called, and every man of the crowd stepped out.

'All right, boys!' says he. 'Now take me up and throw me in. We'll get down that flag, anyhow,' and he pointed to the black flag that the pirates flew on the flagstaff in the fort. Then he took the small flag of the float and put it on his breast, and says he: 'This'll suit better.'

'Won't I do, sir?' said Jack, and the lad laughed a laugh that rang again.

'Oh, my eye!' says he, 'has anyone got a crane to hoist in the Giant?' The lad told us to catch hold of him, and when Jack hesitated, says he: 'We've always been friends, Jack, and I want you to be one of the last to touch me!' So Jack laid hold of him by one side, and Old Land's End stepped out and took him by the other. The rest of us was, by this time, kicking off our shoes and pulling off our shirts, and getting our knives open in our teeth. The two men gave a great heave together and they sent the boy clean over the top of the stockade. We heard across the river a cheer from our boats, as we began to scramble. There was a pause within the fort for a few seconds, and then we saw the lad swarm up the bamboo flagstaff that swayed under him, and tear down the black flag. He pulled our own flag from his breast and hung it over the top of the post. And he waved his hand and cheered, and the cheer was echoed in thunder across the river. And then a shot fetched him down, and with a wild yell they all went for him, while the cheering from the boats came like a storm.

We never knew quite how we got over that stockade. To this day I can't even imagine how we done it! But when we leaped down, we saw something lying at the foot of the flagstaff all red – and the kreeses was red, too! The devils had done their work! But it was their last, for we came at them with our cutlasses – there was never a sound from the lips of any of us – and we drove them like a hailstorm beats down standing corn! We didn't leave a living thing within the Red Stockade that day, and we wouldn't if there had been a million there!

It was a while before we heard the shouting again, for the boats was coming up the river, now that the fort was ours, and the men had other work for their breath than cheering.

Between us, we made a rare clearance of the pirates' nest that day. We destroyed every boat on the river, and the two ships that we was looking for, and one other that was careened. We tore down and burned every house, and jetty, and stockade in the place, and there was no quarter for them we caught. Some of them got away by a path they knew through the swamp where we couldn't follow them. The sun was getting low when we pulled back to the ship. It would have been a merry enough home-coming, despite our losses – all but for one thing, and that was covered up with a Union Jack in the Captain's own boat. Poor lad! when they lifted him on deck, and the men came round to look at him, his face was pale enough now, and, one and all, we felt that it was to make amends, as the captain stooped over and kissed him on the forehead.

'We'll bury him tomorrow,' he said, 'but in blue water, as becomes a gallant seaman.'

At the dawn, next day, he lay on a grating, sewn in his hammock, with the shot at his feet, and the whole crew was mustered, and the chaplain read the service for the dead. Then he spoke a bit about him – how he had done his duty, and was an example to all – and he said how all loved and honoured him. Then the men told off for the duty stood ready to slip the grating and let the gallant boy go plunging down to join the other heroes under the sea; but Old Land's End stepped out and touched his cap to the Captain, and asked if he might say a word.

'Say on, my man!' said the Captain, and he stood, with his cocked hat in his hand, whilst Old Land's End spoke.

'Mates! ye've heerd what the chaplain said. The boy done his duty, and died like the brave gentleman he was! And we wish he was here now. But, for all that, we can't be sorry for him, or for what he done, though it cost him his life. I had a lad once of my own, and I hoped for him what I never wanted for myself – that he would win fame and honour, and become an admiral of the fleet, as others have done before. But, so help me God! I'd rather see him lying under the flag as we see that brave boy lie now, and know why he was there, than I'd see him in his epaulettes on the quarter-deck of the flagship! He died for his Queen and country, and for the honour of the flag! And what more would you have him do!'

Midnight Tales

It was in May 1897 that Bram Stoker published *Dracula* and made his mark on literary history. Though the success of his book, immediately hailed by the *Daily Mail* as a classic of horror fiction, could have enabled Bram to become a full-time writer at once, his loyalty to Henry Irving was such that the idea of quitting his job with the actor never occurred to him. And this despite the fact that Irving declared himself unimpressed by *Dracula* and, when the story was dramatized shortly after publication in order to protect its copyright in the theatre, refused to attend the performance. Maybe Irving recognized something of himself in the blood-sucking count that offended his vanity – but he was certainly one of the very few who failed to agree with the assessment of Bram Stoker's mother. In a letter to her son she declared, 'No book since Mrs. Shelley's *Frankenstein* or indeed any other at all has come near yours in originality or terror!'

Stoker, though, was obviously not upset by the verdict of his Chief, for the evidence reveals that their evening suppers continued as before. At one of these dinners, after the two men had yet again regaled each other with stories, Irving suggested that his manager consider collecting the best of them in a book to be called *Midnight Tales*. Especially, he said, those that were short and dramatic and had a sting in the tail. Stoker was apparently attracted to the idea for he committed three of Irving's favourite yarns to paper some time around the turn of the century. But that was as far as the idea ever got. For whatever reason, no more of these short pieces were written and the proposed book came to nothing.

The stories which follow are, therefore, printed here for the first time in any collection. Had Bram written more, then *Midnight Tales* might well have become a reality. All these years later it has at least become the inspiration for this volume, of which Henry Irving, for all his hostility to *Dracula*, would hopefully have approved.

THE FUNERAL PARTY

THE FUNERAL WAS TAKING place in Dublin of a young married woman whose death had been as sudden as it had been mysterious. Her beauty had been the object of much public gossip, the more so because her husband was a man of advancing years.

On the appointed day for her internment, the undertaker, after the wont of his craft, was early at the home of the deceased arranging the whole funeral party according to the local rules of mortuary etiquette.

With due solemnity and lowered voice he spoke to the widower, 'You, sir, will of course go in the carriage with the mother of the deceased.'

'What! Me go in the carriage with my mother-in-law? Not likely!' the man replied with surprising emphasis.

'Oh, sir, but I assure you it is necessary. The rule is an inviolable one, established by precedents beyond all cavil!' exclaimed the horrified undertaker.

But the widower was obdurate. 'I won't go in that carriage – and that's flat.'

'Oh, but my good sir. Remember the gravity of the occasion – the publicity – the – the – possibility – of *scandal*!' The voice of the man in black faded into a gasp.

But still the widower stuck to his resolution, and the undertaker went away to discuss the matter with some of his intimate friends who were awaiting instructions as to their duties for the funeral service. After some discussion, these men then approached the chief mourner and began to remonstrate with him.

'You really must, old chap, it is a necessity,' said one.

'Etiquette demands it,' insisted another.

'I'll not! Go with my mother-in-law? I'll rot first!' the husband again insisted.

'But look here, old chap . . .'

'I'll not, I tell you! I'll go in any other carriage that you wish – but not that one.'

Finally, one of the circle of undertaker's men who had been silent all the while spoke up.

'Well, of course, if you won't, you won't,' he said. 'But remember it beforehand that afterwards when it will be thrown up against you, it'll be construed into an affront to the poor girl that has gone. You loved her Jack, we all know *that*.'

This argument at last prevailed. The widower signalled to the undertaker and began to pull on his black gloves. But as he moved towards the carriage in which his mother-in-law already sat, a stone-faced woman all in black, he turned to his friends and said in a low voice: 'I'm only doing it because you say I ought to – and for the girl that's gone. But you will spoil my day!'

THE SHAKESPEARE MYSTERY

It was one of those pioneer towns in the Old West where drink started many an argument and guns settled the dispute. The cowboys from the ranges were raw, tough men, but by no means stupid and some were even quite well educated. A fact borne witness to by the subjects that might be found being debated in the town. . . .

One day in the bar of the town's hotel a group of men were discussing Shakespeare, in particular the puzzling question as to whether the Bard had written all the plays attributed to him or if they were actually the work of Francis Bacon. Both sides had their champions and as the evening wore on and the drinks flowed freely the argument grew more heated.

Soon some of the men got greatly excited and as a consequence began drawing their guns on one another. Before tempers were completely lost, however, one forthright man among the group said it was not a question to be settled with bullets but by arbitration.

The other men agreeing to this proposal, all holstered their guns and began looking for an arbitrator. After some time they at last agreed upon a suitable man to settle their disagreement.

The arbitrator selected was an Irishman, who had all the while the debate flew back and forth sat quietly smoking at the bar not saying a word – which circumstance had probably suggested his suitability for the task.

Agreeing to take the office of judge and jury, the man continued to sit quietly smoking while the arguments on both sides were formally stated before him. When the two groups had at last finished he paused a while and then slowly began to speak.

'Well, gintlemin,' he said in a brogue as thick as any to be found back in Ireland, 'me decision is this: thim plays was not wrote be Shakespeare! But they was wrote be a man iv the saame naame!'

A DEAL WITH THE DEVIL

Not so many years ago I knew a rather unusual little boy, one of a large family. He was a mischievous chap, not above a little devilment, and never entirely to be trusted. Though his parents loved him, they were always on their guard against some new prank the boy might perpetrate.

It happened on one evening that the boy asked to be allowed to go to bed at the time he and his brothers and sisters normally had their tea. This was such a unique circumstance as to puzzle the servants who immediately conveyed the request to their mistress.

The mother refused the request with a wave of her hand. Her older sister, the boy's doting Aunt Julia, was expected for the night and would wish to see all the children before they went to bed.

But not to be gainsayed, the child persevered with his request, whimpering and even crying. Finally, he got his way.

In a little while, as night began to fall, the boy's father was sitting in his study at the back of the house when he was suddenly aware of a small figure in the garden. Peering through the window, he made out the figure of his son in his nightshirt.

The father watched somewhat puzzled as the boy stole down the garden steps and hurried to a corner of the garden where there stood a clump of shrubs. In his hand he was carrying a garden fork.

After a lapse of some minutes during which time the father could see nothing of his child behind the shrubs, the boy reappeared and just as stealthily crept back into the house. Naturally curious as to what the youngster might have been doing with a fork, he went out into the garden to see for himself.

Behind the shrubs, the man was just able to make out some freshly turned earth. Using his hands, he began to investigate.

Hidden a few inches down in the ground he found a small, white envelope which the child had evidently buried. Standing up and coming out from behind the shrubs to get a little more light, he tore open the envelope.

Inside were two things. An unused lucifer match and a strip of paper on which the boy had scrawled some words in his childish hand. As the man read what was written he felt a shiver of unease run through his body. For the paper said:

> DEAR DEVIL,
> PLEASE TAKE AWAY
> AUNT JULIA

A Criminal Star

The closing years of the nineteenth century brought mixed fortunes for Henry Irving. In 1895 he was knighted by Queen Victoria (the first actor to be so honoured), while in 1898 a disastrous fire at the Lyceum compelled him to sell the lease (the theatre thereafter became a music hall). His reputation as an actor remained undiminished, however, and aside from further triumphs on the London stage he also carried out several more successful tours of the United States. His faithful manager, Bram Stoker, was as ever by his side, and though there were no longer any more late-night suppers to be enjoyed in the Beefsteak Room, the two men did not give up their habit of dining togther, nor of telling stories to entertain one another. This next tale resulted from what was to prove Irving's last visit to America in 1904.

In November 1903, Irving and his company made their eighth crossing of the Atlantic to appear in a series of plays, culminating in a special performance for President Roosevelt in Washington on 1 January, 1904. Irving had already made the acquaintance of no less than three of the President's predecessors, Chester Arthur, Grover Cleveland and William McKinley, but found his greatest rapport with the friendly and engaging Theodore Roosevelt. Irving and Stoker had first met Roosevelt in New York some years before in 1895, while he was serving as the Commissioner of Police. Bram Stoker recalled that they talked at some length about crime and criminals, and he himself also went by invitation to observe Roosevelt presiding at the Court of Justice in the city. He later wrote in his diary, 'Must be President some day. A man you can't cajole, can't frighten, can't buy.' This prediction came true following the assassination of McKinley in 1901. Irving and Stoker were invited to lunch with Roosevelt in Washington on the first day of 1904 and their dinner-table conversation again returned for a time to criminal matters. The President told the two visitors about an

American actor with an obsession for publicity, whom he had been
forced to prosecute for misleading and defrauding the public, and
this story gave Bram the idea for 'A Criminal Star', which was first
published in America in *Collier's Magazine* in October 1904. The
reader may see a little of Irving – who was well aware of the power of
exaggeration both in his acting and his publicity – in the character
of Wolseley Gartside.

WOLSELEY GARTSIDE, LIKE many others who have risen from the
ranks in the acting profession, was a tiny bit over-sensitive in the
matters of public esteem. In fact, he did not like to be neglected one
little bit.

This was all bad enough when he was engaged by someone else; but when he was out on his own with nothing to check him except the reports of his treasurer, he became a holy terror.

There wasn't any crowding of names off the bill then; there were simply no names at all. Names of other people, I mean; his name was all right so long as the paper was up to the biggest stands, and the types were the largest to be had in the town. Later on he went even further and had all his printing done in London or New York from specially cut types.

When he was arranging his first American tour he wanted to get someone who, as a *persona grata*, could command the Press; who understood human nature to the core; who had the instinct of a diplomat, the experience of a field marshal, and the tact of an attorney-general.

Which is how I came to join his employ. I *thought* my work was going to be easy.

Well, before I started out, which he insisted should be a full week ahead of him, he began to teach me my business. At first I pointed out to him that the whole mechanism of advance publicity wasn't wrong because he hadn't done it. But he took me up short, and expressed his opinions pretty freely, I admit. He gave me quite a dissertation on publicity, telling me that to hit the public you must tell them plenty. They wanted to know all about a man; they didn't care much whether it was good or bad; but on the whole they preferred bad. Then he went on to give me what he called my instructions. That I was to have paragraphs about him every day. 'Make me out,' he said, 'a sort of Don Juan, with a fierce, revengeful nature. A man from whose hate no man is safe; no woman from his love. Never mind moral character. The public don't want it – nor no more do I. Say what ever you please about me so long as you make people talk. Now I don't want argument with you. Do you just carry out my instructions, and all will be well. But if you don't, you'll get the order of the chuck.' I didn't want to argue with him. To begin with, a man like that isn't worth argument – especially about instructions. Instructions! Just fancy an advance agent who knows his business being *instructed* by a star that he has got to boom, and to whose vanity – no, *sensitiveness* – he has to minister. Why, compared with even a duffer at my work the biggest and brightest star in the theatrical firmament don't know enough to come in out of the rain! I was very angry with him, I admit; but in a flash there came to me out of his own very instructions an idea which put anger out of my mind. The top dog isn't angry – though he may bite! 'Very well, Mr Wolseley Gartside,' said I to myself, said I, 'I'll carry out your instructions with exactness. They're yours, not mine; so if anything comes out wrong you are the responsible party.' Before I went to bed I wrote out a mem. of my 'instructions'.

'The public want to know everything about a man. Tell them plenty – all they want. They don't care whether it's good or bad. On the whole, they prefer bad. Give them paragraphs every day. Make me a Don Juan, fierce, revengeful, passionate. No man safe from my hate; no woman from my love. Don't aim at moral character; the public don't want it; no more do I. Say whatever you please about me so long as you make people talk. Make things lively before I come!'

I headed this 'Instructions to Montague Phase Alphage, Advance Agent to Wolseley Gartside, Esquire'. In the morning I brought it to him and asked him to sign and date it, as I wished to carry out his instructions to the full, and to take for myself advantage of his wisdom and his splendid initiative power. He signed it, looking very pleased. The sort of smirk that tragedians use when they're feeling good.

The next day I started out on my travels. The tour was to begin with a week of one-night stands. Wolseley Gartside had insisted on making out the tour himself, and, of course, he knew better than anybody – everybody else. I certainly covered the ground for him that week. I simply lived in trains, and I wore out the stairs of all the offices of what they called newspapers. Do you know, I think there must be a special angelic squad told off to look after advance agents. And if there is, my chap must have had what they call a helluva time. It's a direct mercy that I didn't develop acute DT in letting the penny-a-liners of that group of one-horse towns have the time of their lives. They tumbled to it quick that they would not have to write any themselves, for, of course, I did all that myself. It was best that way, anyhow, for not one of them could have written a decent par. to save his soul.

I filled them all up with Wolseley Gartside; and they filled up as much space as the editorial staff could spare from ads. Generally I paid for the printing, too – though who benefited by it I don't know. I thought Gartside would darken the air when he got my bill; but I did him well – in quantity, at all events. But the quality was good, too; just what the old man liked. I not only painted him as a man of transcendent genius and as an artist that had no peer in past or present, but gave him such a character as a libertine that the local Don Juans began over their drink to talk of reviving lynching, and the womenkind exhausted the dry goods stores for new frocks and fal-lals of all kinds. Why, they tell me that the demand for toupees and false fronts and extensions was such that the New York wholesale hair-houses sent down a whole flock of drummers. The back-numbers were going to have a turn at him as well as the girls and the frisky matrons! I gave him out as having the courage of a lion and the heart of a fiend; the skill at cards of a prestidigitator; the style and daring in the hunt of Buffalo Bill; the learning of an Erasmus; the voice of a De Reske; the strength of Milo – it was before Sandow's time. I finished it all off with a hypnotic gift which was unique; which from the stage could rule audiences, and in the smoking-room or the boudoir could make man or woman his obedient slave. I got most of the newspapers to take up hypnotism as a theme of controversy, and wrote lots of letters on the subject, under various names, which opened people's eyes as to the power of that mysterious craft – or quality, whichever it is – and the consequent danger attendant on their daily lives. I suppose I needn't say that the whole controversy everywhere circled round Gartside and his wonderful powers. I tell you that by the Sunday afternoon when my star came along with his crowd in his special, with his private car at the tail of it, and him on the rear platform, the women of Patricia City, where he opened, were in a flutter. They didn't know whether it was hope or fear. Knowing the sex as I do, I am inclined to think it was hope. To tame and subdue a dragon of voluptuous impurity is the dearest wish of a good woman's heart!

I was fifty miles on my road when the day of opening came; but I ran back – that came out of my own pocket, too! – to see Gartside and hear what he thought of the way I had exploited him. I boarded his train down the line, and came on with him. He was both jubilant and effusive, and said my work in advance was the best he had ever had. 'Go on, my boy, go on, and follow it up. You are on the right tack!' were the last words he said to me. I dropped off at the depot, and got on the outward train, for I didn't want to get pitched into by him when he should find the excitement was less than he expected. I do believe he thought there would be in waiting a murderous crowd, with a rope, intent on a necktie party, with a few regiments of state troops to counteract them.

When I got into the next town the Press was full of what had been said at Patricia City, and wanted me to go at least one better, or they couldn't use my stuff at all. That would be checkmate to me as advance agent, so I was in a real difficulty. I couldn't increase the praise of my star, so the only thing was to go down. I made up my mind to go deeper and deeper into crime. There was no help for it. I knew well that each other town in that group would want its own increase of pressure, and so arranged my plans in the back of my head. I should have to distribute the steps of the downward grade amongst five different towns; so I laid out my work and began to get my copy ready. I never went to bed at all that night, but spent it writing advance matter in shorthand. In the morning I got a smart typist and dictated to her from my stenographic script. I sent off that for Tuesday by mail, and got the rest ready to post when the hour should arrive. I had to be careful not to send matter long enough in advance for the comparison of towns, or of different papers in the same town.

Early on Tuesday morning I got to Hustleville – that was the second town of the tour – and from that moment matters began to hum. All the papers were full, not only of my own matter, but of comments on it. In addition, nearly every one had a leader in which they cut the tragedian to pieces. *The Banner of Freedom* wanted to make out his coming to be nothing short of an international outrage.

'It makes little,' it said, 'for the comity of nations that an ostensibly friendly country like England should be allowed to dump down on our shores a cargo of criminal decadents like the man Wolseley Gartside and his crowd of hooligans. His being left at large so long as seems to have been the case says little for either the morals or the sanity of the people who have permitted his existence. He is a smirch on the fair face of cosmic law, a living germ of intellectual disease, a cancerous growth even in the parasitic calling which he follows; an outrage to man and morals, to fair living, to development of God's creatures – nay, even to God Himself! The people of this State have not in the past lacked courage or energy to terminate swiftly, by the exercise of rough justice in the open courts of natural law, the opportunities of offenders against public good. We have heard of a human pendulum swinging on a giant bough of one of our noble forest trees; there are recollections in the minds of those of our pioneers who happily survive of worthless miscreants riding on rails clad in unpretentious costumes of feathers and tar. It is up to the heroic souls who founded Hustleville to break the long silence of their well-won repose, and, for protection of the city they have won from forest depths, and for the defence of their kin, to raise voice and hand for woman's honour and man's unshrinking nobility! A hint on such a subject should be sufficient. *Verbum sapientiae sufficit*. We have done.'

This reached Gartside after breakfast, and he at once wired me: 'Go on; it is well. *Banner* has struck right note. Shall be ere long living heart of international cyclone!'

I went on the same afternoon to Comstock, which was next on our route. I had, of course, sent on plenty of advance matter, and the editors had written me gratefully about it. But when I called at the *Whoop* – which was, I understood, the popular paper – I was received in a manner which was decidedly chilly. I am not, as a rule, lacking in diffidence but I admit I was a little nonplussed. So I asked the editor if I had hurt or affronted him in any way to cause his greeting to be so different from his written words. He hum'd and haw'd, and finally admitted that he was chagrined that the Comstock *Whoop* had not been treated as well as the Hustleville *Banner of Freedom*.

'How?' I asked. 'I sent you twenty per cent more advance copy.'

'Aye. The quantity was all right; but there were none of the spicy details which worked up the dormant conscience of even a one-horse town like Hustleville. Now, I suppose you know that we young towns can't live on the past. Has-been isn't a good diet for growing youth. Moreover, we're all living on one another's backs, with the nails dug in. What we want in the *Whoop* is anti-soothing syrup; and nothing else is any use to us. So get a move on you and let us have it. We want stronger meat than Hustleville.'

'But there's nothing stronger. To say more wouldn't be true.'

The editor seemed as if struck blind. He raised his hands as if expostulating with the powers of the air, as he said: 'True! Do I live to hear the advance agent of a troupe speak of truth. . . . Now, look here, mister. It's no use talking ethics with you. For either I'm drunk – which would be early in the day for me – or else you've got some sort of freshness on you that I don't understand. And I may tell you for your edification that we don't much care for freshness here. Comstock is a town where we perspire quick; and there's plenty of space in the forest for developing our cem-e-tery. When I got your first letter I told my boys to hold back because this was your funeral, and ye was up in the etiquette. But the boys wasn't altogether pleased. They are good boys, and could knock sparks out of Ananias in making a story. See!

So you'd better get to work. You know your man and they don't; so your story is apt to seem more lifelike. I'll want the copy here by seven. Then, the quicker ye quit the better.'

There was nothing for it but to carry out Wolseley Gartside's *instructions*. It was wife-beating this time that swelled his reputation. I didn't mean to be knocked out by the boys of the *Whoop*, nor to afford an opportunity for exemplifying the sudorific rapidity of Comstock – no, nor to take a part in de-veloping the cem-e-tery either; so the story of W.G.'s experiences as a defendant in the police-court of Abingchester, in the Peak of Derbyshire – that was well out of the way of public prints – was given in full detail, together with a description of the Lord Chancellor who condemned him, and an exciting account of his escape, riddled with bullets, from the county gaol. The editor read it with a beaming face, and said when he had done: 'That's the biggest scoop we ever had. Here, I'll give you a straight tip which will put money in your pocket if you get out your copy right smart. There is every indication that when the play is over tomorrow night there will be an adjournment of citizens to the forest, and that one of the oaks will bear a new sort of acorn. One with a bloated body; but a rotten heart. See?'

I did see; and I sent an urgent letter to W.G. by the driver of the mail train, telling him frankly where his *instructions* were likely to lead him.

He was wise for once, and altered his route. This wasn't a case for vanity, but for skin. So there wasn't any new kind of acorn found in the forest round Comstock, though the search party was all ready!

As for myself, another idea at once dawned upon me. I caught the first available boat to England and abandoned the profession of advance agent. Since then I have succeeded rather well as a writer of sensational novels – and the most sensational of these I dedicated to the estimable Wolseley Gartside. . . .

The Bridal of Death

Although Bram Stoker wrote several more novels after *Dracula*, nothing else achieved the success of that great vampire novel. Indeed, it is probably quite accurate to say that when Irving himself died in 1905, not only was Stoker devastated by the loss of the man to whom he had devoted his life, but he also lost the spark for much of his literary creativity. The last of Bram Stoker's tales to be influenced by Henry Irving was *The Jewel of the Seven Stars* (1903), a novel about the mummy of an Egyptian queen resurrected in England. It is arguably the best of his books apart from *Dracula*, and like the vampire tale has been filmed a number of times.

According to his biographer, Harry Ludlam, this story was the result of talks Stoker had had, more than thirty years before, with Sir William Wilde. Sir William was a famous Dublin eye and ear specialist and Bram met him by courtesy of his son, the notorious Oscar, when both were students at Trinity College. The old man's tales of his adventures and explorations in Egypt made a lasting impression on Bram, and when he was later looking for ideas to follow up *Dracula*, they resurfaced in his mind. An even stronger influence was the novelist Sir Thomas Hall Caine, author of numerous exotic best-sellers including *The Demon Lover* (1894) and *The Eternal City* (1901), who had been a member of the Irving circle, as well as a frequent guest at the Beefsteak Room, for many years. Bram found Caine an attentive ear and useful critic for his own ideas, and actually dedicated *Dracula* to him under the sobriquet 'Hommy Beg', the novelist's nickname in the Gaelic tongue of the Isle of Man where he was born.

In Stoker's biography of Sir Henry Irving he has described how Hall Caine enraptured other dinner guests with his storytelling:

His image rises before me now. . . . His red hair, fine and long, and pushed back from his forehead, is so thin we can see the white line of the head so like Shakespeare's. He is himself all aflame. His hands have a natural eloquence – something like Irving's; they foretell and emphasise the coming thoughts. As he goes on he gets more and more afire till at the last he is like a living flame. We all sit quite still; we fear to interrupt him. The end of his story leaves us fired and exalted, too.

It was in 1902 that Stoker discussed with Caine his plot about the Egyptian mummy, and from the novelist he received a considerable amount of esoteric and occult knowledge which he included in the story. Caine also helped him with the stark and gruesome ending to the book which is narrated by a barrister called Malcolm Ross.

When *The Jewel of the Seven Stars* was issued by William Heinemann in 1903, the publishers found themselves subjected to an outcry from critics and readers. One chapter of the book was felt to be full of dangerous speculation, while the finale, with its attempt to raise a mummy from the dead, was considered so stark and hair-raising as to be offensive. Bram was requested to drop the offending chapter and re-write a happier ending if he wished to see the book reprinted. From that day to this, the book has never been reissued in Britain with these two deleted sections, which are now reproduced here both because of their rarity and because of their association with Henry Irving.

Bram Stoker was not long to outlive his Chief: the years of demanding theatrical work left him physically exhausted and men-tally drained. His health never completely recovered and he died in London on 20 April, 1912, literally worn out. If the newspapers of the day believed that he would be remembered as Irving's manager, time has proved them wrong. Stoker is now known almost exclus-ively as the creator of *Dracula*. And there seems little doubt that it is as the author of this immortal classic that he will be remembered long into the future.

THE TIME WORE AWAY, wondrous slowly in some ways, wonderfully quickly in others. Today, in the new-found joyous certainty of the return of my love, I should have liked to have had Margaret all to myself. But this day was not for love or for love-making. The shadow of fearful expectation was over it. The more I thought over the coming experiment, the more strange it all seemed; and the more foolish were we who were deliberately entering upon it. It was all so stupendous, so mysterious, so unnecessary! The issues were so vast; the danger so strange, so unknown. Even if it should be successful, what new difficulties would it not raise. What changes might happen, did men know that the portals of the House of Death were not in very truth eternally fixed; and that the dead could come forth again! Could we realize what it was for us modern mortals to be arrayed against the gods of old, with their mysterious powers gotten from natural forces, or begotten of them when the world was young. When land and water were forming themselves from out the primeval slime. When the very air was purifying itself from elemental dross. When the 'dragons of the prime' were changing their forms and their powers, made only to combat with geologic forces, to grow in accord with the new vegetable life which was springing up around them. When animals, when even man himself and man's advance were growths as natural as the planetary movements, or the shining of the stars. Ay! and further back still, when as yet the Spirit which moved on the face of the waters had not spoken the words of commanding to come into existence light and the life which followed it.

Nay, even beyond this was a still more overwhelming conjecture. The whole possibility of the great experiment to which we were now pledged was based on the reality of the existence of the old forces which seemed to be coming in contact with the new civilization. That there were, and are, such cosmic forces we cannot doubt, and that the intelligence, which is behind them, was and is. Were those primal and elemental forces controlled at any time by other than that final cause which Christendom holds as its very essence? If there were truth at all in the belief of Ancient Egypt then their gods had real existence, real power, real force. Godhead is not a quality subject to the ills of mortals: as in its essence it is creative and recreative, it cannot die. Any belief to the contrary would be antagonistic to reason; for it would hold that a part is greater than the whole. If then the old gods held their forces, wherein was the supremacy of the new? Of course, if the old gods had lost their power, or if they never had any, the experiment could not succeed. But if it should indeed succeed, or if there were a possibility of success, then we should be face to face with an inference so overwhelming that one hardly dared to follow it to its conclusion.

This would be: that the struggle between life and death would no longer be a matter of the earth, earthly; that the war of supra-elemental forces would be moved from the tangible world of facts to the mid-region, wherever it may be, which is the home of the gods. Did such a region exist? What was it that Milton saw with his blind eyes in the rays of poetic light falling between him and heaven? Whence came that stupendous vision of the Evangelist which has for eighteen centuries held spellbound the intelligence of Christendom. Was there room in the universe for opposing gods; or if such there were, would the stronger allow manifestations of power on the part of the opposing force which would tend to the weakening of his own teaching and designs? Surely, surely if this supposition were correct there would be some strange and awful development – something unexpected and unpredictable – before the end should be allowed to come . . . !

The subject was too vast and, under the present conditions, too full of strange surmises. I dared not follow it! I set myself to wait in patience till the time should come.

Margaret remained divinely calm. I think I envied her, even whilst I admired and loved her for it. Her father, Mr Trelawny, was nervously anxious, as indeed were the other men, Mr Corbeck and Dr Winchester. With Trelawny it took the form of movement; movement both of body and mind. In both respects he was restless, going from one place to another with or without a cause, or even a pretext; and changing from one subject of thought to another. Now and again he would show glimpses of the harrowing anxiety which filled him, by his manifest expectation of finding a similar condition in myself. He would be ever explaining things. And in his explanations I could see the way in which he was turning over in his mind all the phenomena; all the possible causes; all the possible results. Once, in the midst of a most learned dissertation on the growth of Egyptian astrology, he broke out on a different subject, or rather a branch or corollary of the same.

'I do not see why starlight may not have some subtle quality of its own! We know that other lights have special forces. The Röntgen Ray is not the only discovery to be made in the world of light. Sunlight has its own forces, that are not given to other lights. It warms wine; it quickens fungoid growth. Men are often moonstruck. Why not, then, a more subtle, if less active or powerful, force in the light of the stars. It should be a pure light coming through such vastness of space, and may have a quality which a pure, unimpulsive force may have. The time may not be far off when astrology shall be accepted on a scientific basis. In the recrudescence of the art, many new experiences will be brought to bear; many new phases of old wisdom will appear in the light of fresh discovery, and afford bases for new reasoning. Men may find that what seemed empiric deductions were in reality the results of a loftier intelligence and a learning greater than our own. We know already that the whole of the living world is full of microbes of varying powers and of methods of working quite antagonistic. We do not know yet whether they can lie latent until quickened by some ray of light as yet unidentified as a separate and peculiar force. As yet we know nothing of what goes to create or evoke the active spark of life. We have no knowledge of the methods of conception; of the laws which govern molecular or foetal growth, of the final influences which attend birth. Year by year, day by day, hour by hour, we are learning; but the end is far, far off. It seems to me that we are now in that stage of intellectual progress in which the rough machinery for making discovery is being invented. Later on, we shall have enough of first principles to help us in the development of equipment for the true study of the inwardness of things. Then we may perhaps arrive at the perfection of means to an end which the scholars of Old Nile achieved at a time when Methuselah was beginning to brag about the number of his years, perhaps even when the great-grandchildren of Adam were coming to regard the old man as what our transatlantic friends call a "back number". Is it possible, for instance, that the people who invented astronomy did not finally use instruments of extraordinary precision; that applied optics was not a cult of some of the specialists in the colleges of the Theban priesthood. The Egyptians were essentially specialists. It is true that, in so far as we can judge, the range of their study was limited to subjects connected with their aims of government on earth by controlling all that bore on the life to follow it. But can anyone imagine that by the eyes of men, unaided by lenses of wondrous excellence, astronomy was brought to such a pitch that the true orientation of temples and pyramids and tombs followed for four thousand years the wanderings of the planetary systems in space. If an instance of their knowledge of microscopy is wanted let me hazard a conjecture. How was it that in their hieroglyphic writing they took as the symbol or determinative of 'flesh' the very form which the science of today, relying on the revelations of a microscope of a thousand powers, gives to protoplasm – that unit of living organism which has been differentiated as flagella. If they could make analysis like this, why may they not have gone further? In that wonderful atmosphere of theirs, where sunlight fierce and clear is perpetually co-existent with day, where the dryness of earth and air gives perfect refraction, why may they not have learned secrets of light hidden from us in the density of our northern mists? May it not have been possible that they learned to store light, just as we have learned to store electricity. Nay more, is it not even possible that they did so. They must have had some form of artificial light which they used in the construction and adornment of those vast caverns hewn in the solid rock which became whole cemeteries of the dead. Why, some of these caverns, with their labyrinthine windings and endless passages and chambers, all sculptured and graven and painted with an elaboration of detail which absolutely bewilders one, must have taken years and years to complete. And yet in them is no mark of smoke, such as lamps or torches would have left behind them. Again, if they knew how to store light, is it not possible that they had learned to understand and separate its component elements? And if these men of old arrived at such a point, may not we too in the fullness of time? We shall see! We shall see!

'There is another matter, too, on which recent discoveries in science throw a light. It is only a glimmer at present; a glimmer sufficient to illuminate probabilities, rather than actualities, or even possibilities. The discoveries of the Curies and Laborde, of Sir William Crooks and Becquerel, may have far-reaching results on Egyptian investigation. This new metal, radium – or rather this old metal of which our knowledge is new – may have been known to the ancients. Indeed it may have been used thousands of years ago in greater degree than seems possible today. As yet Egypt has not been named as a place where the discovery of pitchblende, in which only as far as is known yet radium is contained, may be made. And yet it is more than probable that radium exists in Egypt. That country has perhaps the greatest masses of granite to be found in the world; and pitchblende is found as a vein in granite rocks. In no place, at no time, has granite ever been quarried in such proportions as in Egypt during the earlier dynasties. Who may say what great veins of pitchblende may not have been found in the gigantic operations of hewing out columns for the temples, or great stones for the pyramids. Why, veins of pitchblende, of a richness unknown in our recent mines in Cornwall, or Bohemia, or Saxony, or Hungary, or Turkey, or Colorado, may have been found by these old quarrymen of Aswan, or Turra, or Mokattam, or Elephantine.

'Beyond this again, it is possible that here and there amongst these vast granite quarries may have been found not merely veins but masses or pockets of pitchblende. In such case the power at the disposal of those who knew how to use it must have been wonderful. The learning of Egypt was kept amongst its priests, and in their vast colleges must have been men of great learning; men who knew well how to exercise to the best advantage, and in the direction they wished, the terrific forces at their command. And if pitchblende did and does exist in Egypt, do you not think that much of it must have been freed by the gradual attrition and wearing down of the granite rocks? Time and weather bring in time all rocks to dust; the very sands of the desert, which in centuries have buried in this very land some of the greatest monuments of man's achievement, are the evidences of the fact. If, then, radium is divisible into such minute particles as the scientists tell us, it too must have been freed in time from its granite prison and left to work in the air. One might almost hazard a suggestion that the taking the scarab as the symbol of life may not have been without an empiric basis. Might it not be possible that Coprophagi have power or instinct to seize upon the minute particles of heat-giving, light-giving – perhaps life-giving – radium, and enclosing them with their ova in those globes of matter which they roll so assiduously, and from which they take their early name, Pilulariae. In the billions of tons of the desert waste there is surely mingled some proportion of each of the earths and rocks and metals of their zone; and, each to each, nature forms her living entities to flourish on those without life.

'Travellers tell us that glass left in tropic deserts changes colour, and darkens in the fierce sunlight, just as it does under the influence of the rays of radium. Does not this imply some sort of similarity between the two forces yet to be identified!'

These scientific, or quasi-scientific discussions soothed me. They took my mind from brooding on the mysteries of the occult, by attracting it to the wonders of nature.

* * *

That night we all went to bed early. The next night would be an anxious one, and Mr Trelawny thought that we should all be fortified with what sleep we could get. The day, too, would be full of work. Everything in connection with the great experiment would have to be gone over, so that at the last we might not fail from any unthought-of flaw in our working. We made, of course, arrangements for summoning aid in case such should be needed; but I do not think that any of us had any real apprehension of danger. Certainly we had no fear of such danger from violence as we had had to guard against in London during Mr Trelawny's long trance.

For my own part I felt a strange sense of relief in the matter. I had accepted Mr Trelawny's reasoning that if the mummy of Queen Tera were indeed such as we surmised – such as indeed we now took for granted – there would not be any opposition on her part; for we were carrying out her own wishes to the very last. So far I was at ease – far more at ease than earlier in the day I should have thought possible; but there were other sources of trouble which I could not blot out from my mind. Chief amongst them was Margaret's strange condition. If it was indeed that she had in her own person a dual existence, what might happen when the two existences became one? Again, and again, and again I turned this matter over in my mind, till I could have shrieked out in nervous anxiety. It was no consolation to me to remember that Margaret was herself satisfied, and her father acquiescent. Love is, after all, a selfish thing; and it throws a black shadow on anything between which and the light it stands. I seemed to hear the hands go round the dial of the clock; I saw darkness turn to gloom, and gloom to grey, and grey to light without pause or hindrance to the succession of my miserable feelings. At last, when it was decently possible without the fear of disturbing others, I got up. I crept along the passage to find if all was well with the others; for we had arranged that the door of each of our rooms should be left slightly open so that any sound of disturbance would be easily and distinctly heard.

One and all slept; I could hear the regular breathing of each, and my heart rejoiced that this miserable night of anxiety was safely passed. As I knelt in my own room in a burst of thankful prayer, I knew in the depths of my own heart the measure of my fear. I found my way out of the house, and went down to the water by the long stairway cut in the rocks. A swim in the cool bright sea braced my nerves and made me my own man again.

As I came back to the top of the steps I could see the bright sunlight, rising from behind me, turning the rocks across the bay to glittering gold. And yet I felt somehow disturbed. It was all too bright; as it sometimes is before the coming of a storm. As I paused to watch it, I felt a soft hand on my shoulder; and, turning, found Margaret close to me; Margaret as bright and radiant as the morning glory of the sun! It was my own Margaret this time! My old Margaret, without alloy of any other; and I felt that, at least, this last and fatal day was well begun.

But alas! the joy did not last. When we got back to the house from a stroll around the cliffs, the same old routine of yesterday was resumed: gloom and anxiety, hope, high spirits, deep depression, and apathetic aloofness.

But it was to be a day of work; and we all braced ourselves to it with an energy which wrought its own salvation.

After breakfast we all adjourned to the cave, where Mr Trelawny went over, point by point, the position of each item of our paraphernalia. He explained as he went on why each piece was so placed. He had with him the great rolls of paper with the measured plans and the signs and drawings which he had had made from his own and Corbeck's rough notes. As he had told us, these contained the whole of the hieroglyphics on walls and ceilings and floor of the tomb in the Valley of the Sorcerer. Even had not the measurements, made to scale, recorded the position of each piece of furniture, we could have eventually placed them by a study of the cryptic writings and symbols.

Mr Trelawny explained to us certain other things, not laid down on the chart. Such as, for instance, that the hollowed part of the table was exactly fitted to the bottom of the magic coffer, which was therefore intended to be placed on it. The respective legs of this table were indicated by differently shaped uraei outlined on the floor, the head of each being extended in the direction of the similar uraeus twined round the leg. Also that the mummy, when laid on the raised portion in the bottom of the sarcophagus, seemingly made to fit the form, would lie head to the west and feet to the east, thus receiving the natural earth currents. 'If this be intended,' he said, 'as I presume it is, I gather that the force to be used has something to do with magnetism or electricity, or both. It may be, of course, that some other force, such, for instance, as that emanating from radium, is to be employed. I have experimented with the latter, but only in such small quantity as

I could obtain; but so far as I can ascertain the stone of the coffer is absolutely impervious to its influence. There must be some such unsusceptible substances in nature. Radium does not seemingly manifest itself when distributed through pitchblende; and there are doubtless other such substances in which it can be imprisoned. Possibly these may belong to that class of "inert" elements discovered or isolated by Sir William Ramsay. It is therefore possible that in this coffer, made from an aerolite and therefore perhaps containing some element unknown in our world, may be contained some mighty power which is to be released on its opening.'

This appeared to be an end of this branch of the subject; but as he still kept the fixed look of one who is still engaged in a theme we all waited in silence. After a pause he went on: 'There is one thing which has up to now, I confess, puzzled me. It may not be of prime importance; but in a matter like this, where all is unknown, we must take it that everything is important. I cannot think that in a matter worked out with such extraordinary scrupulosity such a thing should be overlooked. As you may see by the ground-plan of the tomb the sarcophagus stands near the north wall, with the magic coffer to the south of it. The space covered by the former is left quite bare of symbol or ornamentation of any kind. At the first glance this would seem to imply that the drawings had been made *after* the sarcophagus had been put into its place. But a more minute examination will show that the symbolization on the floor is so arranged that a definite effect is produced. See, here the writings run in correct order as though they had jumped across the gap. It is only from certain effects that it becomes clear that there is a meaning of some kind. What that meaning may be is what we want to know. Look at the top and bottom of the vacant space, which lies west and east corresponding to the head and foot of the sarcophagus. In both are duplications of the same symbolization, but so arranged that the parts of each one of them are integral portions of some other writing running crosswise. It is only when we get a *coup d'œil* from either the head or the foot that you recognize that there are symbolizations. See! they are in triplicate at the corners and the centre of both top and bottom. In every case there is a sun cut in half by the line of the sarcophagus, as by the horizon. Close behind each of these and faced away from it, as though in some way dependent on it, is the vase which in hieroglyphic writing symbolizes the heart – "Ab" the Egyptians called it. Beyond each of these again is the figure of a pair of widespread arms turned upwards from the elbow; this is the determinative of the "Ka" or "Double". But its relative position is different at top and bottom. At the head of the sarcophagus the top of the "Ka" is turned towards the mouth of the vase, but at the foot the extended arms point away from it.

'The symbolization seems to mean that during the passing of the Sun from west to east – from sunset to sunrise, or through the underworld, otherwise night – the heart, which is material even in the tomb and cannot leave it, simply revolves, so that it can always rest on "Ra" the sun-god, the origin of all good; but that the double, which represents the active principle, goes whither it will, the same by night as by day. If this be correct it is a warning – a caution – a reminder that the consciousness of the mummy does not rest but is to be reckoned with.

'Or it may be intended to convey that after the particular night of the resurrection, the "Ka" would leave the heart altogether. Thus typifying that in her resurrection the Queen would be restored to a lower and purely physical existence. In such case what would become of her memory and the experiences of her wide-wandering soul? The chiefest value of her resurrection would be lost to the world! This, however, does not alarm me. It is only guesswork after all, and is contradictory to the intellectual belief of the Egyptian theology, that the "Ka" is an essential portion of humanity.' He paused and we all waited.

The silence was broken by Dr Winchester: 'But would not all this imply that the Queen feared intrusion of her tomb?'

Mr Trelawny smiled as he answered: 'My dear sir, she was prepared for it. The grave-robber is no modern application of endeavour; he was probably known in the Queen's own dynasty. Not only was she prepared for intrusion, but, as shown in several ways, she expected it. The hiding of the lamps in the *serdâb*, and the institution of the avenging "treasurer" shows that there was defence, positive as well as negative. Indeed, from the many indications afforded in the clues laid out with the most consummate thought, we may almost gather that she entertained it as a possibility that others – like ourselves, for instance – might in all seriousness undertake the work which she had made ready for her own hands when the time should have come. This very matter that I have been speaking of is an instance. The clue is intended for seeing eyes!'

Again we were silent. It was Margaret who spoke: 'Father, may I have that chart? I should like to study it during the day!'

'Certainly, my dear!' answered Mr Trelawny heartily, as he handed it to her. He resumed his instructions in a different tone, a more matter-of-fact one suitable to a practical theme which had no mystery about it: 'I think you had better all understand the working of the electric light in case any sudden contingency should arise. I dare say you have noticed that we have a complete supply in every part of the house, so that there need not be a dark corner anywhere. This I had specially arranged. It is worked by a set of turbines moved by the flowing and ebbing tide, after the manner of the turbines at Niagara. I hope by this means to nullify accident and to have without fail a full supply ready at any time. Come with me and I will explain the system of circuits, and point out to you the taps and the fuses.' I could not but notice, as we went with him all over the house, how absolutely complete the system was, and how he had guarded himself against any disaster that human thought could foresee.

But out of the very completeness came a fear! In such an enterprise as ours the bounds of human thought were but narrow. Beyond it lay the vast of divine wisdom, and divine power!

When we came back to the cave, Mr Trelawny took up another theme: 'We have now to settle definitely the exact hour at which the great experiment is to be made. So far as science and mechanism go, if the preparations are complete, all hours are the same. But as we have to deal with preparations made by woman of extraordinarily subtle mind, and who had full belief in magic and had a cryptic meaning in everything, we should place ourselves in her position before deciding. It was now manifest that the sunset has an important place in the arrangements. As those suns, cut so mathematically by the edge of the sarcophagus, were arranged of full design, we must take our cue from this. Again, we find all along that the number seven has had an important bearing on every phase of the Queen's thought and reasoning and action. The logical result is that the seventh hour after sunset was the time fixed on. This is borne out by the fact that on each of the occasions when action was taken in my house, this was the time chosen. As the sun sets tonight in Cornwall at eight, our hour is to be three in the morning!' He spoke in a matter-of-fact way, though with great gravity; but there was nothing of mystery in his words or manner. Still, we were all impressed to a remarkable degree. I could see this in the other men by the pallor that came on some of their faces, and by the stillness and unquestioning silence with which the decision was received. The only one who remained in any way at ease was Margaret, who had lapsed into one of her moods of abstraction, but who seemed to wake up to a note of gladness. Her father, who was watching her intently, smiled; her mood was to him a direct confirmation of his theory.

For myself I was almost overcome. The definite fixing of the hour seemed like the voice of doom. When I think of it now, I can realize how a condemned man feels at his sentence, or at the last sounding of the hour he is to hear.

There could be no going back now! We were in the hands of God!

The hands of God . . . ! And yet . . . ! What other forces were arrayed? . . . What would become of us all, poor atoms of earthly dust whirled in the wind which cometh whence and goeth whither no man may know. It was not for myself . . . ! Margaret . . . !

I was recalled by Mr Trelawny's firm voice: 'Now we shall see to the lamps and finish our preparations.' Accordingly we set to work, and under his supervision made ready the Egyptian lamps, seeing that they were well filled with the cedar oil, and that the wicks were adjusted and in good order. We lighted and tested them one by one, and left them ready so that they would light at once and evenly. When this was done we had a general look round; and fixed all in readiness for our work at night.

All this had taken time, and we were I think all surprised when as we emerged from the cave we heard the great clock in the hall chime four.

We had a late lunch, a thing possible without trouble in the present state of our commissariat arrangements. After it, by Mr Trelawny's advice, we separated; each to prepare in our own way for the strain of the coming night. Margaret looked pale and somewhat overwrought, so I advised her to lie down and try to sleep. She promised that she would. The abstraction which had been upon her fitfully all day lifted for the time; with all her old sweetness and loving delicacy she kissed me good-bye for the present! With the sense of happiness which this gave me I went out for a walk on the cliffs. I did not want to think; and I had an instinctive feeling that fresh air and God's sunlight, and the myriad beauties of the works of His hand would be the best preparation of fortitude for what was to come.

When I got back, all the party were assembling for a late tea. Coming fresh from the exhilaration of nature, it struck me as almost comic that we, who were nearing the end of so strange – almost monstrous – an undertaking, should be yet bound by the needs and habits of our lives.

All the men of the party were grave; the time of seclusion, even if it had given them rest, had also given opportunity for thought. Margaret was bright, almost buoyant; but I missed about her something of her usual spontaneity. Towards myself there was a shadowy air of reserve, which brought back something of my suspicion. When tea was over, she went out of the room; but returned in a minute with the roll of drawing which she had taken with her earlier in the day. Coming close to Mr Trelawny, she said: 'Father, I have been carefully considering what you said today about the hidden meaning of those suns and hearts and "Kas", and I have been examining the drawings again.'

'And with what result, my child?' asked Mr Trelawny eagerly.

'There is another reading possible!'

'And that?' His voice was now tremulous with anxiety.

Margaret spoke with a strange ring in her voice; a ring that cannot be, unless there is the consciousness of truth behind it: 'It means that at the sunset the "Ka" is to enter the "Ab"; and it is only at the sunrise that it will leave it!'

'Go on!' said her father hoarsely.

'It means that for this night the Queen's double, which is otherwise free, will remain in her heart, which is mortal and cannot leave its prison-place in the mummy shrouding. It means that when the sun has dropped into the sea, Queen Tera will cease to exist as a conscious power, till sunrise; unless the great experiment can recall her to waking life. It means that there will be nothing whatever for you or others to fear from her in such way as we have all cause to remember. Whatever change may come from the working of the great experiment, there can come none from the poor, helpless, dead woman who has waited all those centuries for this night; who has given up to the coming hour all the freedom of eternity, won in the old way, in hope of a new life in a new world such as she longed for . . . !' She stopped suddenly. As she had gone on speaking there had come with her words a strange, pathetic, almost pleading, tone which touched me to the quick. As she stopped, I could see, before she turned away her head, that her eyes were full of tears.

For once the heart of her father did not respond to her feeling. He looked exultant, but with a grim masterfulness which reminded me of the set look of his stern face as he had lain in the trance. He did not offer any consolation to his daughter in her sympathetic pain. He only said: 'We may test the accuracy of your surmise, and of her feeling, when the time comes!' Having said so, he went up the stone stairway and into his own room. Margaret's face had a troubled look as she gazed after him.

Strangely enough her trouble did not as usual touch me to the quick.

When Mr Trelawny had gone, silence reigned. I do not think that any of us wanted to talk. Presently Margaret went to her room, and I went out on the terrace over the sea. The fresh air and the beauty of all before me helped to restore the good spirits which I had known earlier in the day. Presently I felt myself actually rejoicing in the belief that the danger which I had feared from the Queen's violence on the coming night was obviated. I believed in Margaret's belief so thoroughly that it did not occur to me to dispute her reasoning. In a lofty frame of mind, and with less anxiety than I had felt for days, I went to my room and lay down on the sofa.

I was awaked by Corbeck calling to me, hurriedly: 'Come down to the cave as quickly as you can. Mr Trelawny wants to see us all there at once. Hurry!'

I jumped up and ran down to the cave. All were there except Margaret, who came immediately after me carrying Silvio in her arms. When the cat saw his old enemy he struggled to get down; but Margaret held him fast and soothed him. I looked at my watch. It was close to eight.

When Margaret was with us her father said directly, with a quiet insistence which was new to me: 'You believe, Margaret, that Queen Tera has voluntarily undertaken to give up her freedom for this night? To become a mummy and nothing more, till the experiment has been completed? To be content that she shall be powerless under all and any circumstances until after all is over and the act of resurrection has been accomplished, or the effort has failed?'

After a pause Margaret answered in a low voice: 'Yes!'

In the pause her whole being, appearance, expression, voice, manner had changed. Even Silvio noticed it, and with a violent effort wriggled away from her arms; she did not seem to notice the act. I expected that the cat, when he had achieved his freedom, would have attacked the mummy; but on this occasion he did not. He seemed too cowed to approach it. He shrunk away, and with a piteous 'miaow' came over and rubbed himself against my ankles. I took him up in my arms, and he nestled there content. Mr Trelawny spoke again: 'You are sure of what you say! You believe it with all your soul?'

Margaret's face had lost the abstracted look; it now seemed illuminated with the devotion of one to whom is given to speak of great things. She answered in a voice which, though quiet, vibrated with conviction: 'I know it! My knowledge is beyond belief!'

Mr Trelawny spoke again: 'Then you are so sure, that were you Queen Tera herself, you would be willing to prove it in any way that I might suggest?'

'Yes, any way!' the answer rang out fearlessly.

He spoke again, in a voice in which was no note of doubt: 'Even in the abandonment of your familiar to death – to annihilation.'

She paused, and I could see that she suffered – horribly. There was in her eyes a hunted look, which no man can, unmoved, see in the eyes of his beloved. I was about to interrupt, when her father's eyes, glancing round with a fierce determination, met mine. I stood silent, almost spellbound; so also the other men. Something was going on before us which we did not understand!

With a few long strides Mr Trelawny went to the west side of the cave and tore back the shutter which obscured the window. The cool air blew in, and the sunlight streamed over them both, for Margaret was now by his side. He pointed to where the sun was sinking into the sea in a halo of golden fire, and his face was as set as flint. In a voice whose absolute uncompromising hardness I shall hear in my ears at times till my dying day, he said: 'Choose! Speak! When the sun has dipped below the sea, it will be too late!'

The glory of the dying sun seemed to light up Margaret's face, till it shone as if lit from within by a noble light, as she answered: 'Even that!'

Then stepping over to where the mummy cat stood on the little table, she placed her hand on it. She had now left the sunlight, and the shadows looked dark and deep over her. In a clear voice she said: 'Were I Tera, I would say "Take all I have! This night is for the gods alone!"'

As she spoke the sun dipped, and the cold shadow suddenly fell on us. We all stood still for a while. Silvio jumped from my arms and ran over to his mistress, rearing himself up against her dress as if asking to be lifted. He took no notice whatever of the mummy now.

Margaret was glorious with all her wonted sweetness as she said sadly: 'The sun is down, Father! Shall any of us see it again? The night of nights is come!'

If any evidence had been wanted of how absolutely one and all of us had come to believe in the spiritual existence of the Egyptian Queen, it would have been found in the change which in a few minutes had been effected in us by the statement of voluntary negation made, we all believed, through Margaret. Despite the coming of the fearful ordeal, the sense of which it was impossible to forget, we looked and acted as though a great relief had come to us. We had indeed lived in such a state of terrorism during the days when Mr Trelawny was lying in a trance that the feeling had bitten deeply into us. No one knows till he has experienced it, what it is to be in constant dread of some unknown danger which may come at any time and in any form.

The change was manifested in different ways, according to each nature. Margaret was sad. Dr Winchester was in high spirits, and keenly observant; the process of thought which had served as an antidote to fear, being now relieved from this duty, added to his intellectual enthusiasm. Mr Corbeck seemed to be in a retrospective rather than a speculative mood. I was myself rather inclined to be gay; the relief from certain anxiety regarding Margaret was sufficient for me for the time.

As to Mr Trelawny he seemed less changed than any. Perhaps this was only natural, as he had had in his mind the intention for so many years of doing that in which we were tonight engaged, that any event connected with it could only seem to him as an episode, a step to the end. His was that commanding nature which looks so to the end of an undertaking that all else is of secondary importance. Even now, though his terrible sternness relaxed under the relief from the strain, he never flagged nor faltered for a moment in his purpose. He asked us men to come with him; and going to the hall we presently managed to lower into the cave an oak table, fairly long and not too wide, which stood against the wall in the hall. This we placed under the strong cluster of electric lights in the middle of the cave. Margaret looked on for a while; then all at once her face blanched, and in an agitated voice she said, 'What are you going to do, Father?'

'To unroll the mummy of the cat! Queen Tera will not need her familiar tonight. If she should want him, it might be dangerous to us; so we shall make him safe. You are not alarmed, dear?'

'Oh no!' she answered quickly. 'But I was thinking of my Silvio, and how I should feel if he had been the mummy that was to be unswathed!'

Mr Trelawny got knives and scissors ready, and placed the cat on the table. It was a grim begining to our work; and it made my heart sink when I thought of what might happen in that lonely house in the mid-gloom of the night. The sense of loneliness and isolation from the world was increased by the moaning of the wind which had now risen ominously, and by the beating of waves on the rocks below. But we had too grave a task before us to be swayed by external manifestations: the unrolling of the mummy began.

There was an incredible number of bandages; and the tearing sound – they being stuck fast to each other by bitumen and gums and spices – and the little cloud of red pungent dust that arose, pressed on the senses of all of us. As the last wrappings came away, we saw the animal seated before us. He was all hunkered up; his hair and teeth and claws were complete. The eyes were closed, but the eyelids had not the fierce look which I expected. The whiskers had been pressed down on the side of the face by the bandaging; but when the pressure was taken away they stood out, just as they would have done in life. He was a magnificent creature, a tiger-cat of great size. But as we looked at him, our first glance of admiration changed to one of fear, and a shudder ran through each one of us; for here was a confirmation of the fears which we had endured.

His mouth and his claws were smeared with the dry, red stains of recent blood!

Dr Winchester was the first to recover; blood in itself had small disturbing quality for him. He had taken out his magnifying-glass and was examining the stains on the cat's mouth. Mr Trelawny breathed loudly, as though a strain had been taken from him.

'It is as I expected,' he said. 'This promises well for what is to follow.'

By this time Dr Winchester was looking at the red-stained paws. 'As I expected!' he said. 'He has seven claws, too! Opening his pocket-book, he took out the piece of blotting-paper marked by Silvio's claws, on which was also marked in pencil a diagram of the cuts made on Mr Trelawny's wrist. He placed the paper under the mummy cat's paw. The marks fitted exactly.

When we had carefully examined the cat, finding, however, nothing strange about it but its wonderful preservation, Mr Trelawny lifted it from the table. Margaret started forward, crying out: 'Take care, father! Take care! He may injure you!'

'Not now, my dear!' he answered as he moved towards the stairway. Her face fell. 'Where are you going?' she asked in a faint voice.

'To the kitchen,' he answered. 'Fire will take away all danger for the future; even an astral body cannot materialize from ashes!' He signed to us to follow him.

Margaret turned away with a sob. I went to her; but she motioned me back and whispered: 'No, no! Go with the others. Father may want you. Oh! It seems like murder! The poor Queen's pet . . . !' The tears were dropping from under the fingers that covered her eyes.

In the kitchen was a fire of wood ready laid. To this Mr Trelawny applied a match; in a few seconds the kindling had caught and the flames leaped. When the fire was solidly ablaze, he threw the body of the cat into it. For a few seconds it lay a dark mass amidst the flames, and the room was rank with the smell of burning hair. Then the dry body caught fire too. The inflammable substances used in embalming became new fuel, and the flames roared. A few minutes of fierce conflagration; and then we breathed freely. Queen Tera's familiar was no more!

When we went back to the cave we found Margaret sitting in the dark. She had switched off the electric light, and only a faint glow of the evening light came through the narrow openings. Her father went quickly over to her and put his arms round her in a loving protective way. She laid her head on his shoulder for a minute, and seemed comforted. Presently she called to me: 'Malcolm, turn up the light!'

I carried out her orders, and could see that, though she had been crying, her eyes were now dry. Her father saw it too and looked glad. He said to us in a grave tone: 'Now we had better prepare for our great work. It will not do to leave anything to the last!'

Margaret must have had a suspicion of what was coming, for it was with a sinking voice that she asked: 'What are you going to do now?'

Mr Trelawny too must have had a suspicion of her feelings, for he answered in a low tone: 'To unroll the mummy of Queen Tera!'

She came close to him and said pleadingly in a whisper: 'Father, you are not going to unswathe her! All you men . . . ! And in the glare of light!'

'But why not, my dear?'

'Just think, father, a woman! All alone! In such a way! In such a place! Oh! it's cruel, cruel!'

She was manifestly much overcome. Her cheeks were flaming red, and her eyes were full of indignant tears. Her father saw her distress; and, sympathizing with it, began to comfort her. I was moving off; but he signed to me to stay. I took it that after the usual manner of men he wanted help on such an occasion, and manlike wished to throw on someone else the task of dealing with a woman in indignant distress. However, he began to appeal first to her reason: 'Not a woman, dear; a mummy! She has been dead nearly five thousand years!'

'What does that matter? Sex is not a matter of years! A woman is a woman, if she had been dead five thousand centuries! And you expect her to arise out of that long sleep! It could not be real death, if she is to rise out of it! You have led me to believe that she will come alive when the coffer is opened!'

'I did, my dear; and I believe it! But if it isn't death that has been the matter with her all these years, it is something uncommonly like it. Then again, just think; it was men who embalmed her. They didn't have women's rights or lady doctors in ancient Egypt, my dear! And besides,' he went on more freely, seeing that she was accepting his argument, if not yielding to it, 'we men are accustomed to such things. Corbeck and I have unrolled a hundred mummies; and there were as many women as men amongst them. Dr Winchester in his work has had to deal with women as well as men, till custom has made him think nothing of sex. Even Ross has in his work as a barrister. . . .' He stopped suddenly.

'You were going to help too!' she said to me, with an indignant look.

I said nothing; I thought silence was best. Mr Trelawny went on hurriedly; I could see that he was glad of interruption, for the part of his argument concerning a barrister's work was becoming decidedly weak: 'My child, you will be with us yourself. Would we do anything which would hurt or offend you? Come now! be reasonable! We are not at a pleasure party. We are all grave men, entering gravely on an experiment which may unfold the wisdom of old times, and enlarge human knowledge indefinitely; which may put the minds of men on new tracks of thought and research. An experiment,' as he went on his voice deepened, 'which may be fraught with death to any one of us – to us all! We know from what has been, that there are, or may be, vast and unknown dangers ahead of us, of which none in the house today may ever see the end. Take it, my child, that we are not acting lightly; but with all the gravity of deeply earnest men! Besides, my dear, whatever feelings you or any of us may have on the subject, it is necessary for the success of the experiment to unswathe her. I think that under any circumstances it would be necessary to remove the wrappings before she became again a live human being instead of a spiritualized corpse with an astral body. Were her original intention carried out, and did she come to new life within her mummy wrappings, it might be to exchange a coffin for a grave! She would die the death of the buried alive! But now, when she has voluntarily abandoned for the time her astral power, there can be no doubt on the subject.'

Margaret's face cleared. 'All right, Father!' she said as she kissed him. 'But oh! it seems a horrible indignity to a queen, and a woman.'

I was moving away to the staircase when she called to me: 'Where are you going?'

I came back and took her hand and stroked it as I answered: 'I shall come back when the unrolling is over!'

She looked at me long, and a faint suggestion of a smile came over her face as she said: 'Perhaps you had better stay, too! It may be useful to you in your work as a barrister!' She smiled out as she met my eyes: but in an instant she changed. Her face grew grave, and deadly white. In a far away voice she said: 'Father is right! It is a terrible occasion; we need all to be serious over it. But all the same – nay, for that very reason you had better stay, Malcolm! You may be glad, later on, that you were present tonight!'

My heart sank down, down, at her words; but I thought it better to say nothing. Fear was stalking openly enough amongst us already!

By this time Mr Trelawny, assisted by Mr Corbeck and Dr Winchester, had raised the lid of the ironstone sarcophagus which contained the mummy of the Queen. It was a large one; but it was none too big. The mummy was both long and broad and high; and was of such weight that it was no easy task, even for the four of us, to lift it out. Under Mr Trelawny's direction we laid it out on the table prepared for it.

Then, and then only, did the full horror of the whole thing burst upon me! There, in the full glare of the light, the whole material and sordid side of death seemed staringly real. The outer wrappings, torn and loosened by rude touch, and with the colour either darkened by dust or worn light by friction, seemed creased as by rough treatment; the jagged edges of the wrapping-cloths looked fringed; the painting was patchy, and the varnish chipped. The coverings were evidently many, for the bulk was great. But through all, showed that unhidable human figure, which seems to look more horrible when partially concealed than at any other time. What was before us was death, and nothing else. All the romance and sentiment of fancy had disappeared. The two elder men, enthusiasts who had often done such work, were not disconcerted; and Dr Winchester seemed to hold himself in a businesslike attitude, as if before the operating-table. But I felt low-spirited, and miserable, and ashamed; and besides I was pained and alarmed by Margaret's ghastly pallor.

Then the work began. The unrolling of the mummy cat had prepared me somewhat for it; but this was so much larger, and so infinitely more elaborate, that it seemed a different thing. Moreover, in addition to the ever-present sense of death and humanity, there was a feeling of something finer in all this. The cat had been embalmed with coarser materials; here, all, when once the outer coverings were removed, was more delicately done. It seemed as if only the finest gums and spices had been used in this embalming. But there were the same surroundings, the same attendant red dust and pungent presence of bitumen; there was the same sound of rending which marked the tearing away of the bandages. There were an enormous number of these, and their bulk when opened was great. As the men unrolled them, I grew more and more excited. I did not take a part in it myself; Margaret had looked at me gratefully as I drew back. We clasped hands, and held each other hard. As the unrolling went on, the wrappings became finer, and the smell less laden with bitumen, but more pungent. We all, I think, began to feel it as though it caught or touched us in some special way. This, however, did not interfere with the work; it went on uninterruptedly. Some of the inner wrappings bore symbols or pictures. These were done sometimes wholly in pale green colour, sometimes in many colours; but always with a prevalence of green. Now and again Mr Trelawny or Mr Corbeck would point out some special drawing before laying the bandage on the pile behind them, which kept growing to a monstrous height.

At last we knew that the wrappings were coming to an end. Already the proportions were reduced to those of a normal figure of the manifest height of the Queen, who was more than average tall. And as the end drew nearer, so Margaret's pallor grew; and her heart beat more and more wildly, till her breast heaved in a way that frightened me.

Just as her father was taking away the last of the bandages, he happened to look up and caught the pained and anxious look of her pale face. He paused, and taking her concern to be as to the outrage on modesty, said in a comforting way: 'Do not be uneasy, dear! See! there is nothing to harm you. The Queen has on a robe – Ay, and a royal robe, too!'

The wrapping was a wide piece the whole length of the body. It being removed, a profusely full robe of white linen had appeared, covering the body from the throat to the feet.

And such linen! We all bent over to look at it.

Margaret lost her concern, in her woman's interest in fine stuff. Then the rest of us looked with admiration; for surely such linen was never seen by the eyes of our age. It was as fine as the finest silk. But never was spun or woven silk which lay in such gracious folds, constrict though they were by the close wrappings of the mummy cloth, and fixed into hardness by the passing of thousands of years.

Round the neck it was delicately embroidered in pure gold with tiny sprays of sycamore; and round the feet, similarly worked, was an endless line of lotus plants of unequal height, and with all the graceful abandon of natural growth.

Across the body, but manifestly not surrounding it, was a girdle of jewels. A wondrous girdle, which shone and glowed with all the forms and phases and colours of the sky!

The buckle was a great yellow stone, round of outline, deep and curved, as if a yielding globe had been pressed down. It shone and glowed, as though a veritable sun lay within; the rays of its light seemed to strike out and illumine all round. Flanking it were two great moonstones of lesser size, whose glowing, beside the glory of the sun-stone, was like the silvery sheen of moonlight.

And then on either side, linked by golden clasps of exquisite shape, was a line of flaming jewels, of which the colours seemed to glow. Each of these stones seemed to hold a living star, which twinkled in every phase of changing light.

Margaret raised her hands in ecstasy. She bent over to examine more closely; but suddenly drew back and stood fully erect at her grand height. She seemed to speak with the conviction of absolute knowledge as she said: 'That is no cerement! It was not meant for the clothing of death! It is a marriage robe!'

Mr Trelawny leaned over and touched the linen robe. He lifted a fold at the neck, and I knew from the quick intake of his breath that something had surprised him. He lifted yet a little more; and then he, too, stood back and pointed, saying: 'Margaret is right! That dress is not intended to be worn by the dead! See! her figure is not robed in it. It is but laid upon her.' He lifted the zone of jewels and handed it to Margaret. Then with both hands he raised the ample robe, and laid it across the arms which she extended in a natural impulse. Things of such beauty were too precious to be handled with any but the greatest care.

We all stood awed at the beauty of the figure which, save for the face cloth, now lay completely nude before us. Mr Trelawny bent over, and with hands that trembled slightly, raised this linen cloth which was of the same fineness as the robe. As he stood back and the whole glorious beauty of the Queen was revealed, I felt a rush of shame sweep over me. It was not right that we should be there, gazing with irreverent eyes on such unclad beauty: it was indecent; it was almost sacrilegious! And yet the white wonder of that beautiful form was something to dream of. It was not like death at all; it was like a statue carven in ivory by the hand of a Praxiteles. There was nothing of that horrible shrinkage which death seems to effect in a moment. There was none of the wrinkled toughness which seems to be a leading characteristic of most mummies. There was not the shrunken attenuation of a body dried in the sand, as I had seen before in museums. All the pores of the body seemed to have been preserved in some wonderful way. The flesh was full and round, as in a living person; and the skin was as smooth as satin. The colour seemed extraordinary. It was like ivory, new ivory; except where the right arm, with shattered, bloodstained wrist and missing hand had lain bare to exposure in the sarcophagus for so many tens of centuries.

With a womanly impulse, with a mouth that drooped with pity, with eyes that flashed with anger, and cheeks that flamed, Margaret threw over the body the beautiful robe which lay across her arm. Only the face was then to be seen. This was more startling even than the body, for it seemed not dead, but alive. The eyelids were closed; but the long, black, curling lashes lay over on the cheeks. The nostrils, set in grave pride, seemed to have the repose which, when it is seen in life, is greater than the repose of death. The full, red lips, though the mouth was not open, showed the tiniest white line of pearly teeth within. Her hair, glorious in quantity and glossy black as the raven's wing, was piled in great masses over the white forehead, on which a few curling tresses strayed like tendrils. I was amazed at the likeness to Margaret, though I had had my mind prepared for such by Mr Corbeck's quotation of her father's statement. This woman – I could not think of her as a mummy or a corpse – was the image of Margaret as my eyes had first lit on her. The likeness was increased by the jewelled ornament which she wore in her hair, the 'disk and plumes', such as Margaret, too, had worn. It, too, was a glorious jewel; one noble pearl of moonlight lustre, flanked by carven pieces of moonstone.

Mr Trelawny was overcome as he looked. He quite broke down; and when Margaret flew to him and held him close in her arms and comforted him, I heard him murmur brokenly: 'It looks as if you were dead, my child!'

There was a long silence. I could hear without the roar of the wind, which was now risen to a tempest, and the furious dashing of the waves far below. Mr Trelawny's voice broke the spell: 'Later on we must try and find out the process of embalming. It is not like any that I know. There does not seem to have been any opening cut for the withdrawing of the viscera and organs, which apparently remain intact within the body. Then, again, there is no moisture in the flesh; but its place is supplied with something else, as though wax or stearin had been conveyed into the veins by some subtle process. I wonder could it be possible that at that time they could have used paraffin. It might have been, by some process that we know not, pumped into the veins, where it hardened!'

Margaret, having thrown a white sheet over the Queen's body, asked us to bring it to her own room, where we laid it on her bed. Then she sent us away, saying: 'Leave her alone with me. There are still many hours to pass, and I do not like to leave her lying there, all stark in the glare of light. This may be the bridal she prepared for – the bridal of death; and at least she shall wear her pretty robes.'

When presently she brought me back to her room, the dead Queen was dressed in the robe of fine linen with the embroidery of gold; and all her beautiful jewels were in place. Candles were lit around her, and white flowers lay upon her breast.

Hand in hand we stood looking at her for a while. Then with a sigh, Margaret covered her with one of her own snowy sheets. She turned away; and after softly closing the door of the room, went back with me to the others who had now come into the dining-room. Here we all began to talk over the things that had been, and that were to be.

Now and again I could feel that one or other of us was forcing conversation, as if we were not sure of ourselves. The long wait was beginning to tell on our nerves. It was apparent to me that Mr Trelawny had suffered in that strange trance more than we suspected, or than he cared to show. True, his will and his determination were as strong as ever; but the purely physical side of him had been weakened somewhat. It was indeed only natural that it should be. No man can go through a period of four days of absolute negation of life, without being weakened by it somehow.

As the hours crept by, the time passed more and more slowly. The other men seemed to get unconsciously a little drowsy. I wondered if in the case of Mr Trelawny and Mr Corbeck, who had already been under the hypnotic influence of the Queen, the same dormancy was manifesting itself. Dr Winchester had periods of distraction which grew longer and more frequent as the time wore on.

As to Margaret, the suspense told on her exceedingly, as might have been expected in the case of a woman. She grew pale and paler still; till at last about midnight, I began to be seriously alarmed about her. I got her to come into the library with me, and tried to make her lie down on a sofa for a little while. As Mr Trelawny had decided that the experiment was to be made exactly at the seventh hour after sunset, it would be as nearly as possible three o'clock in the morning when the great trial should be made. Even allowing a whole hour for the final preparations, we had still two hours of waiting to go through. I promised faithfully to watch her, and to awake her at any time she might name; but she would not hear of resting. She thanked me sweetly, and smiled as she did so. But she assured me that she was not sleepy, and that she was quite able to bear up; that it was only the suspense and excitement of waiting that made her pale. I agreed perforce, but I kept her talking of many things in the library for more than an hour: so that at last, when she insisted on going back to her father, I felt that I had at least done something to help her pass the time.

We found the three men sitting patiently in the dining-room in silence. With man's fortitude they were content to be still, when they felt they had done all in their power.

And so we waited.

The striking of two o'clock seemed to freshen us all up. Whatever shadows had been settling over us during the long hours preceding seemed to lift at once, and we all went about our separate duties alert and with alacrity. We looked first to the windows to see that they were closed; for now the storm raged so fiercely that we feared it might upset our plans which, after all, were based on perfect stillness. Then we got ready our respirators to put them on when the time should be close at hand. We had from the first arranged to use them, for we did not know whether some noxious fume might not come from the magic coffer when it should be opened. Somehow it never seemed to occur to any of us that there was any doubt as to its opening.

Then, under Margaret's guidance, we carried the body of Queen Tera, still clad in her bridal robes, from her room into the cavern.

It was a strange sight, and a strange experience. The group of grave silent men carrying away from the lighted candles and the white flowers the white still figure, which looked like an ivory statue when through our moving the robe fell back.

We laid her in the sarcophagus, and placed the severed hand in its true position on her breast. Under it was laid the Jewel of Seven Stars, which Mr Trelawny had taken from the safe. It seemed to flash and blaze as he put it in its place. The glare of the electric lights shone cold on the great sarcophagus fixed ready for the final experiment – the great experiment, consequent on the researches during a lifetime of these two travelled scholars. Again, the startling likeness between Margaret and the mummy, intensified by her own extraordinary pallor, heightened the strangeness of it all.

When all was finally fixed, three-quarters of an hour had gone; for we were deliberate in all our doings. Margaret beckoned me, and I went with her to her room. There she did a thing which moved me strangely, and brought home to me keenly the desperate nature of the enterprise on which we were embarked. One by one, she blew out the candles carefully, and placed them back in their usual places. When she had finished she said to me: 'They are done with! Whatever comes – life or death – there will be no purpose in their using now!'

We returned to the cavern with a strange thrill as of finality. There was to be no going back now!

We put on our respirators, and took our places as had been arranged. I was to stand by the taps of the electric lights, ready to turn them off or on as Mr Trelawny should direct. His last caution to me to carry out his instructions exactly was almost like a menace; for he warned me that death to any or all of us might come from any error or neglect on my part. Margaret and Dr Winchester were to stand between the sarcophagus and the wall, so that they would not be between the mummy and the magic coffer. They were to note accurately all that should happen with regard to the Queen.

Mr Trelawny and Mr Corbeck were to see the lamps lighted: and then to take their places, the former at the foot, the latter at the head, of the sarcophagus.

When the hands of the clock were close to the hour, they stood ready with their lit tapers, like gunners in old days with their linstocks.

For the few minutes that followed, the passing of time was a slow horror. Mr Trelawny stood with his watch in his hand, ready to give the signal.

The time approached with inconceivable slowness; but at last came the whirring of wheels which warns that the hour is at hand. The striking of the silver bell of the clock seemed to smite on our hearts like the knell of doom. One! Two! Three!

The wicks of the lamps caught, and I turned out the electric light. In the dimness of the struggling lamps, and after the bright glow of the electric light, the room and all within it took weird shape, and everything seemed in an instant to change. We waited, with our hearts beating. I know mine did; and I fancied I could hear the pulsation of the others. Without, the storm raged; the shutters of the narrow windows shook and strained and rattled, as though something was striving for entrance.

The seconds seemed to pass with leaden wings; it was as though all the world were standing still. The figures of the others stood out dimly, Margaret's white dress alone showing clearly in the gloom. The thick respirators, which we all wore, added to the strange appearance. The thin light of the lamps, as the two men bent over the coffer, showed Mr Trelawny's square jaw and strong mouth, and the brown, wrinkled face of Mr Corbeck. Their eyes seemed to glare in the light. Across the room Dr Winchester's eyes twinkled like stars, and Margaret's blazed like black suns.

Would the lamps never burn up!

It was only a few seconds in all till they did blaze up. A slow, steady light, growing more and more bright; and changing in colour from blue to crystal white. So they stayed for a couple of minutes, without any change in the coffer being noticeable. At last there began to appear all over it a delicate glow. This grew and grew, till it became like a blazing jewel; and then like a living thing, whose essence was light. Mr Trelawny and Mr Corbeck moved silently to their places beside the sarcophagus.

We waited and waited, our hearts seeming to stand still.

All at once there was a sound like a tiny muffled explosion, and the cover of the coffer lifted right up on a level plane a few inches; there was no mistaking anything now, for the whole cavern was full of light. Then the cover, staying fast at one side, rose slowly up on the other, as though yielding to some pressure of balance. I could not see what was within, for the risen cover stood between. The coffer still continued to glow; from it began to steal a faint greenish vapour which floated in the direction of the sarcophagus as though impelled or drawn towards it. I could not smell it fully on account of the respirator; but, even through that, I was conscious of a strange, pungent odour. The vapour got somewhat denser after a few seconds, and began to pass directly into the open sarcophagus. It was evident now that the mummied body had some attraction for it; and also that it had some effect on the body, for the sarcophagus slowly became illumined as though the body had begun to glow. I could not see within from where I stood, but I gathered from the faces of all the four watchers that something strange was happening.

I longed to run over and take a look for myself; but I remembered Mr Trelawny's solemn warning, and remained at my post.

The storm still thundered round the house, and I could feel the rock on which it was built tremble under the furious onslaught of the waves. The shutters strained as though the screaming wind without would in very anger have forced an entrance. In that dread hour of expectancy, when the forces of life and death were struggling for the mastery, imagination was awake. I almost fancied that the storm was a living thing, and animated with the wrath of the quick!

All at once the eager faces round the sarcophagus were bent forward. The look of speechless wonder in the eyes, lit by that supernatural glow from within the sarcophagus, had a more than mortal brilliance.

My own eyes were nearly blinded by the awful, paralysing light, so that I could hardly trust them. I saw something white rising up from the open sarcophagus. Something which appeared to my tortured eyes to be filmy, like a white mist. In the heart of this mist, which was cloudy and opaque like an opal, was something like a hand holding a fiery jewel flaming with many lights. As the fierce glow of the coffer met this new living light, the green vapour floating between them seemed like a cascade of brilliant points – a miracle of light!

But at that very moment there came a change. The fierce storm, battling with the shutters of the narrow openings, won victory. With the sound of a pistol shot, one of the heavy shutters broke its fastening and was hurled on its hinges back against the wall. In rushed a fierce blast which blew the flames of the lamps to and fro, and drifted the green vapour from its course.

On the very instant came a change in the outcome from the coffer. There was a moment's quick flame and a muffled explosion; and black smoke began to pour out. This got thicker and thicker with frightful rapidity, in volumes of ever-increasing density; till the whole cavern began to get obscure, and its outlines were lost. The screaming wind tore in and whirled it about. At a sign from Mr Trelawny, Mr Corbeck went and closed the shutter and jammed it fast with a wedge.

I should have liked to help; but I had to wait directions from Mr Trelawny, who inflexibly held his post at the head of the sarcophagus. I signed to him with my hand, but he motioned me back. Gradually the figures of all close to the sarcophagus became indistinct in the smoke which rolled round them in thick billowy clouds. Finally, I lost sight of them altogether. I had a terrible desire to rush over so as to be near Margaret; but again I restrained myself. If the Stygian gloom continued, light would be a necessity of safety; and I was the guardian of the light! My anguish of anxiety as I stood to my post was almost unendurable.

The coffer was now but a dull colour; and the lamps were growing dim, as though they were being overpowered by the thick smoke. Absolute darkness would soon be upon us.

I waited and waited, expecting every instant to hear the command to turn up the light; but none came. I waited still, and looked with harrowing intensity at the rolling billows of smoke still pouring out of the casket whose glow was fading. The lamps sank down, and went out; one by one.

Finally, there was but one lamp alight, and that was dimly blue and flickering. I kept my eyes fixed towards Margaret, in the hope that I might see her in some lifting of the gloom; it was for her now that all my anxiety was claimed. I could just see her white frock beyond the dim outline of the sarcophagus.

Deeper and deeper grew the black mist, and its pungency began to assail my nostrils as well as my eyes. Now the volume of smoke coming from the coffer seemed to lessen, and the smoke itself to be less dense. Across the room I saw a movement of something white where the sarcophagus was. There were several such movements. I could just catch the quick glint of white through the dense smoke in the fading light; for now even the last lamp began to flicker with the quick leaps before extinction.

Then the last glow disappeared. I felt that the time had come to speak; so I pulled off my respirator and called out: 'Shall I turn on the light?' There was no answer. Before the thick smoke choked me, I called again, but more loudly: 'Mr Trelawny, shall I turn on the light? Answer me! If you do not forbid me, I shall turn it on!'

As there was no reply, I turned the tap. To my horror there was no response; something had gone wrong with the electric light! I moved, intending to run up the staircase to seek the cause, but I could now see nothing, all was pitch dark.

I groped my way across the room to where I thought Margaret was. As I went I stumbled across a body. I could feel by her dress that it was a woman. My heart sank; Margaret was unconscious, or perhaps dead. I lifted the body in my arms, and went straight forward till I touched a wall. Following it round I came to the stairway, and hurried up the steps with what haste I could make, hampered as I was with my dear burden. It may have been that hope lightened my task; but as I went the weight that I bore seemed to grow less as I ascended from the cavern.

I laid the body in the hall, and groped my way to Margaret's room, where I knew there were matches, and the candles which she had placed beside the Queen. I struck a match; and oh! it was good to see the light. I lit two candles, and taking one in each hand, hurried back to the hall where I had left, as I had supposed, Margaret.

Her body was not there. But on the spot where I had laid her was Queen Tera's bridal robe, and surrounding it the girdle of wondrous gems. Where the heart had been, lay the Jewel of Seven Stars.

Sick at heart, and with a terror which has no name, I went down into the cavern. My two candles were like mere points of light in the black, impenetrable smoke. I put up again to my mouth the respirator which hung round my neck, and went to look for my companions.

I found them all where they had stood. They had sunk down on the floor, and were gazing upward with fixed eyes of unspeakable terror. Margaret had put her hands before her face, but the glassy stare of her eyes through her fingers was more terrible than an open glare.

I pulled back the shutters of all the windows to let in what air I could. The storm was dying away as quickly as it had risen, and now it only came in desultory puffs. It might well be quiescent; its work was done!

I did what I could for my companions; but there was nothing that could avail. There, in that lonely house, far away from aid of man, naught could avail.

It was merciful that I was spared the pain of hoping.

Peter Owen Modern Classics

If you have enjoyed this book you may like to try some of the other Peter Owen paperback reprints listed below. **The Peter Owen Modern Classics** series was launched in 1998 to bring some of our internationally acclaimed authors and their works, first published by Peter Owen in hardback, to a modern readership. We will also be expanding the Paperback Readers series to include authors such as **Shusaku Endo, Hermann Hesse, Anna Kavan, Anaïs Nin,** and **Cesare Pavese.**

To order books or a free catalogue or for further information on these or any other Peter Owen titles, please contact the **Sales Department, Peter Owen Ltd, 73 Kenway Road, London SW5 0RE, UK tel. + + 44 (0)20 7373 5628 or + + 44 (0)20 7370 6093, fax + + 44 (0)20 7373 6760,** e-mail **sales@peterowen.com** or visit our website at **www.peterowen.com**

Guillaume Apollinaire
LES ONZE MILLE VERGES

In 1907 Guillaume Apollinaire, one of the most original and influential poets of the twentieth century, turned his hand to the novel. He produced two books for the clandestine erotica market, the finer of these being *Les Onze Mille Verges*. One of the most masterful and hilarious novels of all time, it was pronounced owlishly by Picasso to be Apollinaire's masterpiece. For nearly seventy years this book was a legend until it first appeared in 1973.

'A honest, spirited porn job.' – Julian Barnes, *New Statesman*

'Christ!' – Brian Case, *Time Out*

0 7206 1100 8   £9.95

Paul Bowles
MIDNIGHT MASS

Chosen by the author from his best, these superlative short stories reveal Paul Bowles at his peak. They offer insights into the mysteries of *kif* and the majesty of the desert, the meeting of alien cultures and the clash between modern and ancient, Islam and Christianity, logic and superstition.

Set in Morocco, Thailand and Sri Lanka, these stories reverberate with vision and, like Bowles's novels, are universal in their appeal.

'His short stories are among the best ever written by an American.' – Gore Vidal

0 7206 1083 4   £9.95

Paul Bowles
POINTS IN TIME

Here Bowles focuses on Morocco, his home for many decades, condensing experience, emotion and the whole history of a people into a series of short, brilliant pieces. He takes the reader on a journey through the Moroccan centuries, pausing at points along the way to create resonant images of the country and the beliefs and characteristics of its inhabitants.

'His plain and compact prose makes this a wholly satisfying book.' – *Literary Review*

'An impressive book.' – Anthony Thwaite, *Observer*

'Persuasive prose which leaves one with a very strong and distinct flavour of landscape and people.' – *Gay Times*

'I recommend *Points in Time*.' – Anthony Burgess

0 7206 1137 7   £8.50

Paul Bowles
THEIR HEADS ARE GREEN

First published in 1963, *Their Heads Are Green* is an account of Bowles's life and experiences in Morocco, the country that has provided the backdrop to his best novels. He recounts his journeys to the Sahara, which influenced the classic *The Sheltering Sky*, as well as his travels through Mexico, Turkey and Sri Lanka. With his exceptional gift for penetrating beyond the picturesque or exotic aspects of the countries he describes, he evokes the unique characteristics of both people and places.

'Few writers have Paul Bowles's skill in evocation while making of the familiar something new and extraordinary.' – *The Times*

0 7206 1077 X   £9.95

Paul Bowles
UP ABOVE THE WORLD

Dr Slade and his wife are on holiday in Latin America when they meet Grove, a young man of striking good looks and charm and his beautiful seventeen-year-old mistress. An apparently chance encounter, it opens the door to a nightmare as the Slades find themselves slowly being sucked in by lives whose relevance to their own they cannot understand.

Oiled by a dangerous cocktail of drugs and dark relationships, the Slades are lured on another journey: a terrifying trip where the only guides are fantasy, hallucination and death.

Brilliantly written, with the poetic control that has always characterized Bowles's work, *Up Above the World* is a masterpiece of cold, relentless terror.

'Sex, drugs, fantasies and the machinery of derangement . . . Bowles's overpowering void descends on the mind and heart like a hypnotic spell.' – *New York Times Book Review*

0 7206 1087 7   £9.95

Blaise Cendrars
MORAVAGINE

Since its first publication in France in 1926 this ferocious and fantastic masterpiece has established itself as a classic of twentieth-century fiction. The semi-autobiographical story is narrated by a young French doctor who encounters Moravagine in a Swiss lunatic asylum and promptly helps him to escape. Together they travel the world, rally to support the Russian Revolution and fight in the First World War.

Full of tenderness, horror and savage humour, *Moravagine* is a dazzling piece of writing by one of the founders of the modern movement in literature.

'How can I convince the sceptic that I was ravished by Cendrars's *Moravagine*? How does one know immediately that a thing is after one's own heart?' – Henry Miller

0 7206 1098 2   £9.95

Blaise Cendrars
TO THE END OF THE WORLD

The narrative of *To the End of the World* shifts between a Foreign Legion barracks in North Africa and the theatres, cafés, dosshouses and police headquarters of post-war Paris. The central character in this *roman-à-clef* is a septuagenarian actress whose passionate affair with a young deserter from the Foreign Legion is jeopardized by the murder of a barman.

To the End of the World is not pure invention. Like all Cendrars's works it has some basis in his adventures and nomadic life; but this original and often very funny portrayal of the Paris of the late 1940s is obviously the product of an abundant imagination.

'There is nothing like reading Cendrars.' – *Independent*

0 7206 1097 4   £9.95

Jean Cocteau
LE LIVRE BLANC

Le Livre Blanc, a 'white paper' on homosexual love, was first published anonymously in France by Cocteau's contemporary Maurice Sachs and was at once decried by the critics as obscene.

The semi-autobiographical narrative describes a youth's love affairs with a succession of boys and men during the early years of this century. The young man's self-deceptive attempts to find fulfilment, first through women and then by way of the Church, are movingly conveyed; the book ends with a strong plea for male homosexuality to be accepted without censure.

The book is fully illustrated and includes woodcuts by the author.

'A wonderful book.' – *Gay Times*

0 7206 1081 8   £8.50

Colette
DUO and LE TOUTOUNIER

These two linked novels, *Duo* and *Le Toutounier*, are works of Colette's maturity. First published in France in 1934 and 1939 respectively, they have been rated as being among Colette's finest work. In *Duo* Colette observes, with astuteness and perception, two characters whose marriage is foundering on the wife's infidelity. Acting out the crisis, Alice and Michel have the stage to themselves so that nothing is allowed to distract from the marital dialogue.

Le Toutounier continues Alice's story after Michel's death and her move to Paris. There she and her two sisters live in a shabby, homely apartment; fiercely independent, reticent, hard-working, needing men but showing little sign of loving them, they speak a private language and seek comfort in the indestructible sofa (*toutounier*) of their childhood.

'Drenched with her talent at its best.'– *Sunday Times*

0 7206 1069 9   £9.95

Lawrence Durrell
POPE JOAN

In this superb adaptation of a novel by the nineteenth-century Greek author Emmanuel Royidis, Lawrence Durrell traces the remarkable history of a young woman who travelled across Europe in the ninth century disguised as a monk, acquired great learning and ruled over Christendom for two years as Pope John VIII before her sudden and surprising death in childbirth. When *Papissa Joanna* was first published in Athens in 1886 it created a sensation. The book was banned and its author excommunicated. It nevertheless brought him immediate fame and the work established itself securely in the history of modern Greek literature. Subsequently Durrell, one of the most important British writers of the twentieth century and author of the Alexandria Quartet, created a masterpiece in its own right, a dazzling concoction presented with the deftest touch.

'A sharp satire . . . acutely funny . . . salacious.' – *Spectator*

'The most remarkable of his translations and adaptations was his brilliant version of Emmanuel Royidis's novel.' – *The Times*

'A sophisticated literary delight.' – *Publishers Weekly*

'One of the funniest novels ever written . . . A true classic.' – *Punch*

0 7206 1065 6   £9.95

Shusaku Endo
WONDERFUL FOOL

Gaston Bonaparte, a young Frenchman, visits Tokyo to stay with his pen-friend Takamori. His appearance is a bitter disappointment to his new friends and his behaviour causes them acute embarrassment. He is a trusting person with a simple love for others and continues to trust them even after they have demonstrated deceit and betrayal. He spends his time not sightseeing but making friends with street children, stray dogs, prostitutes and gangsters. Endo charts his misadventures with sharp irony, satire and objectivity.

'The perfect guide in the form of fiction to Tokyo and the Japanese experience.' – Grahame Greene

0 7206 1080 X   £9.95

Hermann Hesse
DEMIAN

Published shortly after the First World War, *Demian* is one of Hermann Hesse's finest novels.

Emil Sinclair boasts of a theft that he has not committed and subsequently finds himself blackmailed by a bully. He turns to Max Demian, in whom he finds a friend and spiritual mentor. This strangely self-possessed figure is able to lure him out of his ordinary home life and convince him of an existing alternative world of corruption and evil. In progressing from an orthodox education through to philosophical mysticism, Emil's search for self-awareness culminates in a meeting with Demian's mother – symbol and personification of motherhood.

'One of the most elevated spiritual and ethical allegories I have ever read . . . extremely readable and well-translated.' – *Listener*

'A moving fable of spiritual growth.' – *Observer*

0 7206 1030 X   £9.95

Hermann Hesse
JOURNEY TO THE EAST

The narrator of this allegorical tale travels through time and space in a search of ultimate truth. This pilgrimage to the 'East' covers both real and imagined lands and takes place not only in our own time but also in the Middle Ages and the Renaissance. The fellow travellers, too, are both real and fictitious – Plato, Pythagorus, Don Quixote, Tristram Shandy and Baudelaire all put in appearances.

Like the better-known *Siddartha*, *The Journey to the East* is a timeless novel of broad appeal, particularly among younger readers, stemming from an affinity with the lasting effects of the author's pacifist instincts and his own youthful rebellion against the strictures of a classical education, combined with an easy lyricism and a well-composed symmetry of style.

0 7206 1131 8   £8.50

Hermann Hesse
NARCISSUS AND GOLDMUND

Narcissus is a teacher at Mariabronn, a medieval German monastery, and Goldmund his favourite pupil. Goldmund runs away in pursuit of love, living a picaresque, wanderer's life which brings him both pain and ecstasy. Narcissus remains behind, detached from the world in prayer and meditation. Their eventual reunion brings into focus the diversity between artist and thinker, Dionysian and Apollonian. Thought by some to be Hesse's greatest novel, this is a classic of contemporary literature.

'Deeply moving and richly poetic, this brilliant fusion of concepts is astonishing in its simplicity and power.'
– Birmingham Post

0 7206 1060 5   £12.50

Anna Kavan
ASYLUM PIECE

'If only one knew of what and by whom one were accused, when, where and by what laws one were to be judged, it would be possible to prepare one's defence systematically and set about things in a sensible fashion.'

First published sixty years ago, Asylum Piece today ranks as one of the most extraordinary and terrifying evocations of human madness ever written.

This collection of stories, mostly interlinked and largely autobiographical, chart the descent of the narrator from the onset of neurosis to final incarceration at a Swiss clinic. The sense of paranoia, of persecution by a foe or force that is never given a name evokes Kafka's The Trial, a writer with whom Kavan is often compared, though Kavan's deeply personal, restrained and almost foreign-accented style has no true model. The same characters who recur throughout – the protagonist's unhelpful 'adviser', the friend/lover who abandons her at the clinic, and an assortment of deluded companions – are sketched without a trace of the rage, self-pity or sentiment that have marked more recent 'Prozac' memoirs.

0 7206 1123 7   £9.95

Anna Kavan
THE PARSON

The Parson was not published in Anna Kavan's lifetime but found after her death in manuscript form. Thought to have been written between the mid-1950s and early 1960s, it presages, through its undertones and imagery, some of Kavan's last and most enduring fiction, particularly Ice. It was published finally, to wide acclaim, by Peter Owen in 1995.

The Parson of the title is not a cleric but an upright young army officer so nick-named for his apparent prudishness. On leave in his native homeland, he meets Rejane, a rich and beguiling beauty, the woman of his dreams. The days that the Parson spends with Rejane, riding in and exploring the wild moorland, have their own enchantment, but Rejane grows restless in this desolate landscape. Though doubtless in love with the Parson, she discourages any intimacy, until she persuades him to take her to a sinister castle situated on a treacherous headland . . .

The Parson is less a tale of unrequited love than exploration of divided selves, momentarily locked in an unequal embrace. Passion is revealed as a play of the senses as well as a destructive force. Valid comparisons have been made between this writer and Poe, Kafka and Thomas Hardy, but the presence of her trademark themes, cleverly juxtaposed and set in her risk-taking prose, mark The Parson as one-hundred per cent Kavan.

0 7206 1140 7   £8.95

Anna Kavan
SLEEP HAS HIS HOUSE

A daring synthesis of memoir and Surrealist experimentation, Sleep Has His House charts the stages of the subject's gradual withdrawal from all interest in and contact with the daylight world of received reality. Brief flashes of daily experience from childhood, adolescence and youth are described in what Kavan terms 'night-time language' – a heightened, decorative prose that frees these events from their gloomy associations. The novel suggests that we have all spoken this dialect in childhood and in our dreams, but these thoughts can only be sharpened or decoded by contemplation in the dark.

Kavan maintained that the plot of a book is only the point of departure, beyond which she tries to reveal that side of life which is never seen by the waking eye but which dreams and drugs can suddenly illuminate. She spent the last ten years of her life literally and metaphorically shutting out the light; the startling discovery of *Sleep Has His House* is how much these night-time illuminations reveal her joy for the living world.

Sleep Has His House startled with its strangeness in 1948. Today it is one of Kavan's most acclaimed books.

'Possibly one of her most interesting books, a near masterpiece in the imaginative speculations of those whose paradise simultaneously contains their hell.' – *The Times*

'Anna Kavan's "night-time language" is in no way obscure: on the contrary, her dreams are as carefully notated as paintings by Dalí or de Chirico.' – *New Statesman*

'Her dramas are haunted by a tall woman in black – her mother. There is also a revealing passage of an addict's sordid bedroom, littered with needles and spilled powders . . . Her writing is magnificent. It is a fascinating clinical casebook of her individual obsessions and the effects of drugs on her imagination . . . in the tradition of the great writers on drug literature, de Quincey, Wilkie Collins, Coleridge.' – *Daily Telegraph*

'A testament of remarkable, if feverish beauty.' – Robert Nye, *Guardian*

0 7206 1129 6   £9.95

Anna Kavan
WHO ARE YOU?

Who Are You? is a sparse depiction of the hopeless, emotional polarity of a young couple and their doomed marriage spent in a remote, tropical hell.

She – described only as 'the girl' – is young, sophisticated and sensitive; he, 'Mr Dog-Head', is an unreconstructed thug and heavy drinker who rapes her, otherwise passing his time bludgeoning rats with a tennis racket. Together with a visiting stranger, 'Suede Boots', who urges the woman to escape until he is banished by her husband, these characters live through the same situations twice. Their identities are equally real – or unreal – in each case. With slight variation in the background and the novel's atmosphere, neither the outcome nor the characters themselves are quite the same the second time. The constant question of the jungle 'brain-fever' bird remains unanswered – 'Who are you?'

Kavan's characteristically autobiographical bias

in this novel can be traced to her life in Burma during her first marriage. First published in 1963, *Who Are You?* was reissued to widespread acclaim in 1973.

'To write about this finely economical book in any terms other than its own is cruelly to distort the near-perfection of the original text. There is a vision here which dismays.' – Robert Nye, *Guardian*

'We are indebted to Peter Owen for reissuing Anna Kavan's work . . . *Who Are You?* is accomplished and complete . . . so fully imagined, so finely described in spare, effective prose, that it is easy to suspend disbelief.' – Nina Bawden, *Daily Telegraph*

'Lots of fun to read, sprouts with a macabre imagination and is, no question, a classic.' – *Sunday Telegraph*

0 7206 1150 4   £8.95

Yukio Mishima
CONFESSIONS OF A MASK

This autobiographical novel, regarded as Mishima's finest book, is the haunting story of a Japanese boy's homosexual awakening during and after the Second World War. Detailing his progress from an isolated childhood through adolescence to manhood, including an abortive love affair with a classmate's sister, it reports the inner life of a boy's preoccupation with death. This fourth reprint attests to the novel's enduring themes of fantasy, despair and alienation.

'A terrific and astringent beauty . . . a work of art.' – *Times Literary Supplement*

0 7206 1031 3   £11.95

Boris Pasternak
THE LAST SUMMER

By the author of *Dr Zhivago,* and his only other completed work of fiction, *The Last Summer* is set in Russia during the winter of 1916, when Serezha visits his married sister. Tired after a long journey, he falls into a restless sleep and half remembers, half dreams the incidents of the last summer of peace before the First World War, 'when life appeared to pay heed to individuals'.

As tutor in a wealthy, unsettled Moscow household, he focuses his intense romanticism on Mrs Arild, the employer's paid companion, while spending his nights with the prostitute Sashka and others.

In this evocation of the past, the characters are subtly etched against their social backgrounds, and Pasternak imbues the commonplace with his own intense and poetic vision.

'A concerto in prose.' – V.S. Pritchett

0 7206 1099 0   £9.95

Cesare Pavese
THE DEVIL IN THE HILLS

The Devil in the Hills is the most personal of Pavese's novels, an elegiac celebration of lost youth set in the landscape of his own boyhood: the hills, vineyards and villages of Piedmont.

Three young men spend away their sun-drenched summer talking, drinking – rarely sleeping, and there is an overwhelming sense that it is the last summer that they will be able to indulge such idle pleasures. In contrast to their feelings of transience, the prolonged leisure of their new, wealthy acquaintance, Poli, fascinates them. For a while they linger in his world, in his decaying villa, half appalled by his cocaine addiction, his blasphemy, his corrupt circle of friends, but none the less mesmerized until autumn creeps upon the hillside, and the seasonal moment of leave-taking arrives . . .

'In this remarkable author, the compassionate moralist and the instinctive poet go hand in hand.' – *Scotsman*

'The Devil in the Hills shows how ahead of his time he [Pavese] was.' – *The Times*

'Erotic, but extraordinarily delicate and controlled.'
– *Guardian*

0 7206 1118 0   £9.95

Cesare Pavese
THE MOON AND THE BONFIRE

Anguila, the narrator, is a successful businessman lured home from California to the Piedmontese village where he was fostered by peasants. But, after twenty years, so much has changed. Slowly, with the power of memory, he is able to piece together the past and relates it to what he finds left in the present. He looks at the lives and sometimes violent fates of the villagers he has known from childhood, setting the poverty, ignorance or indif-ference that binds them to these hills and valleys against the beauty of the landscape and the rhythm of the seasons. With stark realism and muted compassion Pavese weaves the strands together and brings them to a stark and poignant climax.

'Wonderfully written and beautifully translated.'
– *Sunday Times*

'Reminds us again how good a writer Pavese was.'
– *Sunday Telegraph*

0 7206 1119 9   £9.95

Mervyn Peake
A BOOK OF NONSENSE

'I can be quite obscure and practically marzipan.' From the macabre to the brilliantly off-beat, Mervyn Peake's nonsense verse can, like marzi-pan, be enjoyed by young and old alike. This collection of writings and drawings was selected by his late widow, Maeve Gilmore, and it intro-duces a whole gallery of characters and creatures, such as the Dwarf of Battersea and Footfruit.

'Deserves a place among the eccentrics of the English tradition alongside Sterne, Blake, Lear, Carroll and Belloc.'
– *The Times*

0 7206 1059 1   £7.95

Edith Piaf
MY LIFE

Taped in hospital shortly before her death, 'to set the record straight', this is the dramatic and often tragic story of the legendary French singer Edith Piaf. She recalls her early years in the Paris under-world, her rise to international stardom, her long fight against alcohol and drugs, and her succession of stormy love affairs – and defiantly asserts the message of her most famous song, *Non, je ne regrette rien*.

0 7206 1111 3   £9.95

Marcel Proust
PLEASURES AND REGRETS

This was Proust's first published work, appearing when he was only 25, and it consists of stories, sketches and thematic writings on a variety of sub-jects. The attitudes reflect many characteristics of the turn of the twentieth century, yet Proust illu-mined them with the unique shafts of observation and gift of analysis that he was later to perfect in *The Remembrance of Things Past*. This book is a period piece of intricate delights and subtle flavours that will be relished by the author's many admirers.

'How do you get a flavour, first-hand, of the only writer who could compete, in the 20th century, with the intimidating geniuses of Joyce and Beckett? I would suggest this little volume.' – Nicholas Lezard, *Guardian*

0 7206 1110 5   £9.95

Joseph Roth
FLIGHT WITHOUT END

After many adventures, a young Austrian soldier returns home after the Great War. Having fought with the Red Army during the Russian Revolutionary War and worked as a Soviet official, he arrives back in bourgeois Vienna to find that it no longer has a place for him. His father has died and his fiancée, who had waited many years for his return, has married another man and left for Paris; there is nothing for an ex-soldier in Austria at the end of the Habsburg empire. He travels Europe searching in vain for a place to belong, not with his estranged brother in Germany nor with his former fiancée in Paris. This is the story of a young man's alienation and his search for identity and home in a world that has changed out of all recognition from the one in which he grew up.

'Almost perfect.' – *Rolling Stone*

0 7206 1068 0   £9.95

Joseph Roth
THE SILENT PROPHET

This story grew out of Roth's visit to the Soviet Union in 1926, at a time when speculation was rife about the fate of Leon Trotsky. Roth referred to this book as his 'Trotsky novel', but the experiences of the book's hero, the Trotsky-like Friederich Kargan, are also recognizably those of a less well-known Jewish outsider, a perpetual exile in post-First World War Europe – Joseph Roth himself

Not strictly a historical novel nor personal analysis, *The Silent Prophet* is a beautifully descriptive journey from lonliness into an illusory worldliness back into lonliness, and a haunting study of alienation.

A novel one should not wish to be without . . . Roth is a very fine writer indeed.' – Angela Carter, *Guardian*

'With his striking elliptical style, which can evoke despair through real wit it would be only mildly flattering to view him as a compassionate, laconic Conrad.' – *Time Out*

0 7206 1135 0   £9.95

Joseph Roth
WEIGHTS AND MEASURES

At the insistence of his wife, Eibenschutz leaves his job as an artilleryman in the Austro-Hungarian army for a civilian job as Inspector of Weights and Measures in a remote part of the Empire near the Russian border. Attempting to exercise some proper rectitude in his trade duties, he is at sea in a world smugglers, profiteers and small-time crooks. When he discovers that his wife has become pregnant by his own clerk, he spends less and less time at home, preferring to frequent a tavern on the border. Here, he becomes hopelessly drawn to a gypsy woman, Euphemia; she, however, is prepared to share the bed of the landlord and Eibenschutz's enemy, Jadlowker, an unprincipled profiteer, who has made the tavern a beacon for local smuggling activity.

'Written with the melancholy wit and grace of Gogol, with passages of electrifying beauty.' – *The Times*

'An absorbing fable, dark, beautifully written and with a physical immediacy in the prose . . . I want to read more.' – *New Statesman*

'Weights and Measure gave me the purest reading pleasure.' – Robert Nye, *Guardian*

0 7206 1136 9   £9.95

Bram Stoker
MIDNIGHT TALES

Horror stories never lose their popular appeal and Bram Stoker is a master of the genre. In the last decades of the nineteenth century, the Lyceum Theatre in London was the scene for brilliant gatherings hosted by the great actor Sir Henry Irving. There Irving and his guests talked of the theatre and told strange tales of far distant places. Bram Stoker was Irving's manager during these years and such dinner-table conversations provided him with inspiration both for his immortal classic of horror fiction, *Dracula*, and for the chilling stories in this book.

Opening the collection is a terrifying encounter

with a werewolf, a scene from an early draft of *Dracula*. Here, too, is 'The Squaw', Stoker's most blood-curdling short story, set in a medieval torture chamber. The theatrical world features in 'Death in the Wings', a tale of brutal revenge. Also included is the dramatic finale from the 1903 novel *The Jewel of the Seven Stars*, with its raising of a mummy from the dead, which so shocked Edwardian readers that it was later expurgated. Some of the stories in this collection have not been reprinted since their original magazine publication, and all display the fascination with the strange and the gruesome that made Bram Stoker a master of the macabre.

'A head-on collision between horror and sexuality.'
– *The Times*

'Compelling . . . strictly for vampire lovers.' – Robert Nye, *Guardian*

0 7206 1134 2   £9.95

Tarjei Vesaas
THE BIRDS

A tale of delicate beauty and deceptive simplicity by one of the greatest Scandinavian writers of the twentieth century, *The Birds* tells the story of Mattis, who is mentally retarded and lives in a small house near a lake with his sister Hege who ekes out a modest living knitting sweaters. From time to time she encourages her brother to find work to ease their financial burdens, but Mattis's attempts come to nothing. When finally he sets himself up as a ferryman, the only passenger he manages to bring across the lake is a lumberjack, Jørgen. But, when Jørgen and Hege become lovers, Mattis finds he cannot adjust to this new situation and complications abound.

'True visionary power.' – *Sunday Telegraph*

'Beautiful and subtle.' – *Scotsman*

'A masterpiece.' – *Literary Review*

'The Birds is a delight.' – *The European*

'A spare, icily humane story . . . The character of Mattis, absurd and boastful, but also sweet, pathetic and even funny, is shown with great insight. The translation conveys successfully a concentration of style and feeling that seems to Vesaas's characteristic mark as a novelist.'
– *Sunday Times*

0 7206 1143 1   £9.95

Tarjei Vesaas
THE ICE PALACE

The Ice Palace is the story of two eleven-year-old girls, Unn and Siss. Unn is about to reveal a secret, one that leads to her death in the palace of ice surrounding a frozen waterfall. Siss's struggle with her fidelity to the memory of her friend, the strange, terrifyingly beautiful frozen chambers of the waterfall and Unn's fatal exploration of the ice palace are described in prose of lyrical economy that ranks among the most memorable achievements of modern literature. In 1973 Tarjei Vesaas was awarded the Nordic Council Prize for this novel.

'How simple this novel is. How subtle. How strong. How unlike any other. It is unique. It is unforgettable. It is extraordinary.' – Doris Lessing, *Independent*

'It is hard to do justice to *The Ice Palace* . . . The narrative is urgent, the descriptions relentlessly beautiful, the meaning as powerful as the ice piling up on the lake.
– *The Times*

0 7206 1122 9   £9.95